A voice sounded through the flames, and hands reached out to rescue her. "Miss Layton. Miss Layton!"

Ophelia came awake with a gasp. She wasn't in a wall of flame, but in the inn's garret room, surrounded by darkness. Wide eyes and golden hair swam before her, illuminated by the moon. Mr. Drake was holding her, leaning over her in the bed.

"Miss Layton, you were having a nightmare," he said. "Please, be calm."

Her throat hurt when she swallowed, as if she'd been trying to scream in her sleep. "There was a fire," she said, though barely any sound came out. Her throat ached as if it had been shredded by glass.

"There's no fire here. It was only a dream. We're safe now." He stroked her long, loose hair, still damp from her bath. His touch felt so gentle, so soothing, that it took her a moment to think of the impropriety. She wore only her thin chemise, and he was in shirtsleeves, his legs fully bare. She ought to tell him he must leave, that he should not be in here, but the words wouldn't come because she was too befuddled. She'd never been so near a man in his state of undress.

"Are you awake now?" He moved closer to put a steadying arm around her. "Miss Layton?"

"Yes, I..." She was half in a world of fire, and half in this world where Mr. Drake embraced her, his strong, muscular body so near beside hers.

"It was f-fearsome," she whispered. "My nightmare."

"Don't worry, please. You're safe here. Shall I light the candle?"

She didn't want him to. She felt better in the darkness, but he reached beside her bed and lit it anyway. He looked back to her and his expression altered, his eyes widening as he stared. *He's seeing me without the wig and makeup*, she thought. *Seeing that I am blonde and small, not dark-haired and powerful like Armide.* Mr. Drake was so close to her. Was this how common ladies and gentlemen conducted themselves, with this easy proximity?

"Would you like me to stay here with you?" he asked. "To keep the nightmares away?"

Rival Desires

by

Annabel Joseph

Properly Spanked Legacy, Book One

A Guide to the Properly Spanked Families
(and the characters you'll meet in this new series)

The Marquess of Wescott
(the hero of this book)
eldest son of the Duke and Duchess of Arlington,
aka Arlington and Gwen from
Under A Duke's Hand
He is commonly called Wescott due to his title, although he is also
known by his Christian name, John (or more usually Jack).
His two youngest sisters, Hazel and Elizabeth, appear in this book.

The Earl of Augustine
eldest son of the Marquess and Marchioness of Barrymore
aka, Minette and Augustine from
My Naughty Minette
Now that the previous Lord Augustine has inherited his father's title
of Barrymore, his oldest son now bears the name and title of Augustine.
His Christian name, Julian, is rarely used.

Viscount Marlow
eldest son of the Earl and Countess of Warren
aka Warren and Josephine from
To Tame A Countess
His given name is George, but he goes by Marlow due to his
inherited title.

The Marquess of Townsend
eldest son of the Duke and Duchess of Lockridge
aka Hunter and Aurelia from
Training Lady Townsend
Now that Hunter has inherited his father's dukedom of Lockridge,
his oldest son now bears the name and title of Townsend.
His Christian name, Edward, hasn't been used since childhood.
Townsend's sister Rosalind is close friends with Wescott's sisters
Hazel and Elizabeth.

Chapter One:
A Fire

London, 1822

The Marquess of Wescott leaned away before his victim's fuchsia-pink slipper could connect with his forehead. It caught the edge of his gold-blond hair instead, which had long since straggled free of its velvet tie.

"Don't be naughty, Ellie," he scolded, delivering a few more spanks to the quivering backside balanced upon his lap. "If you can't behave yourself, I'll have to tie you up."

"Oh, you wouldn't be so cruel, sir," she cooed, twisting herself upright until she managed to straddle his thighs. She tugged one of his wavy locks, not at all intimidated by his stare.

"I think we both know I can be considerably crueler." He taunted the buxom courtesan with a hard twist of her nipples, reveling in her pain-filled moan.

Across the room, his friend Viscount Marlow tightened his fingers in Berta's hair, urging her to take his cock deeper in her humming throat. She wiggled her ample arse while she serviced him, showing off the cane welts he'd made minutes earlier.

"If only Lord Townsend was here, my sweet," he said, thrusting between her lips. "He'd have been pleased to add a few more stripes to your bottom while you suck me off."

"Ooh." She paused long enough to simper with theatrical alarm. "He'd bugger me too, wouldn't he, milord? Right up my sore arse, hard and rough like?"

"You'd love that, wouldn't you?" Marlow pushed back his riotous, white-blond hair and favored her with a grin. "And Towns would love to do it. Too bad he's off pining over someone."

"Pining over who? Some society lady?" Ellie sniffed. "Such a faithless customer. He hasn't been here in weeks."

"Tedious, to be in love, and miss out on such glorious perversions," said Wescott, arranging Ellie back over his lap.

"More tedious still to be in love with someone he can't tell us about," said August from the silk-draped bed. The dark-haired man was more formally known as the Earl of Augustine, but he didn't look very formal now as he stroked his rigid cock, waiting his turn. "I bet he's burning for Lady Pissy Pot."

"Good God, not her." Wescott spanked Ellie's cheeks for emphasis, then pointed at his friend. "And it's *Lady Priscilla Pott* to you, you perverse bull calf. She's got money and class, even if she hasn't the best temper. You wish you had half a chance at courting her."

"I wish no such thing. Unlike you, I don't have anyone on the hook, and I prefer it that way."

Wescott rolled his eyes. Everyone in the *ton* knew he was all but betrothed to the beautiful Lady June, not that he wished to think about that now, with a famously lewd courtesan draped across his lap.

"If you ask me, Miss Priss would be perfect for Towns, with his love of proprieties," said Marlow. "As for me, all I want is right here." He fondled Berta's full, round arse, then bent her over a chair for more caning. The lass danced and whined at each stroke, but also arched her back with the grace of a quality professional.

10

No, talk of engagements and marriages didn't belong in high-class brothels like Pearl's Erotic Emporium, where duties fell away and fantasy reigned. Townsend's secret sweetheart might cut into his randy activities, breaking up their foursome for a while, but there was still plenty of fun to be had. Wescott sent Ellie over to tend to August's waiting erection and settled in to watch Marlow flick a cane against Berta's reddening arse. Why did he enjoy the frantic struggling and crying of women? Why did he enjoy punishing them, and watching them go wild?

And what would happen once he won the hand of Lady June, and settled down into a society marriage? All his life, women had thrown themselves at him with lusty abandon, earning him a reputation as a rake. His handsome features, combined with his bold height and stature, had been more a curse than blessing. His parents, the Duke and Duchess of Arlington, hoped a marriage would improve his reputation, but life would be dull without forays to the brothel.

At Marlow's invitation, Wescott gave Berta a few stripes of his own, flicking the cane mercilessly against her already tender cheeks. She gave a tormented squeal at each stroke, her feigned agony rousing him to full staff for the third time that night.

"Go on and take her cunny, you horny bastard," Marlow offered. "I'll have her mouth."

Wescott shoved into the courtesan's soaked quim, fucking her steadily enough that she could still fellate his friend, but firmly enough to elicit some ball-tightening groans. Meanwhile, August alternated between spanking and diddling Ellie on the bed, until her giggles and cries rose to moans of ecstasy.

Suddenly, a gruff male voice interrupted them, and a fist pounded on the door. Charlie, one of the house bruisers from downstairs, shouldered it open and entered, gasping for breath.

"There's a fire coming this way, milords, a terr'ble fire burning up Parker's Lane," he cried. "We're getting everyone out, right now.

Berta, Ellie, put on clothes and run for yer lives, quick like. Take yer money and yer coats!"

Wescott helped Berta to her feet while Marlow ran to the window. The women scrambled to grab gowns, perfume, and baubles, the pleasing erotic tableau of moments ago exploded into panicked activity.

"Don't stop to collect things," scolded Charlie. "Gents, you must go too, with the clothes on your back." He waved the women out as August fumbled to button his shirt and Marlow did up his trousers.

"Leave your damn cravat," Wescott shouted to August. "We've got to get away, get to the coach."

They herded frightened, half-dressed harlots as they went, and avoided the eyes of their fellow customers, lords, and some ladies, who'd come to Pearl's for a pleasurable night. When they made it down the stairs and through the door into the open air, a flood of people had already filled the streets, fleeing surrounding buildings. The dry, warm fall had primed London for a spark to catch flame. Smoke poured toward them, advancing like a wall.

"Such a fire," a rasping man croaked beside them, "and the wind's blowin' toward Drury Lane."

"We'll take the horses," Wescott said, his senses sharpened despite the smoke in his eyes.

August covered his mouth with his shirtsleeve, his words muffled. They'd left their tailored coats and waistcoats behind. "It's spreading south," he said. "No way to go home."

"Getting away will be enough." Wescott wove between panicked groups, pulling his friends to the side lane where his coach-and-four waited. His groom stood near the shifting horses, watching anxiously in the direction of Pearl's.

"Release the horses," Wescott shouted as they arrived. "We must get away quickly."

The groom untethered the beasts with dexterous speed, aided by Wescott and his friends. They were finely trained stallions, standing still for the men to swing onto their backs, even amid the crowds and threatening flames. The groom paused at the last horse and shouted to Wescott. "I'll take the reins now, my lord, and try to roll the coach home."

"Nonsense. Ride the horse and leave the coach to burn."

"But my lord—" He coughed through billowing smoke.

"You'll never get the coach through the crowds, damn it. I can buy another. Go, and I'll meet you at the house."

The fire brigade clattered past, their massive carriages parting the crowds as they made their way back toward the flame and smoke. Men labored over pumps and levers, many of them half dressed and half asleep. Wescott's friends were already away.

"Go on, then," he yelled at his groom, and to his relief, the man obeyed, freeing the lead horse and riding him bareback through a break in the crowd.

Wescott patted his stallion's mane, taking care to give the animal clear signals as he navigated the chaos. The fire advanced at a terrifying pace, so he was forced to turn east as another engine arrived with groaning cisterns of water. He urged his mount in the direction of Broad Street, leaving the straighter path of escape to those on foot, but the fire followed, crackling and hissing in the dry night air.

"The theaters," a gentleman bellowed in the middle of the exodus. "If the brigade can't stop the fires, they'll burn."

Indeed, the evening's opera would just be ending at this hour. As Wescott came to Exeter Square, the crowds ballooned as London's upper crust poured from the theaters' ornate doorways into soot-filled roads. Many carriages had gotten away to rattle down the street, but others were abandoned by their owners, left to burn. He spared a thought for his luxurious coach, with its custom interior and painted doors. This very moment, the silk-paneled walls might be melting under the flames.

He patted his horse's neck to calm him, keeping a firm, easy grip with his thighs. He'd learned to ride bareback on the wild Welsh moors of his mother's childhood manor. He wished he were there now, in the open, fresh air, rather than this flame-choked corner of the city. People fled *en masse*, peers and commoners alike, their mouths covered and heads bowed against the smoke. Ladies pressed their pristine gloves to coughing lips, running, however unladylike, across crowded streets to cleaner air. The menfolk guided them, urging them forward when they wilted. This was no time to fall out in a swoon.

Amidst the clamor of exodus, Wescott noticed a woman cowering against one of the theater's grand columns, as if she might find shelter there. She was a performer, perhaps an operatic actress, considering her bright, Italianate costume and hip-length black curly wig. She coughed, clutching at her clumsy skirts, looking about for rescue, but everyone around her had already fled. Behind him, he could hear the advancing crackle of fire and the shouts of the brigade. They were chasing the flames, which were still heading this way.

"Come with me," he said, leaning down to offer his arm.

"I can't," she sobbed. "A driver is coming for me."

"He won't make it. He's likely stuck somewhere."

The poor, frantic actress was garishly made up. On closer perusal, he could see blonde wisps escaping the bounds of her heavy black wig. Her tears smudged the theatrical kohl lining around her eyes, lending her an otherworldly look.

"I don't know where to go," she said. "I was to meet the carriage here, by the stage door."

"You can't wait for it. The fire's just behind me, and they haven't yet got it in check."

She stared at him, frightened to numbness. He imagined he looked less than trustworthy, with no coat or hat, and his clothes disarranged. His horse started to dance, so Wescott braced himself and leaned farther, and pulled the woman up, depositing her in his lap, gown, wig, and all. She clutched at his shoulders, then at her wig as he galloped across the now empty square toward Parker's Lane. Once he arrived there, he found the fire had circled around, cutting off his path to the north. He turned south again, cursing beneath his breath. Whoever'd begun this damn fire was causing a terrible lot of destruction.

"I c-can't br-breathe," the woman cried, choking on the words.

"Turn your face into my chest," he said. "Cover your mouth and nose with that hair if you must."

He covered his face too, drawing his collar higher against the smoke and ash in the air. She mumbled something else about her carriage, but he couldn't help her locate it now. He had to find somewhere the two of them could breathe, and where his faltering horse could take water and rest. He turned east when he was able, praying the flames would die down, and the fire extinguish itself in the Thames before it made its way to Charles Street.

"How are you doing?" he asked the woman.

She didn't respond, but he could feel her breathing in and out against his chest. He held her with one arm, guiding the horse with the other, disregarding propriety in service of keeping her safe. Her long performer's wig covered her back like a cloak, and reminded him she wasn't precisely a lady, so propriety needn't be foremost in his mind. Still, he was a gentleman, a peer of the realm. He wouldn't take advantage of an actress in a desperate situation.

She lifted her face and tried to speak, her voice catching.

"What?" he asked.

"There's so much smoke. Where are we going?"

"Hold on to me, miss. I won't let you come to harm."

He rode with his trembling, sniffling passenger for half an hour, urging his mount eastward, until the ringing bells and shouts of the fire brigade faded and they found calmer, cleaner night air. His horse rallied, and the actress didn't cough as spasmodically as she had, but he didn't know where he was, or where he should go. He only knew he couldn't turn homeward, not with the fire still burning, covering the streets in smoke.

"Hell and the devil," he said, pausing at a trough outside a quiet pub to water his horse.

The woman stirred against him, roused by clearer air.

"Pardon my language," he said as she peeked up at him. "I believe we're out of danger. How are you faring, miss?"

In answer, she burst into tears. He stared down at his half-buttoned shirt—of excellent quality—now ruined by the smeared stage paint she wore. Despite the paint, he could see she had a pretty face, with wide eyes and elegant cheekbones, and full, appealing lips. He also could not fail to notice she possessed particularly alluring curves. She must have found it easy to make the stage with such *accoutrements*, and wondered how many admirers she had. Perhaps, like many actresses, she had a gentleman sponsor who spoiled and kept her. The thought displeased him as soon as it crossed his mind.

Why, do you wish to take her as your mistress?

A ridiculous idea to entertain as the actress leaked tears in her wig and ruined makeup, with both of them covered in smoky grime. He was of an age and status where he might take a mistress if he wished, sponsor a dancer or actress and buy her pretty things. He might even retain such a mistress after his eventual marriage, but that couldn't be his focus tonight. He buttoned his shirt and made a loose knot of his cravat, a clumsy attempt to improve his piratical appearance.

"Don't cry," he said, being so bold as to run a finger down one of her sullied cheeks.

She shrank from the affectionate gesture, glancing around nervously. "I don't know where we are."

"I'm not sure either."

"I waited for the carriage. I thought it would come."

"You can't worry about that now." He wondered whose carriage had been coming to pick her up. Some gentleman who'd been waiting to spend the night in her arms? "It's likely the driver couldn't get through," he said. "The theater had emptied by the time I got there."

"This is terrible," she said through her tears. "What if the carriage caught fire? Or was overtaken by the crowds? Or...or..." She sniffled, struggling for breath. "What if they're still there looking for me?"

"I don't think that's possible, as the smoke would have driven them away. In fact, I fear it may be some time before it's possible to ride back. Where is your home, miss? Where do you live?"

She hesitated before she told him. "West of the theater, near Grosvenor Square."

Grosvenor Square? This pretty young actress had a serious sponsor then, a wealthy one. No doubt the man was someone he knew, someone who moved in aristocratic circles.

"I know that area," he said aloud. "Your name?"

She balked, as if he might be some charlatan prying for information. Well, his hair was loose and wild, and he was riding bareback through London in his shirtsleeves, fresh from a sex parlor.

"You needn't tell me your real name," he said with a shrug. "Your stage name will do."

"I don't have a stage name." She touched her cheeks, the theatrical creature. "I'm La—Miss Layton."

Silly, that she didn't trust him enough to reveal her real name, but the popular novels of the day were all about murder, mayhem, and kidnapping for ransom, actresses and infamous ladies being the victims of choice. He had no liking for murder, and no need for ransom money, so she needn't have worried. He only wished to get her somewhere warm and less smoky. Even here, curls of ash wafted on the wind.

"Will the fire still come?" she asked in a shaky voice.

"I don't think so. They'll run it toward the river, and it'll burn itself out before it reaches these streets." Now that Wescott's horse was refreshed, he guided it into a walk along a quiet lane.

"I've never been in a fire before," she said.

"Nor have I, nor do I ever wish to be again."

"The smoke was terrible. I thought I would die." She held his stallion's neck as she spoke, apparently at ease on horseback. Indeed, now that she wasn't sniveling, her elocution marked her as a woman of elegant manners, which might explain how she'd secured such a wealthy patron. "Thank you for helping me, and escorting me from danger."

"You're welcome, Miss Layton. I was raised to assist those in need."

"And...sir...who are you?" she finally asked.

He was used to meeting women in formal introductions, at dinner parties, or in ballrooms. No need for such pomp here.

"I'm Jack," he said, giving her his childhood nickname. "Mr. Jack Drake." He decided not to intimidate the chit with his full, toplofty name and title, although he wondered if he outranked her rich patron. Why did he care? *Because you're playing the hero, Wes, and she's charming.*

And talented, probably in more ways than one.

If only he knew the name of her patron, he'd have an idea if this woman was the type to suit him in bed. Now that they'd made their dramatic escape, he pictured an inn, a small room, the two of them together, and her eager to thank him for rescuing her from the fire...

By God, what was wrong with him? At times like this, he understood why the society gossips had fun changing his surname from "Drake" to "Rake." This wasn't an opportunity for flirtation or seduction. Both of them were filthy and tired, and he'd already had plenty of sex for one night.

They rode awhile in silence, his well-trained horse stepping delicately on the unevenly cobbled road.

"Where are we going, Mr. Drake?" his actress asked. "If we can't return to our homes?"

"We'll stop at an inn, as soon as we come across a reputable one."

"I don't..." She looked on the verge of tears again, brushing at the soot-stained ruching that festooned her theatrical skirts. "I can't stay at an inn, sir. It...it wouldn't be proper."

He subdued the urge to chuckle. Playing the proper lady, was she? With her garish costume and wig, and the carriage meeting her outside the stage door, to escort her to her lover's nest near Grosvenor Square? "It's hard to be proper in such circumstances," he countered. "Would you rather sleep outside in the lingering smoke?"

She started trembling again, whether from fear or embarrassment, he didn't know. Did she worry he'd take advantage of her? Tempting as it was to plan a seduction, no fantasies could be acted out this night.

"You'll have your own room, Miss Layton," he assured her, "if that's what you're worried about."

"I haven't any money for a room. I've just come from—from onstage."

"I'll pay for the rooms, and a warm bath too. Please, calm yourself. You'll be kept perfectly safe until the air clears and we can return to our respective homes. I'll deliver you to Grosvenor Square by morning light, if that will do."

"That would be...that would be very kind." She blinked at him. "Thank you, Mr. Drake." Her voice was roughened, perhaps by tears, perhaps by damage from the smoke. "I promise you'll be repaid for your assistance."

"The only repayment I require is your safe conduct home."

She lowered her face, reassured, while he scanned the area, trying to divine their location. If he had to guess, they were somewhere near Bishopsgate, but all the family homes and shops were dark and quiet compared to West London. By the time he found a respectable inn with rooms to let and adequate accommodations for the horse, he felt enormously tired.

He gave the innkeeper news of the fire near Covent Garden, and told the man Miss Layton was his sister. The good innkeeper stared suspiciously at her opera costume, but as they'd requested separate rooms, he held his peace.

As for Miss Layton, she seemed too tired to object to the false pretense, or indeed to anything. Refusing the offer of a cold dinner, she allowed Wescott to see her upstairs to a small garret beneath the rafters, where the servants were already setting up a bath. No, it was not a venue for a seduction, which was unfortunate, for an assignation with this actress would have made a fine tale to share with his friends.

"I'll be next door," he told her. "Please wake me if you rise before me in the morning. We'll do well to return home as soon as we can."

"Yes, I will. Thank you, Mr. Drake."

He left her reluctantly, then asked for a dinner tray and his own bath to distract him from preposterous thoughts. What would his mother think if he took a mistress from the stage? An actress? The whispers might eventually reach her ears, or God forbid, his father's. His parents were terribly faithful, and ridiculously in love with one another, so his poor reputation pained them. There would be another uncomfortable conversation about respect and morals, and the expectation of marital fidelity, now that he was practically engaged to Lady June.

He soaked in the dented hip bath for nearly half an hour, washing away smoke and smut, and the lingering scent of the girls at Pearl's Emporium, then he dried off and sprawled naked upon a narrow cot, imagining the clean, downy blankets that comprised his bed at home. His valet would have turned down the covers, awaiting his return, but there was no such coddling here. Nearly an hour elapsed before servants came to take the bathtub and dinner tray back down.

He wondered how Miss Layton was faring in her adjacent room, but resisted the urge to look in on her. A warm fire, a stiff drink, and comfortable surroundings filled his thoughts just before he tumbled into a bone-tired sleep.

Chapter Two:
A Nightmare

Lady Ophelia Lovett sat shivering in the tin bathtub, huddled against the stale night air that seeped in the windows. She'd finished with her bath, but there were no attendants to bring her a towel, which she'd left just out of reach on the edge of the bed. Nor did she have a clean, warm chemise to change into. She had only the garish, soot-stained opera costume, and the tangled black wig, which was likely ruined beyond repair.

Her father could replace them for the theater company. Such an expense wouldn't touch the Earl of Halsey's deep pockets. In fact, her father was so wealthy that her rescuer could kidnap her and demand a ransom beyond his wildest dreams, if he discovered who she was.

And would you mind so much if he stole you away, Ophelia?

She stood in the tub and let the cool air attack her skin. It was what she deserved, because she'd sort of, a little bit, been imagining what it might be like to be kidnapped by the dashing Mr. Jack Drake. He was so tall and strong, and so virile in a way she wasn't accustomed to. It had given her a protected, excited sort of feeling when he held her against his massive body.

Oh, what kind of lady was she, to harbor such thoughts?

She was no lady at all. She pretended to be one because her parents expected it, but inside her mind, where no one could see, she always wished for more adventure than her narrow place in society would allow. She wished for freedom, for space to breathe outside the dutiful cage her parents had created for her. She would have offered up her "God-given voice" in an instant if she could have traded it for some chance at novelty and excitement.

Like a kidnapping? Ophelia, you are the very worst of women.

How awful of her to dwell on lurid, ridiculous kidnapping fantasies when there were so many more serious things to worry about. Were her parents safe? Had they escaped the fire? Did they search for her? And what had happened to Jacqueline? It smarted to think her maid had deserted her, run away with the panicking crowds, when the woman was expressly charged with her care.

Now she was alone with a man she didn't know, and while he didn't seem threatening, her reputation, at least, was endangered. Lurid fantasies aside, there would be gossip if anyone of import saw her in his company, for Mr. Drake seemed the sort of man proper ladies would gossip about. The way he looked, the way he carried himself, she was sure he couldn't walk by anyone without attracting attention.

She'd never encountered a man like Mr. Drake at her all-girls music school in Vienna, or on stage in any classical recital or opera. Goodness, she'd been back in England for nearly two months now, and she hadn't encountered a man like Mr. Drake in any drawing room or tea parlor either. He wasn't like the gentlemen who'd courted her older sister Nanette, or the mousey viscount she'd finally settled upon.

No, Mr. Drake was like the Vikings she'd learned about in her history books, before her famed soprano voice lifted her from her childhood schoolroom and landed her in Vienna. His hair was long and golden-blond like a Viking's, and his eyes were a startling, vivid green. When he held her atop his horse, his giant hands seemed formed to wield great broadswords rather than teacups.

Oh, she was a wanton dreamer, full of imaginings, and at such an inappropriate time. Such thoughts burst forth when she least wanted them. She deserved another five minutes of shivering in the night air, but instead she reached for the rough, thin towel to pat herself dry.

He must be a working man, she thought, a man of trade or commerce who could buy a fine stallion, but hadn't yet saved enough money for proper tack. He was too clean to be a low sort of laborer. Nor was he a refined gentleman, for no gentleman would ride about in his shirtsleeves with his collar all undone. She'd never seen a man in that sort of undress, not in all her eighteen years.

Being so close to Mr. Jack Drake and his non-refinement had piqued a certain curiosity, but she needed to govern her thoughts. As her mother often told her, she had to be the most proper lady in all of London society, since God had gifted her with a voice that necessitated a life on stage. *You cannot silence such talent,* her mother had argued when her father pointed out that theater circles were not the place for his highborn daughter. God had given her an angel's voice.

And so Ophelia must behave like an angel, and remain above reproach, or Papa would force her to abandon her singing. That would doom her chance at adventure for good, for then she'd have to marry some terribly boring suitor like the one her sister had chosen, and settle down in some stuffy country house to be a wife and mother for the rest of her life. She didn't believe she'd done anything really sinful yet, aside from harboring Viking fantasies. She should not be in the company of such a man, of course, but he'd been kind enough to pay for separate rooms.

She lifted the opera costume with disdain, and instead put on her own cotton chemise she wore beneath it. It smelled less of ash and was mostly clean. The smoke, the fire, the fleeing crowds, she had to put all that away, or she wouldn't be able to sleep. Her mind turned on fears of her parents burning in the flames as they searched for her.

When she refused that horror, it was replaced by thoughts of her heavy wig on fire as she tried to outrun the advancing inferno. So many images she couldn't tolerate at the moment, and her empty stomach was churning because she'd been too worried to eat.

Even if her parents hadn't been harmed, they'd be beside themselves with worry. Her father might send out riders to search for her, but they'd never find her in this far-flung room. How was she to sleep now, with so much to worry about? Her performance in *Armide* seemed a million hours ago. She hardly remembered if she'd sung well, or whom she'd performed with, or who had been in the audience to watch.

She pulled the covers up to her chin, wishing her mind would be still, because her body was exhausted and needed rest. And tomorrow... tomorrow she'd need to get home without Mr. Drake learning how highborn she was. She didn't dare tell him her true address, for then he'd know who she was. Worse, someone might see them together, right outside her father's house.

Oh dear, that mustn't happen. She'd have to ask her rescuer to drop her off at some nearby establishment. Perhaps in the park? How humiliating this all was.

She blew out the candle and lay in the dark, listening to unfamiliar noises and the settling of the old inn, and felt even more homesick than she'd felt in Vienna. She missed her Mama and Papa, and even her faithless French maid Jacqueline. She only had the ability to say a very short prayer through the ache in her smoke-scorched throat. *Please, God, let them all be safe.*

Alas, sleep brought no respite from her worries. She dreamed of fire almost the minute she closed her eyes. The flames flew at her like birds, hissed at her like snakes, and seared wherever they touched her. *Mama, Papa, I'm waiting here. Where are you? Jacqueline, you were to have waited with me. How could you leave me alone?*

She called out for them, and told them she was so, so sorry, although she didn't know for what. Still, the flames grew as high as the buildings looming over her, threatening to enfold her and turn her into fire. Unlike Armide, the warrior-sorceress she'd played in the opera that evening, she had no power, no strength to save herself. The fire was hot and suffocating, alive with the shrieks and screams of those around her. Was she on stage? Was this a dream? No, it was real life, real fire, all over again. No, no, no...

A voice sounded through the flames, and hands reached out to rescue her. "Miss Layton. Miss Layton!"

Ophelia came awake with a gasp. She wasn't in a wall of flame, but in the inn's garret room, surrounded by darkness. Wide eyes and golden hair swam before her, illuminated by the moon. Mr. Drake was holding her, leaning over her in the bed.

"Miss Layton, you were having a nightmare," he said. "Please, be calm."

Her throat hurt when she swallowed, as if she'd been trying to scream in her sleep. "There was a fire," she said, though barely any sound came out. Her throat ached as if it had been shredded by glass.

"There's no fire here. It was only a dream. We're safe now." He stroked her long, loose hair, still damp from her bath. His touch felt so gentle, so soothing, that it took her a moment to think of the impropriety. She wore only her thin chemise, and he was in shirtsleeves, his legs fully bare. She ought to tell him he must leave, that he should not be in here, but the words wouldn't come because she was too befuddled. She'd never been so near a man in his state of undress.

"Are you awake now?" He moved closer to put a steadying arm around her. "Miss Layton?"

"Yes, I..." She was half in a world of fire, and half in this world where Mr. Drake embraced her, his strong, muscular body so near beside hers.

"It was f-fearsome," she whispered. "My nightmare."

"Don't worry, please. You're safe here. Shall I light the candle?"

She didn't want him to. She felt better in the darkness, but he reached beside her bed and lit it anyway. He looked back to her and his expression altered, his eyes widening as he stared. *He's seeing me without the wig and makeup,* she thought. *Seeing that I am blonde and small, not dark-haired and powerful like Armide.* Mr. Drake was so close to her. Was this how common ladies and gentlemen conducted themselves, with this easy proximity?

"Would you like me to stay here with you?" he asked. "To keep the nightmares away?"

She trembled at his softly spoken suggestion. *It wouldn't be proper for you to do so, sir.* That was what she meant to say, but instead she answered, "Yes, I'm frightened. Please..."

For the fire frightened her still. It had been so loud and hot, so out of control, that it seemed to have imprinted itself upon her psyche, so it still blazed in her mind. She could still smell traces of smoke on Mr. Drake's skin, although he'd clearly bathed and washed his Viking's hair. As he bundled under the covers beside her, she wondered if she smelled of smoke, too.

Next she knew, they were lying quite together beneath the blankets, his warm legs right against hers. He leaned on one arm and stroked her hair with the other, studying her with a kind, almost fond expression. She shouldn't allow it, she knew. She ought to tell him not to touch her, but it felt so reassuring. Perhaps he'd had nightmares too. Would he only touch her hair? No, now he stroked her face, and she realized she was still shedding tears.

"It's been such a fraught night," he said. "I don't want to be alone either."

She leaned into his touch, even though she knew this was against the rules of decency and God's will. "I'm not sure how to feel," she whispered. "I wish I were at home, and none of this had happened."

"I wish that too."

His eyes were deeper green by candlelight, a strange, enticing shade of green she'd never encountered before. His jaw was square and strong, textured with a shadow of stubble. He was so close to her, this strange, fascinating male, and she thought, why not touch that stubble to satisfy her curiosity? How did such rough, masculine features feel? When she traced light fingertips along his jawline, his expression changed again, grew more intent. His hand covered hers, stroking it, gentle and rough at the same time.

"Miss Layton, I must tell you—you're so much more beautiful without the wig."

"Oh." Her mind spun at his compliment. She had no idea what to reply. "I don't like wearing that wig," she whispered. "I'm made to wear it, to sing the character Armide. She's a dark sorceress in the opera's story."

"A dark sorceress?" He let out a small sigh. "And you're a soft, sweet sorceress in real life, aren't you? You're so pretty, I'd like to kiss you."

"I don't know if you should," she said quickly. "I'm no sorceress, not really." She was babbling in a whisper, for her voice wouldn't work. "I'm not a practiced kisser, either. I don't think you'd like to kiss me."

But she wanted him to, secretly, guiltily, because she'd never been kissed by a man before. So when he leaned his face toward hers, his eyes full of questions, she lifted her chin and pressed her lips to his.

And oh, what happened then was so lovely, so unexpected. As their lips met, his arms tightened around her, drawing her close against his entire frame. Ophelia felt so many sensations, all of them warm, comforting, and delicious. This close, she could tell he'd used the same soap she'd bathed with, and also smell that bit of smoke, so the danger stayed between them, the danger they'd escaped. As his hands moved over her, exploring her body's curves, she thought of him sweeping her up from the stage door, the way he'd plucked her right up with one arm and settled her onto his horse.

He was very strong to do such a thing. Why, she might have perished if he hadn't come along. They embraced with deep feeling and abandon, and as her pleasure grew, his attentions began to feel necessary, not improper. His kisses were a whirlwind, falling on her lips, her cheekbones, her chin, her eyes. He smoothed back her hair, murmuring that she was so beautiful, so lovely beneath her costume, then pressed a firm hand down her back, along her spine. She wondered why she'd been taught a man's touch was so frightening and forbidden, when it felt so marvelous.

For this was forbidden. She was a lady, the daughter of a powerful earl, and no man ought to even touch her hand without proper introduction and a chaperone's permission.

But she was so far outside the bounds of propriety and her strict upbringing that she began to feel unhitched from that part of herself. This was the freedom she'd longed for all her life. Mr. Drake said she was beautiful and lovely, and she felt for the first time that she *was*, that she was a desirable woman, and it made her feel happy and excited, and a little wild. She returned his kisses with a reckless enthusiasm that surged the more he caressed and fondled her. When he slid his palms down and cupped her bottom, she gasped, not in outrage, but pleasure.

He made a soft sound, somewhere between a moan and a grunt, and rubbed his fingers over her round cheeks through the thin cotton of her chemise. She'd always been short in stature, and not at all voluptuous, but he sighed as if her bottom was the most glorious creation on earth. One of his legs wrapped about hers, drawing her closer. His chest and stomach were hard as a wall, and there was something else poking beneath the hem of his shirt, a thick shaft, but part of his body. His man's part. She'd never seen one before, or imagined it would feel like this. He moved the hard thing against her pelvis with their clothing between them. Her hips arched toward the pressure as a curious longing built at the apex of her thighs.

"You stunning creature," he whispered. "How elegantly you're made. I want to stroke you all over."

She didn't protest as he inched up the hem of her chemise. Soon the light garment was pushed up her body and over her head, and he'd stripped her naked, all with her panting cooperation. She didn't feel like Lady Ophelia Lovett anymore. She wasn't even the fictitious Miss Layton. She was an aching, wild sorceress throwing aside the rules she'd been taught, because this touching and kissing was so powerful that she must be powerful, too. Mr. Drake touched his tongue to one of her bare nipples, and she arched at the heady sensation.

"You like that," he said with a smile in his voice.

She couldn't answer. She grasped his hair and tried without success to be still as he teased her other nipple with his tongue, but the sharp pleasure was too much. She ought to stop him, but she couldn't stop him. Her fingers skittered over his shoulders and down his arms, looking for a place to hold. He tore open his shirt's buttons and shrugged it away, and then she had his entire naked, hard chest to explore with her greedy fingers. She squeezed his tensing muscles, amazed at the force of him, his intensity. She stroked his neck, fascinated by the texture of his skin and the glorious beat of his pulse.

"Miss Layton." His rough voice drew her attention, and he held her gaze. His green eyes were not soft and kind now, but alive with desire. "God help me, I want you. Perhaps it is the situation. The fire."

"Sir, you have me. I'm here." Why couldn't she speak above a whisper? All her energy was elsewhere, in the teeming tips of her breasts, in the aching throb between her legs. "I feel as if I'm on fire right now."

"I do, too." He slid a hand down to touch her quim just where it throbbed, and it felt too good to stop him, or protest about proprieties. He traced his finger over a tiny, needful bit of her flesh in such a way that she wanted to bite and scratch him, and eat him whole.

"Are you sure you want this after all you've been through tonight?" he asked. "If you prefer, I'll leave you to your peace."

Peace? It was senseless to speak of peace while he worked such magic with his touch. One of his fingers traced about her wet, hot opening, a place that had never felt so swollen with sensation before.

"Please, sweet lady..." His voice was so strained it was difficult to hear. "You're so bright, so lovely."

"Yes, please," she agreed, and his finger eased inside her, there, where she was wet and excited. She was so shocked that she gasped. His finger felt big and strange there, but exciting at the same time.

"I'll be careful," he promised.

She was glad, because this intimacy was unexpected. Did men and women do these things? They must, because it felt so good.

"Please," she said again, even though she knew she shouldn't. He said he would be careful, and oh, his finger inside her felt naughty and stretching, and he was kissing her again, making it even more exciting. He shifted, coming over her. His knees spread her thighs, and then his thick rod was at that wet place, and then...

He pushed it inside her with a slow, aching stretch. She hissed from the pain, although it wasn't really pain as much as surprise that he would do such an unexpected thing.

"I'm sorry." He kissed and nuzzled her, arching over her but holding her close. "I know I'm a lusty size, and you so small. I'll take care. I'll go slow."

Oh, she thought. She wondered if going slow would help, because he'd begun this thing, and she was confused and a little injured, and he was pushing deeper still. *This is too much. This is not what I meant when I said "please" to you.*

But even as her mind rebelled, her body opened for him, accepting his part inside her, accepting that the adventure she'd wished for had taken this novel turn. As he moved in her, she grew wetter from the sensation and pressure of his thrusts. His hair fell down against her face, a soft, sweet distraction. His eyes held hers as he paused within her, seated as deep as her body would let him go. "All right, my sweet?" he asked. "Does it feel good for you?"

It felt...unsettling. She had let him go too far, without realizing. She was certain this was terribly wrong, perhaps the worst thing a proper lady could do with a man. She knew it, but she still wanted him to continue moving inside her.

"I'm a little bit afraid," she admitted, even as she arched against him. "I'm afraid I shouldn't have done this."

"I'll take care of you." He spoke through gritted teeth. "I promise I won't spend inside you."

She didn't know what that meant, only that she wanted him to continue stroking her and kissing her, and yes, pressing his thick, stretching length inside her while she clung to his broad shoulders. She craved the heat of his body against hers. She needed the ache and pulsing in her breasts and quim to be satisfied. *There was a fire*, she thought. *And now there's this...*

The two events might have been one and the same in her mind now. Both spawned worry, confusion, and unbearable heat. *Rescue me again*, she thought. *Help me, please.*

When he commenced again, the shock was a little less. What had felt enormous inside her now felt tight and hot, and exciting. This was a man, then, when his proper clothes were off: urgent, powerful, mysterious, a little magical, because he brought pleasure that overrode any discomfort or pain she might have felt at the circumstances. She lay back and relaxed her thighs, and as he surged in her, she experienced sensations she'd never felt before. Squeezing. Pulsing. Tingling. Was this desire? A tightness or pressure built in her middle, not the pressure of Mr. Drake inside her body, but a restless pressure that desperately needed release.

She didn't mean to guide him with her moans and sighs, but somehow he read them anyway, and touched her just as she needed to be touched, just where she needed to be touched. He squeezed her breasts, which she liked, then tweaked her nipples, which made her tense all over, but in a nice way. When she ground her pelvis against his, he reached between them and circled his finger over that sensitive button again. Now that he was inside her, thrusting within her, it made her feel like she might explode.

"Ah, yes," he said in approval, as her cries turned to pleas. "Yes, my sweet sorceress. Exactly like that."

Exactly like that. Exactly like that... Even though she was acting like an undisciplined, lustful creature, he said *exactly like that*, and she felt safe and protected, and not afraid to reach for more. She bucked her hips, full of his power, dancing to his touch, and within moments, the anxious pressure inside her released like a rising wave finding its crest. A surge of sensation washed over her, spreading from the place they joined out over her entire body. She rode upon undulations of ecstasy, shocked once again by this new development. When this bliss was over, she'd be ashamed of herself, scandalized and disappointed that she'd let herself go so far, but for now, she basked in the pleasure that overtook her.

By the time the astonishing paroxysms passed, she felt wrung out, sated and limp like a rag doll. Mr. Drake thrust within her a few more times, then surged deep. With a whispered curse, he jerked away from her, leaving her body. Tonight had been shock upon shock, and here was another, as he knelt over her and pumped his thick rod until it spilled a pale fluid upon her bare stomach. He growled like an animal as the stuff spurted onto her. It felt hot and sticky against her skin.

She lay still, because her confusion was too deep by this point, and satisfaction had made her tired. He pumped his rod a few more times, looking down in the candlelight. "There's blood," he said, looking at his hands. "You're on your courses?"

She thought of race courses, stupidly. What did he mean? "I don't know," she said in a soft voice.

"Less likelihood of a child, if you are. But I took care, as you see." He wiped away the fluid on her stomach using the rough sheets, then lay beside her with a great sigh of satisfaction. "My dear, thank you for this lovely interlude. You excited me beyond bearing." His smile widened to a grin. "That's one way to chase away nightmares. A very pleasant way, I think."

Her mind was spinning with the remnants of pleasure, and sudden exhaustion. "I think I must... I must..."

"Yes, use the necessary." He gave her a boost out of bed, when it seemed her legs would fail her. She went behind the screen to use the chamber pot, and wished for water to clean herself. A moment later, Mr. Drake was there, offering the pitcher of water that had been warming by the dying fire. She took some time to wash, and a few extra moments to think. *What have I done? What now?*

When she finally summoned the courage to emerge, he was watching from the bed, the man who'd done those amazing, and probably awful things, which she'd very much enjoyed. She returned his smile in spite of her misgivings.

"May I stay here with you?" he asked, beckoning her back under the covers. "Only in case the nightmares come back. I promise I won't trouble you again, unless you wish it."

She didn't understand what that meant, to trouble her again. She moved into his warm embrace and curled up against him, remembering everything he'd done to her, trying to understand what had gone on between them, while he fell almost instantly to sleep.

On the side table, the candle had burned almost to its end. She felt like that in a way, like all of her had been consumed, until she was nothing. But oh, like the candle, there had been so much flame, so much brightness along the way.

Chapter Three: Morning's Light

Wescott woke from a disordered dream of fire and flames, and an exotic, black-haired sorceress. For a moment, he didn't recall where he was. The room was dim, the small window above admitting only muted light. He finally remembered as he became aware of the soft, pale tresses trailing over his arm.

He was curled up with the blonde—not black-haired—actress. Their legs intertwined beneath the tangled sheets, reminding him of the previous night's intimacies. He knew he must wake her soon so he could return to his residence, and she to hers. This time out of reality and responsibility must come to an end, but first...

Ah, first, he would enjoy a few final moments studying her pert, delicate nose and rosebud lips. Ah, those lips. They could sing, surely, but what else could they do? What lucky gentleman had regular use of them? Her coquettish manner of innocence and earthiness had driven him wild the night before, had sparked such intense lust he

34

could hardly govern his actions. Now, he was loath to tear himself away from her.

Dear God, how he wished to take her now, in the quiet light of morning. How he wished to tease open those enthralling pink lips with his stiffening cock, or perhaps rile her up with a sound spanking on her perfectly formed arse cheeks. They'd look so beautiful and red, marked with his handprints. Did her gentleman patron spank this sweet girl? A damnable waste if he did not.

He drifted into a warm, arousing reverie, imagining her pretty blue eyes filling with tears as the spanking continued. She would writhe on his lap and clutch his legs, begging for respite, not that she would get it...

Next he knew, she stirred beside him, jostling him awake. He was as hard as he'd ever been in his life with the virile humors of sleep. Oh, how he ached to fuck her again, but he dared not partake of any more of her charms. They'd slept too late, in their exhaustion. His family must have learned of his absence by now, and would send out searchers in a panic.

"Miss Layton." He moved his hips so his unfortunate erection wouldn't be the first thing she felt upon waking. "Miss Layton, I'm sorry to disturb you, but..." He nudged her shoulder and brushed back a tangled lock of her hair. "Miss Layton, we must rise and make ourselves ready to leave. I must take you home—"

She came awake with great abruptness, clutching his arm. "No," she said in a harsh whisper.

"No?"

She blinked at him, her eyes still blurry with sleep. "I— You—" She seemed to have trouble getting the words out. "You cannot take me home."

"But I must." He frowned in concern. "Have you lost your voice?"

Her hands flew to her throat, then reached to pull the blankets up high, covering her naked shoulders. "Yes. My throat must be swollen...from the smoke and fire...last night. It hurts."

"Don't speak if it hurts you. I'll be ready in just a moment, if you'd care to rise and dress yourself as well as you may." He glanced at her brightly colored costume. What a spectacle they'd make, trotting across town, the Duke of Arlington's son and a disheveled opera actress. There was nothing for it. He would not abandon her here, in the poorer streets of town, where one might mistake her profession. She might be a stage creature, but she was too clean and mannerly to be a common whore.

"Please, Mr. Drake. You needn't see me home." She sat up and massaged her throat again. "Oh, no," she said. "I shall not be able to sing."

Don't worry, he thought. *With those lips of yours, there will always be someone willing to take care of you.*

Perhaps it would be him. He would see where she lived, learn who paid for her niceties, and see if they might pass her off to him in the near future. Though, how could any man tire of such a lovely specimen of femininity, who was also, apparently, possessed of a marvelous voice?

"You'll sing again." He embraced her, doing his best to hide his engorged cock beneath the tails of his shirt. If she didn't let him up soon, he'd lose control and bed her a second time, and a third. Perhaps that was her aim in clinging to him.

No, she was truly upset, and truly bereft of voice.

"Don't try to speak," he said again. "My voice has roughened too."

"I—I must speak," she whispered. "I— Please— I cannot inconvenience you to see me home."

"How else will you get there? You've no money, no manner of conveyance, and, I dread to mention, no reasonable clothes."

She gazed in dismay at her outlandish costume. Perhaps she could hide her face within the wig, if she was so ashamed to be seen in his company. Was she worried her special patron, or one of his friends, might glimpse them near Grosvenor Square, and make trouble for her?

"If you like," he said, caressing her arm soothingly, "I can take you to your place and explain to your...your relations...exactly what has happened."

"Oh, goodness, no." The vehemence of her denial clearly hurt her voice further.

"Well, I'll not leave you here, mute and penniless, to fend for yourself. Not after the, ah..." How to put it without causing her to blush deeper? "The affectionate encounter we enjoyed last night."

"Take me to Hyde Park then," she whispered, her gaze troubled. "If you deliver me to the east side of the park, near King Street, that is very close to my home."

"If that's what you wish, I'm happy to comply."

She clearly did not want to flirt or reminisce, and he was tired of arguing with her. That part of town would be safe enough, if she would not allow him to see her to her doorstep. "Now, please, Miss Layton, we must ready ourselves to depart."

And I must find a private place to relieve this pressure in my cock before I climb atop a horse with you, he added in his mind. *Or you'll find yourself having an entirely different sort of ride.*

* * * * *

Mr. Drake was a rumpled mess in the daylight, but somehow appeared twice as attractive, with the sun glinting off his gold hair and striking eyes. She could hardly look upon him without coloring deeply. She was so befuddled from the night before, so confused and ashamed she could barely focus her thoughts. Seeing the virile shape of him in the day's light only upset her more. The man was determined to make her ride home with him. She'd wear the costume and wig, yes, but if one of her Mama's friends recognized her from the performance, she'd be ruined beyond repair.

Not that she wasn't already ruined.

She couldn't remember now when she'd lost control of herself the previous evening. She'd been tired, yes, and light-minded from hunger, but to let him do such things to her... Why, she hadn't just let him, she'd participated fully. If only it hadn't felt so exquisite, so free and adventurous, she could have gathered her wits and implored him to stop.

As it was, she feared she only implored him to go further, and further, until things went too far. She was reasonably certain he'd breached her maidenhead, an expression she'd not understood until she felt the sharp pain of his thrust between her thighs. So, there was her maidenhead, it seemed, and that maidenhead had been breached repeatedly, causing both consternation and pleasure.

What now? She tried to recall what happened to young ladies whose maidenheads had been breached. She'd only ever been told it was a bad thing. She wasn't told of the consequences of such. Mr. Drake had said he'd protect her, that there would be no consequences, but he'd been breathless with lust at that moment, so who knew if he spoke truth?

She sighed and put on the smoky-smelling costume, which looked far less elegant away from the theater's lights. It looked farcical, in fact. She didn't want to don the long, black wig, but she knew she must, to disguise herself as well as she could.

There was no question of lingering at the inn to take a meal, even though she felt weak with hunger. Anyway, her throat hurt too much to tolerate anything but tea and custard. As soon as she got home, she'd beg her Mama for sweet, hot, comforting foods.

Oh, Mama, if you knew what I've done, you'd be so disappointed.

She could never, ever tell her proper, God-fearing mother the truth of last night. She risked a glance at Mr. Drake as he lifted her atop his horse. He was so very handsome, yes, but so common. His shirt was filthy, and his boots scuffed. He'd probably done what he did with her to other women, seducing them with his whispers, and his intent green eyes. How else could he be so skilled at it?

She straightened her shoulders and held herself stiff as he settled behind her. She would not perch on his lap like a wanton, even though she must look scandalous in her wig and costume.

"Comfortable?" he asked.

She nodded, since it hurt to speak. Her dress provided ample padding for her riding muscles, which were sore from last night. Or perhaps she was sore from...

Oh, no. She couldn't think about it. She arranged her skirts to cover her soft-soled stage slippers and bowed her head. She intended to ride all the way to Hyde Park with her eyes down, but there were so many novel sights in London that she was hard-pressed not to lift her head and stare now and again. Busy streets, carriages and merchant carts, animals and children and all manner of signs to read.

She'd been so sheltered in Grosvenor Square, and Vienna too, so focused on her vocal studies. At home in the summers, she was kept quietly in the parlor, to do ladylike things. She'd been so constrained her whole life, compelled to be proper and perfect. Maybe that explained her lapse in behavior last night.

She stared down at Mr. Drake's hands. They, at least, were not dirty and common. In fact, his nails were clean and clipped, his fingers strong and sure as he guided the horse through the streets with subtle movements of his knees. How competent he was, how utterly manly and—

For all that was good, she could *not* still be dreaming about Mr. Drake! She'd be a lucky girl indeed if she suffered no consequences from this adventure, as he promised.

In time, they arrived in quieter and more fashionable streets. The lingering smell of smoke grew thicker and sickened her. The terrifying fire would be difficult to forget.

"We're almost there," he said, tightening his arms as if to comfort her. She tried her best to shield her face. There were too many people out and about, any of whom might recognize her. "Are you sure you don't want me to take you to your doorstep, Miss Layton? It's no difficulty at all."

She tried to picture uncouth, seductive Mr. Drake escorting her into her father's courtyard, and knocking at the Earl of Halsey's door. She shook her head hard to banish the thought.

"The park, please," she whispered. "You've been too kind already." She remembered, cringing, that she'd offered him repayment for the lodgings. He could not expect that now; she didn't want any connection to him after today.

When they reached the lane beside the park, she wished she might leap from his horse, but he prevented any quick escape by seizing her hand. "Miss Layton, there is something I must tell you," he said, holding her startled gaze. "If there is any...any result from our time together, or any need of...anything, you need only inquire of your friends at the theater after Mr. Jack Drake. One of them will surely recognize the name and tell you where to find me."

She nodded, taken aback by the gravity in his tone. "I'm sure I shall be fine." She blinked, pushing back the black wig to get a better look at him this last moment. His hair was so golden and wild. "Thank you for rescuing me," she whispered. "I would not have enjoyed perishing in a fire."

"Few enjoy such things," he said with a charming smile. His quick, impassioned kiss caught her by surprise, then he jumped down to assist her from his horse, being careful not to disorder her wig or dress.

"You must go now," she said in a begging rasp, and he complied, swinging back atop his great black stallion and wheeling away, toward the other side of town. He did not look back, even though she stood there a full minute watching the man who had breached her maidenhead disappear forever. She must forget all that now, forget such an ill-advised adventure had ever happened, or she'd be ruined in truth. When he turned onto Mount Street, she gathered her gaudy skirts and hurried toward her father's stately home.

* * * * *

Wescott arrived at his town house to find it in an uproar. The street was clogged with carriages, the horses stamping impatiently. His groom took his exhausted stallion, promising to bathe and rest the panting mount. His butler, renowned for his never-changing demeanor, looked visibly relieved when he let him in the door.

"My lord, we thought—" Color rose in his sunken cheeks. "Indeed, welcome home."

"Thank you, Jensen. Sorry it took so long. There was a fire."

The servant trailed behind him as he headed for the stairs. "My lord, there was some fear that you had come to harm. If you please, your parents are here, as well as Lady Hazel and Lady Elizabeth. Lord Augustine, Lord Marlow, and Lord Townsend have been awaiting your arrival as well. Shall I announce you in the front parlor?"

Wescott turned from the stairs with a sigh. A proper hot bath, shave, and change of clothes would have to wait. "How long have they been here?" he asked.

"Since early morning, when Lord Marlow alerted your family that you hadn't returned home after the fire. Have you taken any injury? Shall I call for a physician?"

"I'm perfectly well," he assured him.

His mother, hearing his voice, burst from the doors of the parlor before the butler could announce his arrival. She threw her arms around him, her copious dark hair in disarray, as if she'd dressed just out of sleep.

"My darling son," she cried, hugging him close. "We feared the worst when your friends came to see us. I've been so terrified." He held her as she shook against him. "Oh, Jack, are you all right?"

"I'm fine, Mama."

The Duchess of Arlington was no shrinking woman, so it pained him to see her weeping. Hazel and Elizabeth, his two youngest sisters, flung their arms around him also, crying and wailing that they'd been too worried for words, so he was momentarily stuck in the doorway, enveloped by three of the most precious women in his life.

"That's enough," said his father, arriving to rescue him. "You see he's fine, my loves. Let him sit with us and take some refreshment. He looks as if he's spent a trying night."

Wescott smiled at him in gratitude and took a seat on the divan, nodding to his three gentlemen friends as they greeted him. August, Townsend, and Marlow looked as haggard as he felt. His mother sat beside him, still sniffling, while his friends brought their chairs near. August and Marlow looked particularly peaked. He wondered if they'd slept at all.

"So where've you been?" asked Marlow with typical bluntness. "We thought you were coming behind us when we left."

"I stopped to talk to my groom. It took some convincing to get him to leave the carriage."

"The carriage did not survive," his father confirmed. He waved a hand. "But it's replaceable, and your groom arrived safely home."

"I hoped he would. The fire advanced quickly once the winds started up. I tried to go around it to come home, but I got caught up in the crowds near the theater, so I headed east. I rode with the fire at my heels for some time before we—I—came to a place I could rest."

He decided he wouldn't tell them about Miss Layton. Rescuing an actress, and proceeding to seduce her in the middle of the crisis, wasn't an act of which to be proud.

"The horse was too tired to return amidst the smoke, as was I," Wescott continued, "so I took a room at an inn near Buxton Street and spent a restless night." He squeezed his mother's hand. "I'm sorry for your worry."

"Oh, Jack." Elizabeth insinuated herself between him and their mother, and leaned into his arm. "I cried when you didn't come home. Your friends said you'd only gone the wrong way and couldn't get back, but I worried you had burned alive."

"Elizabeth," chided his father. "There's no need for such dramatics. You see your brother is well."

"I cried too," said Hazel. His sisters were a full decade younger than him, the babies of the family, though, at seventeen, Hazel would be coming out the following year. He kissed them both and thanked them for their tears of concern.

"Did you see or hear anything of Lady Ophelia Lovett?" Townsend interrupted the siblings' affection, his voice tense with worry.

Before Townsend could say anything else, his father cleared his throat, looking at Elizabeth and Hazel. His mother sent the two girls on an errand to the kitchen to fetch their guests some sweets. Once they were gone, his father paced to the window with a somber expression and looked out into the street.

"The Earl of Halsey's daughter went missing in the fire as well, Wescott. Our search parties encountered one another near the theater, where she was separated from her family. No one's seen or heard from her since last night."

Townsend started pacing, which wasn't like him. He was typically the calmest and most level-headed of their group. Wescott sent a questioning glance at Marlow and August. Could this missing Lady Ophelia be the woman Townsend had been mooning over the past few months? Wescott had never heard of her, but Towns seemed beside himself. Horrible, to think she might have gone to the theater with her family, then been lost in the roaring, spreading fire.

His father turned from the window, his imposing air of authority lending even more gravity to the discussion. "Now that you're found," he said, "we must let the Halseys know, so the searchers can focus on Lady Ophelia alone."

"I'll go," said Townsend, his face pale with lack of sleep. "Then I'll head down to search the area of the fire again."

"We'll go with you," August offered.

Marlow agreed. "Yes, three are better than one. We'll find her." He gave Townsend a fortifying nudge on the shoulder. "She might have turned up at home now that it's morning, just as Wescott's done."

"Yes," said August. "It's likely the lady found shelter and was waiting for morning's light."

The men saw themselves out, leaving Wescott alone with his parents. Their expressions were grim.

"Poor child." His mother blinked back tears. "She'd only just returned to London from abroad. Lady Halsey must be worried sick for her safety."

"I didn't know the Halseys had a daughter besides Lady Nanette," Wescott said. Nanette had been courted by scores of bachelors the year before. Halsey had money, lots of it, as well as a respected and distinguished title, which brought out the *ton*'s marriageable men in droves. If Halsey had another daughter, she'd be an apt match for Townsend, especially since he seemed full gone with love.

"There were so many people fleeing the theaters when the fire came," he said to his mother. "They must have swept Lady Ophelia along with them. Surely they wouldn't leave a fine lady to manage on her own."

"She'd just come from the stage," his father said, "and the opera house is so large. There are so many doors letting out this way and that. Perhaps, being new to the theater, she got lost finding her way out."

"How awful." The duchess shook her head. "How will her parents forgive themselves if the worst has happened?"

Her voice trailed off as his sisters returned bearing sweet buns and biscuits, which they dumped onto the tea tray in front of their brother.

"Thank you," he said, but his mind was turning on other things. "She'd just come from the stage...?" he echoed. "Lady Ophelia?"

"Yes, she performs in operas. Society is changing, isn't it?" his mother said, glancing at her daughters. "There was a time no cultured woman would appear on stage, no matter how talented. Now, titled ladies perform regularly in the salons in Bath. And Lady Ophelia's voice is surpassingly lovely, I hear. The coloratura soprano of a generation, if gossip is to be believed."

"Gossiping is bad, Mama," said Elizabeth. "You've told me many times that I'm to pay gossip no heed."

"This is good gossip," her mother said. "Lady Ophelia apparently sings so much more beautifully than...well..." She cleared her throat delicately. "Than the other women of the opera company, that she was invited to sing with Domino Nicoletti in *Armide*, and well as another opera later this fall."

"I don't know that I would have allowed it, no matter how lovely her voice is," the duke said, displaying the famous Arlington frown. "Ophelia is Hazel's age, not even out yet, and making appearances onstage. And now..."

His mother gave a quick shake of her head, wishing the topic dropped, but Wescott was thinking back over the night's events with rising anxiety.

"What does she look like?" he asked. "What does Lady Ophelia look like?"

"You might ask Townsend," his mother said. "He's carried a torch for her ever since she returned from her Viennese music school this spring."

How had his mother known of Townsend's love, when none of the rest of them had? Probably because she attended the society balls they didn't deign to appear at.

"Please, what does she look like?" His voice gained urgency, enough to capture his parents' notice.

"Do you believe you've seen her?" his mother asked.

"She is petite in stature, I believe, with pale coloring. But she would have been in costume last night," said his father. "She is blonde, isn't she, dear?" he asked his wife. "Quite blonde, like her mother?"

"She has elegant, smooth blonde hair," Hazel chimed in, proud to know something her parents didn't. "My friend Fiona saw her at a ball and said she had long, white-blonde plaits upon her head like a crown, light and shining like a princess. She's pale and tiny as a china doll, and has pretty blue eyes. She also said Townsend asked her to dance at five different balls before he got a place on her card."

"That's gossip," Elizabeth said, frowning at her sister.

Meanwhile, Wescott tried to shove down rising panic. Why, half the women in England were blonde with blue eyes. *But with smooth, white-blonde hair? Tiny like a doll?*

Lost outside the theater in a fire?

"I think..." His voice trailed off with the weight of what he had to admit, the weight of what he'd done the previous night. "I think..."

"You think what, darling?" his mother prompted.

"I think I may have seen Lady Ophelia outside the theater. But something awful has happened. A terrible mistake has been made."

His parents exchanged shocked looks. "What do you mean?" asked his father. "What sort of mistake?"

He couldn't speak for the enormity of the situation. Lady Ophelia, making her debut in the opera. The inn, his seduction...

By God, the blood on his cock. His hands curled into fists. She hadn't been on her courses. He'd seduced away her virginity thinking she was some willing trollop, then dropped her off on the edge of a park in a goddamned opera costume and wig.

"Darling?" his mother said in a soft voice. "What has happened to Lady Ophelia? You must tell us."

He gave a pointed look at his sisters. "Perhaps...in private."

"Must we go to the kitchens again?" Elizabeth asked, not at all happy.

"I think that might be best. We haven't eaten all morning, from worrying about your brother. Ask cook for a delicious pie," their mother said, shooing them to their feet.

As his sisters left, Wescott sat with his head in his hands, wondering how to begin his confession. He had a reputation as a rake, yes, but this was several steps beyond.

"The good news..." He sighed, lifting his head to meet their concerned stares. "The good news is that I'm quite certain Lady Ophelia wasn't harmed in the fire."

The bad news was that he'd harmed her another way, and would pay the price for his undisciplined behavior. He'd had no business seducing her, whether actress or lady or both.

Chapter Four: Necessary Arrangements

An hour later, Wescott sat across from his parents in his father's ducal carriage, freshly bathed, groomed, and attired in his finest embroidered coat and whitest, most starched cravat. His unfashionably long hair was pulled back in a neat queue, and he wore the diamond tiepin and solid gold rings he always took care to remove before a rollicking night at Pearl's.

He and his parents didn't speak to one another as they rode toward Grosvenor Square. What was there to say? He'd told them everything, from Lady Ophelia's rescue to his misconceptions about her state in life, to the fact that he'd done an "unforgivable thing" during their stay at the inn, which his parents understood without him going into detail.

They were embarrassed, he was ashamed, and now things must be put right, no matter how delicate and humiliating a situation it was. It showed the depth of their parental love, that they accompanied him on this errand to the Earl of Halsey's, where he must offer to marry the daughter he'd disgraced. He'd seduced away Lady Ophelia's virtue with the greatest pleasure. Now he must put up with a great deal of pain.

And this pain would not stop with him, or his parents. No, the pain and embarrassment would extend to Lady Ophelia and her well-respected family, and to Lady June, whom he could no longer marry, when he'd given her every expectation he would. It would extend to Townsend, who'd nursed a deep *tendre* for Ophelia for months now. All of this, because she'd looked so lovely and needful after her nightmare. A sigh escaped his lips.

His mother looked up at him. "You mustn't seem reluctant to do your duty, dear," she said quietly. "No matter the circumstances."

"Yes," his father agreed. "Don't be a churl."

"I'm only..." He cast about for the right word to describe his feelings. "Beside myself. I'm so sorry for what I did."

"It's not us to whom you must apologize." He heard the sharp edge to his father's comment. "You must make amends to the lady. Going forward from such a misstep...it will require great attention to her feelings."

"I know." He resisted the urge to bury his head in his hands. "I acted in such grievous misunderstanding. I had no idea who she was." He didn't know why he repeated it again. He'd told them already. "I didn't know. I didn't mean any harm."

"You're certain you didn't force her?"

His father's words hung in the air, suffocating him within the coach. He hadn't, had he? He reached to open the window, to let in some air, as he thought back over the previous night's seduction.

"I didn't. She never tried to stop me. It's only that...well..." He tried to relax his hands, but ended up fisting them again. "I'm not sure she knew what she was trying to stop me from. But she was not upset. She didn't... I swear that I didn't..." His voice cut off; he was unable to say more.

"My dear." His mother placed her fingers over his. "Whatever happened between you, it cannot be undone. You're doing what you must to protect her from the repercussions."

"If she'll even want that. Perhaps she wished to marry someone else. Perhaps she and Townsend had an understanding."

"I believe Townsend was one of many vying for her affections."

He hoped his mother was right. "I don't want to hurt her any more than I already have," he said.

"You must take care you don't," said his father. "Or you'll have me to answer to. You shall walk into Halsey's house and offer for her hand with the greatest respect and sincerity, and hope that he accepts your suit without boxing you upside the head, or taking a cane to your back."

"As for Lady Ophelia..." His mother straightened her shoulders. "I shall welcome her to our family with such affection that all the rest shall be forgotten. She'll be happy as your wife, I'll make sure of it. She'll not know a moment of regret."

"I believe it shall be Wescott's job to keep her happy," his father said. "And I trust he'll manage it, starting with your behavior toward her this day. It's best to begin a marriage in accord. Although..." He gave his wife a wink. "We began in the worst of circumstances, didn't we, Gwen? And we survived well enough."

"Indeed." She smiled in reply. "You see, Jack, good marriages start in all sorts of unfortunate ways."

He'd been a young man when he first heard the story of his parents' marriage, the way they'd met a mere day before they were to wed. His mother, according to the oft-repeated tale, had written a hysterical letter to her father only a few days later, begging him to come fetch her.

"One positive note in this debacle is that you must hold some attraction to the young lady," said Wescott's father.

There seemed no need to answer, considering what had transpired between them. He flattened his lips in a line.

"I'm sure she's lovely." His mother squeezed his arm. Wescott wished he shared their positivity. The truth was, he hardly knew Lady Ophelia. He'd fallen for her in darkness and whispered fears. In morning's light, all of it had seemed a dream.

When they pulled up in front of Halsey's Grosvenor Square mansion, the dream became all too real. Riders and carriages dotted the courtyard, the remnants of a nightlong search for the young lady of the house. The Arlingtons were met inside the door by a red-faced father, before any of them could produce calling cards.

"If it isn't *Mr. Jack Drake*," Lord Halsey said in a grating voice. "My son has just left to visit your town house, Wescott, and slap a glove in your face."

"That won't be necessary, sir." Wescott spoke in conciliatory tones, even as a flush heated his cheeks. "I've come to offer my deepest apologies to your daughter, and to make things right."

"Make things right, indeed." Halsey was spitting mad. "As if such a thing is possible. My daughter is hiding upstairs, destroyed by the shame and ignominy of her experience last night. You took her to an inn, then rode her home through London in the morning for every Tom, Dick, and Harry to gawp at."

"Sir, I—"

"What's more, you were too cowardly to bring her to her doorstep. What sort of gentleman drops a lady off unaccompanied at the edge of Hyde Park and continues on his way?"

"Sir, she asked me to take her there. I didn't know—"

The Duke of Arlington's deep voice sounded from beyond his shoulder. "My son did save your daughter from the fire, Halsey. Perhaps we might sit down and discuss things, since nothing at this point can be changed."

The earl had no choice but to usher them down the eerily silent hallway of his mansion and guide them into the front parlor. "Guthwright," he barked at his butler. "No damn tea trays. No interruptions. Let no one in, particularly Viscount Murdock," he added, naming his son.

Wescott sighed inwardly. He'd had no problem with Murdock before. Now, he was to gain a brother-in-law and enemy all at once. Lady Halsey sat stiffly on a chair by the fire, staring at him with equal parts revulsion and fury. *This is the pain you deserve*, he thought. *This is what your rakish habits have wrought.*

"It all started with a terrible misunderstanding," his father began.

"Let your son speak," Halsey said. "It's him I wish to hear from, if you please, Your Grace."

The Duke of Arlington was not used to being addressed so rudely, but in this case, he let it pass and looked at his son.

Wescott tugged the sleeve of his coat, subtly, hoping his nerves didn't show. As a marquess of the realm and a future duke, he'd been taught right from wrong, and trained to handle himself in delicate situations. He'd learned elocution and etiquette from his parents and tutors, and been drilled in the ways of polite conduct in society. It was time to put those lessons to use.

"You see, sir, I was leaving the area of the theater when I saw your daughter in need of assistance. The fire was approaching and she stood alone in her costume. I worried she wouldn't be able to escape in time because of her heavy skirts, so I brought her atop my horse to carry her. She gave her direction as Grosvenor Square, but I couldn't deliver her home with the fire spreading toward the Thames, so we turned east and rode for some time. My horse began to falter from the smoke, and I thought it best to stop at some safe place."

"And she accepted this?" her father asked in disbelief.

"She was exhausted and frightened. We barely exchanged words. I did assure her I would provide her with her own room, and that I would bear the cost, as she hadn't any money." He spread his hands. "I didn't know who she was. She gave her name as Miss Layton when I questioned her. I thought she was an actress, and I could tell she was giving me a false name, so I...I also withheld my full name and title."

"Why?" Lord Halsey's teeth were set in a line. "Why not give your real name, if you didn't intend her harm?"

"I'm sorry now that I didn't. I wasn't sure of her intentions, you see, of what might transpire if she knew my station. I thought she was an actress," he repeated, although it seemed stupid of him now. "You must understand, it was such an irregular situation."

"And you are a degenerate knave," Lord Halsey snapped.

"Halsey." His father's voice held a note of warning. "If you want his story, he will tell it, but you won't abuse him with name calling."

"Is it name calling, Your Grace? Your son and his cohort are not known about town for their moral rectitude."

"My son would have acted differently toward your daughter if she'd told him her true name and station. He's never insulted a lady or conducted himself unlawfully."

"Hasn't he?" asked Halsey, turning a deeper shade of red.

"Gentlemen," his mother said. "You are upsetting Lady Halsey."

At this, Halsey turned to his wife and, rather than offering sympathy, attacked her with vicious scolding. "This is your fault, Greta. You couldn't be happy until she was up there on stage before the entire *ton*, bringing you laud and recognition."

Lady Halsey held a handkerchief to her lips and shook her head. "You must not speak so. It was God's plan. God gave her that voice—"

"And you used it to ruin her. If she hadn't been at that theater, singing that blasted opera with Signore Whatever-His-Name-Is—"

"And if you'd let me wait for her backstage, rather than dragging me to the carriage, none of this would have happened," she cried. "Why couldn't you stay to watch your own daughter, with her beautiful soprano?"

"I couldn't stay because of all the disgusting men in the audience gawking at her, and I wasn't leaving you behind. It's bad enough my daughter is on stage, without my wife milling by the alley doors, amidst all those dancers and musicians."

His mother rose and moved to Lady Halsey, who was crying copious tears now. "Please, I'm sure neither of you meant for Lady Ophelia to come to harm. And she hasn't come to harm. My son encountered her in her moment of need and very likely saved her life. What is that, if not God's plan?"

Wescott glared at his future in-laws, wondering what God had to do with any of this. "At any rate, sir, I've exposed your daughter to the danger of unsavory gossip, and I beg you to let me repair my mistakes. With your permission, I'll marry Lady Ophelia and afford her all the honor and privilege my title allows." He saw the glint of approval in his mother's eyes and pressed on with his speech. "Sir, your daughter is not to be held responsible for the events of last evening, nor you, Lady Halsey. The trespass was mine."

He stood in company with his shame and faced them all: the tearful mother, the angry father, his own conflicted parents. His father spoke first.

"Well said, Wescott. Now, provided Lady Ophelia is in agreement, we should begin making marital arrangements." The duke gave a diplomatic flourish to the succinct request. "My son will be honored to unite the Arlington peerdom with the esteemed Halsey line."

"Lady Ophelia shall be in agreement," said her father. "Now that you've left her no other choice."

The negotiations that followed were complex, fraught, and frequently testy, but within an hour's time, they'd drawn up a preliminary contract of marriage, including gifts, dowries, settlements, and plans for the procurement of a special license, so the wedding could take place within the week.

There was, after all, no time to delay. They'd been seen together, and gossips would talk. A story could be spun of rescue and romance, but only if they wed quickly and disappeared to the country, before the finer details were brought out. He'd been inside Lady Ophelia, had stripped her of her virginity, even if he'd pulled away before he'd spent. She must have the security of marriage.

After they put signatures to paper to seal the accords, Wescott stood and faced Lord Halsey.

"Sir, is it possible to speak with Lady Ophelia before I go?"

Halsey practically growled his rebuttal. "What for? Even if she wanted to see you, she's in no condition to receive visitors after last night, particularly gentlemen callers."

"He's hardly a gentleman caller," his father said. "They're to be married. Let Wescott speak with his fiancée."

Lord Halsey wasn't happy about it, but his wife offered to accompany Wescott to her daughter's rooms. It was a relief to leave the drawing room after so much antagonism. For him, the experience had been nearly as bad as escaping the fire.

"I'm not sure you'll receive a warm reception," she said as she led him up the stairs. "My daughter's mind is quite...unsettled...from her...your...adventure."

Like him, Lady Halsey barely knew how to handle the situation. He thought longingly of a time years in the future, when this awkward betrothal would be forgotten, or at least never mentioned.

Lady Halsey went into her daughter's room first. After an uncomfortably long time, during which Wescott expected to be dismissed, she reemerged and beckoned him into the outer drawing room. It was a private, feminine space, a smaller echo of the larger parlor downstairs. His bride-to-be stood looking out the window, dressed in a maidenly white gown with a pale sage sash. Her blonde, braided hair was pinned atop her head in the crown Hazel had described, baring her neck and slumping shoulders. She looked so bereft his heart thumped in sympathy.

"So...you've told her we're to be married?" he whispered to her mother. He'd expected more of a reaction, at least for her to turn around.

"I've told her," the woman replied through tight lips. She took up a chair near the fireplace. Wescott approached Lady Ophelia, remembering the bewigged sorceress of the night before, with her bright, full dress. Now she looked small and fragile, in her gauzy, understated column of a gown. How could this be the same woman? He clasped his hands and stopped a few paces behind her.

"My lady."

54

She turned her head to the side, running small fingers over her pale throat. "I'm sorry, but I can't speak," she said in a whisper. "My voice has not returned."

"I'm sorry to hear that."

His own voice sounded too loud in the silent room, especially after her whisper.

"I'm sure your lost voice is only temporary. At least I hope so. At any rate..." He cleared his throat, feeling like an ass. "Thank you for seeing me. I must begin by apologizing with the most abject regret for my behavior last night."

"Last night..." She repeated the words in a pained murmur. "I cannot think of it. I cannot even look at you."

He frowned at her exposed nape. "Nevertheless, I am here."

"Yes, you are here to perform your duty, and ask for my hand. My mother says you are a gentleman, but I can hardly believe it."

Her whisper held as much rancor as a shouted insult. "Lady Ophelia," he replied, as calmly as he could. "Neither of us wished for this to happen. The unorthodox circumstances, the fire—"

"Fire or no, it has ended in disaster. I should have refused your assistance." She shook her head. "I'm ruined now. That's the word, though no one is using it."

"You're not ruined, because I'm here." He grasped for patience in the face of her disdain. "Lady Ophelia, please accept my deepest apologies for my conduct last night. It was wrong of me to lie down with you. That was my fault."

She pressed her forehead to the window, letting out a breath. "I wish I'd made you leave," she whispered.

"I worked very hard to ensure you wouldn't. It's pointless to dwell upon it at this point. We must be married and make the best of things."

"The best of things."

He barely heard her peevish exhalation. Her shoulders drew up tight.

"Yes, the best of things," he repeated. "There's nothing else to do. My lady, I wish you would turn to look at me. Otherwise, you won't recognize me at the altar. I'm not much like Jack Drake, not on a typical day."

For a long moment, she made no movement. Then finally, slowly, she turned, her gaze faltering and lighting somewhere in the middle of his chest, upon his shining coat buttons. She looked so different now, here, in her childhood room, clean and wan, with her appearance so terrifyingly ladylike. Her blue eyes looked vivid as cornflowers in May.

He must look different to her too, with his hair tamed and his stubble shaven, turned out in his best finery from head to toe. Did it offer any solace that she was marrying a member of the peerage rather than a common mister off the street?

"My real name is John Daniel Worthington Drake," he began, when her gaze finally traveled to his face. "I'm the eldest son of the Duke of Arlington, titled the Marquess of Wescott, although my mother and sisters still call me Jack on occasion, when they wish to make me feel like a boy."

But he was no boy, and she was no actress. He was a rake, and she his offended victim. She exuded delicacy and refinement—and helpless anger. He could hardly believe they'd lain together with such tender abandon. He'd made love to her mere hours ago, enjoyed her breathless caresses, and now she regarded him with vitriol and shame. He wished to reach for her, to see if she could possibly be the same woman, but he didn't dare. Her expression and stance didn't welcome familiarity, however they'd conducted themselves the night before.

"It's my pleasure to meet you," she whispered in her barely-there voice, in a tone that let him know the sentiment was not true. She did not offer her hand. "You *are* quite different than I remember, and I suppose you must realize by now that I'm not who I said I was."

"If only we'd been honest," he said, attempting a smile.

"I chose not to be honest," she whispered. "And now..."

Now, she was clearly aghast at the prospect of marrying him. She was devastated by the situation, as he was. He believed she downright loathed him for his part in her ruination. He could see it in the way she held herself, in the way she wouldn't meet his gaze.

"My lord, if you please..." She rubbed her forehead as her rosebud lips pursed in a frown. "I'm very tired from...from last night. Perhaps you might call upon me some other time." She was already turning away when the door burst open.

"Lady Ophelia, I wish to marry you!"

Wescott and his betrothed spun as one toward the other side of the room, where a disheveled and wild-eyed Townsend stood ramrod straight, breathing full-on, as if he'd run across the whole of London to make his declaration.

"You may think I'm being impulsive, but I'm not." Lord Townsend gazed, transfixed, at Lady Ophelia, his hand pressed to his heart. "I love you, dear lady, more than anyone in the world, and it would be my honor to marry you without question or hesitation, no matter your current situation."

Ophelia turned to Wescott, her eyes wide, and whispered, "Who, my lord, is that?"

Chapter Five:
For Better or Worse

Ophelia stared in shock as the young man strode toward her, running his fingers through disordered black hair.

"My lady," he began, halting a respectable distance away. "My deepest apologies for frightening you. It is only that I must—" He paused, out of breath. Had he sprinted up the stairs? "It is only that I must speak my heart, and offer you an option besides marriage to this—this— If I may be frank, my lady, he is a creature of the lowest moral habits, an inveterate scoundrel."

The man gestured toward Mr. Drake. No, the Marquess of Wescott. He drew himself up in return.

"A 'scoundrel,' Townsend?" he repeated, with a taut edge to his voice.

"No, Wescott." He held up a hand. "I will speak without interruption from you, you blackguard. I have only just become aware of what transpired last evening, of the disrespectful and scurrilous way you conducted yourself whilst Lady Ophelia was in your care. It was wrong of you to ride with her through London and expose her to gossip, and imperil her good reputation with your—your selfish manipulations."

"You're saying a lot of big words," the marquess retorted, "but making very little sense."

"I used to regard you well, but no longer. Anyone who would carelessly risk such a worthy lady's reputation—"

"Her reputation shall survive, Townsend. Lady Ophelia and I are betrothed to be married."

He shook his head. "A betrothal can be broken. This betrothal *must* be broken, for she deserves far better than you."

"Let me guess," said Wescott acidly. "She deserves you?"

"Yes. I love her. I'll treat her with the respect that is owed her, every day of her life."

"Strong feelings for a woman who doesn't even know who you are," Wescott snapped back.

Ophelia watched as they argued, and had the sense the two men, in less fraught circumstances, might be friends. In fact, the man named Townsend looked much the way the marquess had appeared last night. His coat was mussed and his cuffs not quite clean. His ebony hair, while not as long as Wescott's, looked equally straggled and wild.

Townsend turned back to her, taking a step forward in appeal. "Lady Ophelia, you must break your betrothal to this man. Please understand, he does not have the tenderness of feeling, the concern and admiration that I carry in my heart."

"For me?" she whispered.

Wescott snickered beside her. She wished him to be quiet, for he was not being kind.

"I'm sorry, Lord Townsend," she said, rubbing her throat. "I know we've made an acquaintance. We danced, didn't we? Once?"

"Indeed, only once, to my dismay. Before then, I admired you at other balls and dances, and observed your vocal recital at Lady Garland's party in June. Your voice bespelled me. Since then, I've attended every one of your performances at the theater. If only I'd been the one to rescue you last night, you would not have been so disrespected, I assure you."

"See here," Wescott said. "You did not rescue Lady Ophelia. I did. You don't understand the circumstances. I suggest you stop your ridiculous exclamations of love and see yourself out of the lady's drawing room, since this entire situation has nothing to do with you."

Townsend turned to her mother. "Lady Halsey, you must want better for your daughter. You must sense, with your maternal instinct, the absolute sincerity of my love."

Lady Halsey wrung her hands. "My daughter has already been promised to Lord Wescott," she said. "The contract has been signed."

"By her?" Townsend held out a hand to Ophelia. "Have you signed it, lady?"

"Don't touch her," Wescott growled.

Ophelia was taken aback by the possessiveness in his threatening words. As for Lord Townsend, she'd never seen a man behave so, spouting love talk and soulful declarations as if they'd courted one another for years.

"Have you signed it?" Townsend pressed her, his voice like a plea.

She shook her head. She had not read it, signed it, or learned anything of what was in it.

"I'm a marquess, you see, the same as him." When he gestured toward Wescott, Ophelia noticed that the other man's hands looked ready to strike. "I'm a duke's son."

"So am I, you utter buffoon."

Lord Townsend ignored him, speaking only to her, and occasionally darting a look toward her mother. "I'll be Duke of Lockridge one day, my lady, with a holding as great as his, and you can be my duchess. Unlike him, I adore you. I have adored you since I first laid eyes on you, and reflect often on your lightness and grace."

"Are you quite finished?" Wescott's voice sounded like a warning, but Townsend was not cowed. He moved toward the man, who was just a little bit taller and broader than him.

"I am not finished." Townsend tipped up his chin. "I don't care about the damage you caused to her reputation, Wescott. I don't care if people gossip. I am prepared to marry her nonetheless."

"I rescued her, so I shall marry her. If the gossips——"

"Damn the gossips. They can just as well gossip about me instead of you. At least I will love and respect the lady in a way you never can. I know you, Wes. I know your moral shortcomings, and your wicked, damnable habits."

Her mother gasped. Wescott's spine snapped even tighter and straighter than before. "Continue that line of argument, and you'll regret it." His voice sounded low and sharp as a knife. "I know you, too, Townsey. I have plenty of stories to tell regarding your own 'wicked habits,' but I won't, to protect the ladies' sensibilities. Have some manners, you mad, lovesick calf, or I'll use my fists to teach you some."

"That's your way, isn't it? You're unfailingly brutish and rude."

"No, brutish and rude is intruding on a lady's privacy and behaving in this manic fashion."

"My lady." Now he did take Ophelia's hand, and went down on one knee. "Tell Wescott you will not marry him, that you prefer to make a life with me."

Ophelia's thoughts spun. Townsend's gaze was so intense, his eyes a vivid amber-gold beneath dark lashes. Wescott was at her other side, his hovering presence radiating anger. If the men had been friends once, she feared they never would be again. As for which she would choose for a husband—at the moment, she didn't want either one.

"I don't know," she whispered.

"Why won't you speak aloud?" Townsend asked. "What have they said to silence you?"

"She's lost her voice. Get off your knees. Lady Ophelia cannot marry you, because she's betrothed to me. We're to marry within the week, by special license." He paused and stared very intently into Lord Townsend's eyes. "She cannot marry you, Towns. It's not possible."

"What do you mean?"

"Damn it, Townsend, it's not possible at this point."

For the first time since he'd entered, Townsend was silent.

"It's *not possible*," Wescott repeated. "Do you understand?"

Townsend looked disbelieving, then so furiously angry that Ophelia took a step back. The next events happened so quickly, she could hardly separate them in her mind. Townsend lunged at Lord Wescott and next she knew, fists were flying. Her mother screamed and went to the door, calling for help. The men shouted curses and insults as they pushed back and forth.

In the midst of the fracas, Wescott's sleeve ripped, along with Townsend's collar. Her mother shrieked at them to stop fighting, but they only shed their coats and threw them aside, and tussled like common boys in an alley, throwing punches and shouting more profane oaths. *Blackguard, devil, damnable whoremonger.* Ophelia stood with her back to the window, her hand pressed to her mouth. The things they said shocked her, but the sound of their fists striking one another shocked her more.

"Please stop," she whispered. "Please stop."

Her mute pleas had no effect. The men didn't stop brawling until Lord Halsey and the Duke of Arlington strode into the room, flanked by the house's heftiest footmen. They pulled Wescott and Townsend apart as her mother led her away from the chaos. She realized then that she was crying, tears soaking her cheeks.

Her mother guided her to her bedroom and sat with her on the edge of the bed.

"Mama," she whispered, "I don't want to wed either of those men. I'm not ready to be married. I've barely begun my singing career."

"Your singing career is over for now. There'll be a scandal if you don't wed the marquess. People saw you together, and they'll talk because you're the Earl of Halsey's daughter. Didn't I tell you for years how important it was to adhere to proprieties?" She gripped her arm to the point of pain. "You've done this to yourself."

"I could go to Europe and sing there for a couple of years, until the scandal's forgotten!" Desperation—and fear—made her rasping voice tremble. "I could go back to Vienna and study a bit longer, until all this is forgotten."

"There's no 'forgetting' what you've done." Her voice was not kind, not gentle the way she needed at that moment. "You've got to marry Lord Wescott, Ophelia. You haven't any other choice."

"But Lord Townsend..." Her chin trembled. "Wouldn't he be better? He seems kinder and more loving than Lord Wescott. He said he loves me and would marry me."

"I don't think he will anymore," she said tightly. "You must marry Lord Wescott now, for better or worse. As for a career onstage, you must forget that dream. It's ruined for you now, daughter. He will not allow you to perform publicly after this, if he permits you to sing at all."

* * * * *

Wescott wed Lady Ophelia in a small, private ceremony in his parents' garden, looking as dignified as anyone might with two somewhat-healed black eyes. Since his best coat had been ruined in the fight with Townsend, he wore his second best, a dark blue coat that clashed with Ophelia's daffodil-yellow gown.

As for his bride, she cried through the entire service. He tried not to take it personally, but she appeared so miserable, so completely devastated that it was hard for him to stand beside her throughout the charade. She said her vows in a bitter, tremulous tone, her contempt for him perfectly clear to all in attendance, now that her voice was restored.

Well, nearly restored. He'd saved her from the fire, but apparently the smoke had weakened her sensitive, Vienna-trained vocal cords. He was sorry about that, sorry about so many things. He was sorry Townsend wasn't at his wedding, that his old friend had left London in a fury after swearing he'd never speak to him again. Marlow and

Augustine were here though, supporting him through one of the most appalling days of his life.

When the ceremony was finally over, there was the wedding luncheon to endure. His parents opened their town house to hundreds of guests so they could pretend there'd been a normal, happy wedding between two people in love. He and Ophelia circulated to greet everyone, but managed not to speak a word to each other. As the guests thinned out, it became harder to avoid his sulky bride.

"Darling." His mother joined him, taking his hand. "Your sisters are leaving with Louisa and her husband soon, to visit the children. You ought to say goodbye."

All four of his sisters, two of them happily married, gathered around, wishing him well.

"Lady Ophelia is so pretty," said Louisa, the eldest. "She seems...very sweet."

"Thank you," he replied. "I'm happy that we've wed."

It wasn't the truth, but well-mannered gentlemen followed the script. His father joined them, along with Wescott's only brother, Gareth, who'd taken a rare day away from his studies to attend the "happy event." So many kind wishes, so many congratulations from his family, and all Wescott could think about was how much he didn't want to be married, and how mournful Ophelia looked.

"I cried on my wedding day too ," his mother confided, once her other children had left.

"I know, Mama."

"Some brides can't help the tears. There's so much anxiety, so many emotions. Once your father and I came to understand one another, there was plenty of room for love to develop between us."

"Once we 'came to understand one another,'" the duke echoed with a half-smile. "Was it as easy as all that?"

His mother's smooth skin deepened in a blush. "Marriage is never easy, but it's worth it to try your best. I agree with Louisa. Ophelia seems a lovely girl."

"She is lovely," said Wescott, watching her across the hall, chatting with some members of her family.

"And she'll adore Wescott Abbey. Oxfordshire is so pretty at this time of year. The two of you will have time to learn more about each other as you set up your home."

He wasn't sure Ophelia would adore doing anything with him, but his parents had been kind enough to refurbish his ancestral estate several years ago, when they first started hounding him about marriage. Wescott Abbey was the original seat of the Arlington holdings, a castle-like stronghold that had served as a religious retreat in ancient times. It was considered one of the most striking manors in England, with multiple towers, hidden rooms, winding stone staircases, and expansive gardens and meadows.

"I'm sure Ophelia will love the Abbey," he agreed. "It's the perfect time to go there, now that the Season's nearly over."

"And now that you're married." She tapped him lightly with her fan, then snapped it open, fluttering it in a rare show of nerves. If only a marriage could succeed on his mother's hopes alone, but he feared it wouldn't be so easy.

As he turned with her, he saw Marlow and Augustine lingering by the door. "Excuse me, Mama."

"Yes, go say goodbye to your friends. Oh, Jack, what a shame Townsend couldn't be here today." Her gaze flitted over what remained of the bruises on his face. He wished the damned things would fade away. He walked to his friends, affecting a light, easy manner. Knowing him as they did, they weren't fooled.

"Good show, Wescott," said August. "You played the contented groom very well. I only saw one or two instances of the Arlington frown."

"I tried my best." He glanced across the room at Ophelia. She too was forcing a smile, conversing with some of her parents' friends.

"Uh-oh, there's the frown a third time," said Marlow, elbowing August. "Honestly, Wes, she seems a good sort, your new wife. Augustine and I conversed with her for some time, and to me, she seems the kind of bride who won't cause a lot of trouble. She's thoughtful, well-spoken, and polite."

"Indeed she is." August kept his voice low, but Wescott caught the note of reproof. "Don't see how you mistook her for a strumpet."

"Are you here to support me or scold me?"

"A little of both. See here, Wes." Now Marlow's tone darkened, too. "What were you thinking, bedding that lady while London was burning? Does nothing dampen your libido? Now you're getting married before any of us were ready for it, and you've betrayed Townsend—"

"Didn't betray him," Wescott said. "I didn't realize he was in love with her. Ophelia had no idea who he was."

"Not betrayal then, but you've angered him to the point he's bolted for France. We'll be lucky if he doesn't join the godforsaken army, the mood he's in. Now August and I are on our own, when there used to be four of us."

"With Pearl's closed by the fire," August added morosely. "There's no point even staying in town."

The damned fire. Wescott wished he knew who'd started it. He'd run him through with a sword a dozen or so times, or if it was a woman, give her a hiding she'd never forget. Now he was married, his best friends were cross, his parents were disappointed, his in-laws were embarrassed, and his bride... Well, she cared for him about as much as one cared to slop through a pile of muck in the gutter.

"You're welcome at Wescott Abbey over the winter," he said. "It's an old, drafty place, but there are beautiful views from the towers."

Marlow shuddered. "Yes, I'm sure I'll enjoy those views while I'm shivering under a pile of blankets before the fire."

"Don't come then." He shrugged. "Go to France and keep Townsend out of the army. He'd make a terrible soldier."

"We can't go anywhere until after my parents' ball," said Marlow. The Earl and Countess of Warren always threw a grand bash near the end of the Season. "I wish the two of you weren't running off to the country so quickly. Lady Wescott could have graced the gathering with a song."

He shook his head. "She can't sing right now, or practice. The fire's done something to her voice. She says she may never sing again."

"Does she want to sing again, now she's married?" asked August. "Will you let her?"

"Not in damned Drury Lane." He doubtless produced the fourth Arlington frown. "No public stages, no lights, no madmen like Townsend running after her declaring their love. It's just as well she's lost her voice. I hope it stays away until our nursery's full, and she loses interest in performing."

"Spoken like a true domineering husband." Marlow raised a brow. "Does she know who she's marrying? Does she know anything about your affinity for disciplinary pleasures?"

"I should hope not."

"Perhaps she does," said August. "Maybe that's why she sobbed as she said her vows. It was rather uncomfortable to watch."

"It's his wedding day, for God's sake. Don't say things like that." Marlow bumped him on the shoulder. "He's the first of us to marry, poor fellow. I dread *your* wedding day, Lord Augustine, and pity whatever lady has the misfortune to marry you."

"Not as much as I pity your future bride, Mad Marlow."

Heat rose in the blond viscount's cheeks. "I've told you how much I hate that name."

"If only it wasn't so fitting."

Before Marlow and August could start arguing in earnest, Wescott held up a hand. "It's been a long and trying day, but I suppose it's what I deserve. Thank you for coming to the ceremony, either way."

"Wouldn't miss it," said Augustine. Marlow nodded, but Townsend's absence hung unspoken between them. The four of them had been friends for as long as they could remember, spending dinners and playtimes and holidays together, because their parents were close friends. All of them were the oldest, the first-born sons, sharing the pressures of tutors, rules, and expectations for the future. They'd fallen out before, over little things, but they always came back together. This rift with Townsend went deeper. He'd up and left the country.

"We'll come to the Abbey, too," Marlow promised. "When winter's most bleak. We'll try to bring Townsend if he comes home from France."

"Of course, if you like. If he wants to."

Nearly everyone had left the wedding luncheon by now. From the busy chatter of voices and congratulations, only quieter conversations remained. His friends would leave soon, too. They were searching for the words to excuse themselves. After that, it would be him and Ophelia, and an entire life to figure out together.

"Just because it started badly..." Wescott paused, pulling at his cuffs. "Well, that doesn't mean it will continue badly, does it? The lady will come around."

"How it starts means nothing," said August. "It's how you go on from here."

"I agree," said Marlow. "The marriage will be what you make it. If she starts crying again in the bedroom tonight, just spank the tears out of her."

"That's terrible advice." August turned on Marlow. "We're all miserable that Wescott's married now, but we don't want him to fail, because that would make everything even worse."

As if things could be worse. As August and Marlow started to bicker again, Wescott thought he'd already failed beyond repairing. When his friends took their leave, he crossed to his bride and reached for her hand, trying to ignore the coolness in her expression.

"Lady Wescott," he said. "What an extraordinary day it's been."

"Indeed," she agreed. "An extraordinary wedding day."

And it's not over. He didn't say it aloud, but surely she realized there was more to come. A wedding night, though she'd not come to his bed a virgin. He wondered if that would make it easier or harder to consummate this marriage of necessity.

"Shall we take our leave?" he asked. "I'll be pleased to escort you to your new home in town."

"If you wish, my lord." She met his eyes just for a moment.

"You needn't 'my lord' me now that we're married. You may call me Wescott, or Jack if you prefer." He could see the name Jack reminded her of their illicit night together, and everything that had led them to now. He doubted she would ever call him by that name. "I'll call you Ophelia," he said when she didn't answer, "and starting tonight, we shall try to make the best of things, my dear."

Chapter Six:
Starting Tonight

Ophelia lay in her new bed, wondering what would happen if she locked the door against her husband. Was she brave enough to do that?

No. She'd avoided him as much as she could to this point, but her choices were at an end. She was married to Lord Wescott because he'd swept her away at the inn with his capable virility. He'd made her his marchioness, so she now outranked her parents and siblings, even as her dreams of novelty and adventure were ended. She would be a proper English wife to a proper English peer, and that would be her life forever after. She didn't even know the man, not really, and here she was in his house.

Her prison, more or less.

She barely noted her surroundings, although her new suite of rooms was luxuriously appointed with flowers and furnishings, and candles that barely smoked. The bed was soft and inviting, the fireplace warm, and the adjoining dressing room larger than her entire suite of rooms had been in Vienna. All her clothing and personal items had already been set out and organized by Lord Wescott's bevy of efficient servants, so she might decide what must be packed for their journey to Oxfordshire.

She had nothing to complain about, except that she'd been forced into a marriage she didn't want, because he'd taken advantage of her so easily. He stripped her of her virtue like she was a mere plaything, so she must marry him and let go of her freedom, her singing career, and the chance to perform and travel. He'd taken away all her hopes and dreams. Just looking at him brought intense feelings of regret, anger, and shame. She wished he would not come to her, but he'd said that awful thing about starting tonight. *Starting tonight, we shall make the best of things.*

It was the second time he'd said they would "make the best of things," but she didn't care for that sentiment. She would rather blame him and hate him, and mourn for all she'd lost. Now she would become exactly like her mother, stifling in a marriage she didn't want to a man she'd never really loved.

And that man had a lawful right to her body. Her mother had touched briefly on that topic, had told her she must perform her "marital duties" once she and the marquess were wed. Ophelia had hinted that she needed more information, but her mother's lips had wrenched closed as soon as she spoke of it. "I would think you already know enough," she'd said under her breath.

Her mother and father had argued about her after the marquess came to offer marriage. She'd heard their shouting through the walls, and all the servants had, too. Her Mama said she'd "fallen" because she'd been too sheltered, and her father yelled she'd been too long away from polite society, off training at that "damned opera school."

But her music school had been strict and proper, her Viennese chaperones unbending in the pursuit of proper etiquette. She'd hardly had a chance to talk to the other girls, much less a gentleman of Lord Wescott's age and experience. No one had ever spoken the slightest word of what a man might do to a woman after he comforted her from a nightmare. If they had, she might not be in this situation.

Now she was fallen, and married, with everything in her life gone awry. When her husband knocked, she pulled the sheets and blankets up to her chin, her fine silken sleep gown tangling between her trembling legs. If she didn't speak, perhaps he would go away.

"Ophelia?"

Of course he wouldn't go away. His voice came through the door between their bedrooms, and then he appeared, tall and forbidding. Mr. Jack Drake, the Marquess of Wescott. Her husband. He walked toward her bed, clothed in a robe of dark, embossed silk. It made his hair look darker, his shoulders wider and more intimidating. His eyes moved over her huddled form.

"Are you cold, Lady Wescott?"

He used the new title to remind her they were married, that he had power over her. She felt threatened, and did not answer him. She wished there were more candles. She wished it wasn't night.

"What do you think of your new rooms?" he asked. "Of course, we'll leave for the country soon, but this is my favorite house to use in the city. Have you settled in? Is the bed comfortable?"

He sat on the edge of it, watching her, expecting an answer. She clenched her fingers on the blankets and managed a bleak, "Yes, my lord."

His lips curved in a taunting smile. "Come, Ophelia. You're not afraid on your wedding night, are you? The one bright spot in this hasty marriage is that we're known to one another, at least in this way. You can't be afraid of something you've already experienced, and, I daresay, enjoyed."

Enjoyed? She'd barely known what he was about that night. Perhaps she'd found some pleasure at the end, but that was when she was caught in his spell, before she realized how very badly he'd behaved toward her.

"So you want to do...that...again?" Now that she'd found her tongue, the question came out cloaked in bitterness.

He made an impatient sound, tugging down the bed sheets. "It's customarily done after a marriage. You can't have children any other way. Do you like children, Ophelia?"

"Would it matter if I didn't?"

He'd pulled the sheets down enough to reveal her chest and shoulders. Her sheer, beribboned nightgown had been purchased especially for her wedding night, but she felt like an imposter wearing it. She didn't feel pretty, or wifely. She brought her hands up to shield her breasts, lest he see the pink tips of her nipples.

"Don't hide from me," he said. "Why are you cross? You liked my touch enough the night of the fire."

"I don't want to talk about the fire." She scooted back from him, pulling the sheets with her. The rush of emotion startled her even as she blurted out her thoughts. "I hated the night of the fire and I'm ashamed of what you did to me. I never wanted to be married in this hurried, embarrassing fashion, by special license. I especially didn't want to marry you."

"Is that so?" He held her gaze, his regard unsympathetic. "Then you ought to have stopped me when I nudged your thighs apart."

"I didn't know what you were doing. How was I to know?"

He sighed in irritation. "We can't do anything about it now. Am I such an awful prospect? Women competed for my affections on the marriage market. Am I not handsome enough? Rich enough for your tastes?"

"It has nothing to do with that."

"But you don't wish to be married to me?"

"No, I don't. I don't wish to be married at all." To her horror, she burst into tears, her voice breaking as she tried to hold herself together. "I don't think I can forgive you for what you did to me at the inn, or forgive myself. I feel so...so ashamed about everything."

He frowned at her tears, as if they made him angry. At the same time, he pulled her into his arms so firmly that she couldn't resist him. He was warm, solid, but still, really, a stranger. It made her cry harder, even as he held her close.

"You needn't feel ashamed anymore, my little songbird," he said. "I've made you an honest woman."

She hated that expression, *an honest woman,* and shuddered at the pet name, *little songbird,* which seemed kind and insulting at once. She tried to push away from him, but he wouldn't let her. Now that she'd begun crying, the tears gushed out of her, along with all the feelings she'd tried to keep at bay.

"I don't like that I am one of *those* women," she sobbed.

"You aren't. By God, I wish you wouldn't feel that way. We're married. You're my wife."

"But I don't want to be your wife. I don't want to be anyone's wife, not after all of this. I should have told you who I was that night," she cried, hating the fear she felt. "You should have told me who you were."

"But I didn't, and you didn't, and here we are. My dear girl, what shall we do with all this guilt and angst?" He tilted her head up, forcing her to look at him. "Would it help if I punished you for what you did?"

She blinked into his wide, green eyes. "If you *punished me*?"

"Yes. If your guilt is so great you can't get past it, it doesn't bode well for our marriage or our intimate life. I believe the best solution is for me to punish you for your perceived transgressions at the inn, so you can forgive yourself, as I have. A good spanking should do the trick."

He looked bigger and scarier than ever, saying those words.

"A spanking?" she said, trying again to pull away. "I don't want you to spank me. I wouldn't like that at all."

"That's the point," he said, terrifyingly sure of himself. "A proper spanking, one that hurts you to an adequate degree, will allow you to express true remorse. And once you've paid that price for your bad behavior, both of us will be able to move on."

Move on? To what? Her marital duties, which he clearly intended to demand of her? She shook her head. "No. I don't like that idea."

"Well, I do. It's rather late to cut a switch or fix a birch rod. Come with me." Before she knew what he was up to, he'd plucked her from her bed and walked her toward her dressing room. "I'm sure you've an adequate hairbrush we can use."

"A hairbrush? Lord Wescott!" She should have resisted, or dragged her feet or something, but that seemed childish, and he surely didn't mean to...

"Ah, this will work." He lifted the largest wooden hairbrush from her dressing room table and sat in the chair. "Come, lie over my lap."

With those words, he tugged her over to him and bent her across his knees. She resisted now, shocked by this turn of events. He couldn't truly intend to spank her. Girls had been disciplined with the occasional cane stroke or two at the music school, girls who tested the rules, but never her. "My lord, please," she said, struggling to right herself. "You can't do this."

"As your husband, I can do it. In fact, it's my duty." He held her easily, for he was so much larger and stronger. "You'll feel much better when you've been properly spanked."

With those words, he lifted the hem of her nightgown, folding it above her waist. Her face flooded with heat. She couldn't believe he was doing this. She pressed her thighs together, too humiliated now to try to squirm away. The marquess circled her waist with one arm, then brought the flat, polished side of the hairbrush to her bottom with a sharp, crisp *thwack*.

Ouch. Oh, no. She reared across his lap, because it hurt even more than she'd imagined it would. A hot, throbbing ache suffused her arse cheeks, and then another blow fell, and another, one on top of the other like molten rain.

"Oh, please, my lord, that's enough."

"Enough?" He scoffed. "I've just begun, and I'm hardly using my strength." He said this conversationally, even as the spanking continued.

"Please, Wescott, it hurts so much." She jerked about without even meaning to, until he was forced to tighten his arm around her middle. "Ow, it hurts, *it hurts*."

"It's supposed to hurt."

She peered back at him in a panic, beating her arms upon the floor. His expression was stern, his bearing upright. Her new, spacious dressing room had become a very painful and unfriendly place. She'd certainly never be able to sit in this chair after being spanked like this.

"You must stop, my lord, please. I can't bear anymore."

"Remember why you're being punished. It must hurt a little, don't you think, in light of your shame and regret?"

"It hurts a lot." She kicked a leg back at an especially hard smack. Oh, she must look a sight with her bare bottom exposed to his gaze, and her carefully arranged hair going tousled as she bucked upon his lap. "Please, I can't survive anymore. A husband...a husband should not hurt his wife like this."

The smacks stopped, but he didn't release her. She was breathing hard, almost crying.

"Lower your feet, if you please." His stern voice was the antipathy of all her pleading. "You nearly kicked me, Ophelia. Put your toes on the floor."

"I can't," she sobbed. "Why are you doing this? It's our wedding night."

She twitched, then trembled, as his warm hand cupped her arse. His palm rubbed back and forth, replacing the stinging pain of the hairbrush. His gentle touch only seemed to intensify the lingering sting. "Indeed, it's our wedding night, Lady Wescott," he said in that same stern voice. "And as your husband, it's my right to discipline you when you require it. I shall take that charge seriously and guide you when I need to. You all but begged for punishment to expiate your guilt."

It was true she'd felt trapped by guilt, stuck in a never-ending spiral of anxiety about the way they'd met. But how could this help? She hung her head and squeezed her eyes shut.

"Once you've been punished," he went on, "you'll find it easier to move past your guilty feelings. Now, you must submit to the rest of your spanking so you can feel better afterward."

"How...how much longer will it be?"

"I'll stop when you feel punished enough. You must trust me, now that we're wed."

God save her. Of all the men to marry, why did it have to be him? Now she must submit to his discipline, because screaming or crying for help wouldn't work, not in his house, where the servants were loyal to him. With an aggrieved sigh, she lowered her feet to the floor as he'd instructed her.

"That's better," he said. "Hold this position, if you please."

"I don't please." She braced herself for the pain to begin again. "But I don't suppose I have a choice."

A moment later, the spanking resumed. Oh, the hairbrush stung so badly. Perhaps it would be possible to wash away her sinful behavior through this agony alone, for it was the worst pain she'd ever felt. Another blow, and another. Sometimes he alternated cheeks, landing a sharp smack right in the middle, and she'd smother a shriek and think how much she despised him. Some servant, somewhere, had to be hearing this spanking, and her crying, which only added to her punishment's shame.

* * * * *

Wescott shifted in the chair so his new wife couldn't feel his jutting erection. He was spanking her for earnest reasons, to mitigate her guilt, but he was enjoying himself in the process. Her pert, round arse was so perfectly formed, he was half tempted to lift her and impale her immediately upon his cock.

But no, that would be bad form. He was punishing her for a reason, and he had to take care to do it right. He had to hold her just so, enough to support her, but not restrain her in a frightening way. He had to temper each spank to a specific degree, for if he spanked her too hard, her arse would go numb, and the pain would be less effective. Too softly, and she wouldn't receive the punishment she needed in order to feel changed.

Her hairbrush was the perfect tool for the occasion, just the right weight for a proper spanking. Now and again, his bride kicked and struggled, but for the most part, she submitted, and he began to hope their marriage might work out after all.

When her bottom reached a uniform, splotchy red, he noticed her sobs growing less resentful and more pitiable. When she cried without decorum or reservation, he knew she'd been punished enough. He put down the hairbrush and gave her a few final spanks with his palm, just to experience the feeling of doing so. Her arse cheeks were so soft, so hot. There would be bruises tomorrow to remind her of her punishment. He'd show them to her in a mirror if she said anything else about feeling guilty. Now, definitely, she'd paid her price.

As for his part in their encounter at the inn, he did not feel guilty. He'd married her, for God's sake. He would take care of her, be a good husband as far as he was able, and that was his punishment— the lack of his former freedom, and the loss of Townsend's friendship. It was a heavy price, but one he was obliged to pay.

He brushed her nightgown back down over her scarlet bottom and hoped he hadn't gone too hard this first night. He helped her to her feet, then drew her into his lap when she tried to back away.

"A proper spanking's not over until we talk about it," he said.

She turned her head against his shoulder. "I don't want to talk to you."

"Why? Because I punished you? You needed it." He rubbed her back as she still shuddered with the occasional sob.

"It hasn't worked as you said," she accused. "I still don't want to be married, and I'm still ashamed you took away my virtue. I wish you'd leave me alone."

He shushed her and pushed her hair from her eyes. She looked a mess, tearful and red-faced and messy-haired, ready to scream at him if only she had the courage to do it. "There, now," he murmured. "It's over. You must calm down."

She squirmed on his lap, his hard thighs doubtless increasing the pain in her spanked bottom. He told her to be calm, but he knew she wouldn't be for some time. A woman's first punishment took a bit of time to digest.

As for spanking his own wife, instead of a painted courtesan in a flagellation parlor, that was an entirely new thing. A rather interesting thing. Her disordered gown, her pouting, trembling lips, her indignant expression...all of it was true and real, and incredibly arousing. His cock ached for her, pounded with a more intense desire than he'd ever felt after spanking the harlots at Pearl's.

"Enough squirming and sniveling, Ophelia." He guided her against his chest, stroking her back and shoulders. "You took your punishment well for a beginner. You are a beginner, aren't you?"

She sniffled, her cheek sliding against his robe. "Of course I'm a beginner. I've never been spanked before, because I've always been very good. I'm sure I didn't need to be spanked by you, of all people. I don't feel better, or less guilty, and I think... I think you merely enjoyed hurting me."

"Shall I spank you again?" He joked, but she jerked back and stared at him. She didn't recognize his dry humor. How little they knew one another.

"What is your favorite color?" he asked, because he thought he ought to know something, anything, about his wife.

She shifted with a grimace. "Pale yellow, I suppose. The color of daffodils."

"Ah, the color of your gown today. That's exactly what I thought when I first saw it—daffodils. And you wore it to become my bride.

How wonderful." He touched her chin, then her cheek, meaning to comfort her. "I'm sorry today was difficult for you. I'm sorry you had to submit to a spanking on your wedding night, but you mustn't say it was because I enjoy hurting you. If I truly enjoyed hurting you, I wouldn't have married you at all."

"You had no choice," she said peevishly. "Nor did I."

"I had more choice than you. I could have made it seem you were the responsible one, rather than taking responsibility myself."

She crossed her arms over her chest, hunching her shoulders. "No one would have believed you, since you're the acknowledged rake."

"I wish you wouldn't call me names, Ophelia. If you make a habit of it, I shall have to make a habit of taking this hairbrush to your bottom."

She gave him a look of icy reproof. "How uncivilized you are. I wish I could have married Lord Townsend. He'd never think of spanking me."

It took all Wescott's strength not to laugh at that, since out of all of them, Townsend had the greatest fondness for exacting strict discipline.

"Lord Townsend is not your husband," he told her. "I am, with all the rights and privileges that entails. So, dear wife..." He set her on her feet. "I believe we ought to be getting to bed."

She followed him into her bedroom calmly enough, and got under her covers to await him, but when he started to remove his robe, she burst into tears.

"Must we do that?" she asked. "Must we lie together and repeat what we did at the inn?"

He froze, surprised by her outburst. "Why wouldn't we?"

"I can't. Not yet, please. My bottom hurts. You just spanked me, and you married me when I didn't want to get married, and now...now you want to do *that* to me again?"

"Curse you, woman, you enjoyed it before." His memories of that night were scattered at best, after all that had come afterward, but he was certain she'd enjoyed herself in the moment. He remembered her shaking in his arms, not the bad, frightened shaking she was doing now, but warm, wild shaking. "Do you remember how things went that night? You clung to me, flush with satisfaction."

"Please don't remind me of that. I didn't know how sinful it was."

Sinful. Wescott's spirits sank. She felt guilty as ever, spanking or no.

"See here," he said, raising his voice. "What happened that night was a mistake, yes, but we've moved past it. We're married. I'm your husband, you're my wife."

"I know." Her tears increased, her voice rasping as it rose. "But I can't... I can't yet. Not tonight. I don't know how I would manage it. Please, you must understand that I'm not ready. I just...can't."

Scoundrel and pervert that he was, his tastes did not extend to rape. His erection ebbed, because these weren't the type of tears that aroused him.

"What can I do to soothe you?" he asked, tying his robe closed.

"You can leave me alone. Please, you must understand. I did not want this marriage."

"So you've said several times, but it's happened, so what shall we do now? Sleep apart, as if we aren't married at all?"

"Yes. At least for now. At least...tonight."

She was crying, practically weeping, for fear he would exercise his marital rights. How his friends would laugh if they could see him now.

"Very well," he said, not very kindly. "I'll leave you alone if that's what you wish."

"It is what I wish, especially since we must travel tomorrow. Thank you."

He had more to say on the subject, and many misgivings to express, but he held his tongue and left the room. He'd been trained in statecraft and governance since birth, due to his father's high station, and one thing he'd learned early on was when to stay silent and bide his time. She would not be swayed tonight, it seemed, especially since he'd taken a hairbrush to her arse.

For now, he would retreat and consider his options, and take solace in the fact that he was the husband, and at some point in the near future, he would eventually get his way.

Chapter Seven: Another Lesson

Ophelia came awake to the sounds of a large house preparing for travel. Servants called to one another downstairs, loading baggage carts that would go before them to Wescott Abbey, her husband's country estate.

She sank down beneath the covers, pulling them over her head. If she was quiet enough, and hid here in the bedroom, might they all leave without her?

"Lady Wescott?"

Her new maid's voice quashed that daydream. Rochelle was English, not French, and while French maids were considered more fashionable, her own had run off and deserted her, so Ophelia was glad for Rochelle's English manners and kindly smile. Jacqueline had been a bit tart in her interactions, as if she hadn't found Ophelia worthy of her service.

Jacqueline is gone now, she reminded herself, *and you're a married woman.* She was Lady Wescott, rather than Lady Ophelia. She was stuck with her husband's name forever and ever, which was unfortunate, since she didn't like him very much. He'd spanked her on their wedding night, which had to make him one of the worst husbands of all time.

"Lord Wescott has sent you a note, my lady," Rochelle said, presenting it to her in bed, propped on a shiny silver platter.

She took the folded card, embellished with a gold-embossed *W*, and opened it with some trepidation. Would he scold her for last night? Would he threaten more spankings? Would he be pleasant, as a husband should?

Dear Ophelia,
I trust you've slept well. I'd like to leave by noon.
Wescott

So he would do neither thing, but be so bland and polite that it unsettled her.

"Could you have a breakfast tray brought up?" she asked Rochelle. "I'd rather not go down."

"Indeed, my lady. I'll send a footman at once."

Her husband wished to leave by noon, did he? Perhaps she'd dawdle over breakfast until 11:59. Perhaps she'd ask the maid for an intricate chignon that would take the better part of an hour to execute, and then be indecisive over which gown to wear.

But the memory of the previous night's punishment came to her when she shifted her still-sore hindquarters, and she sighed and rose to get ready. After picking at her breakfast tray with little appetite, she donned a pale blue gown with a matching bonnet. Rochelle kept her to schedule, her agile hands pinning hair and fetching gloves with none of Jacqueline's sullenness.

So Ophelia found herself handed up into the carriage a full hour before noon. Her husband greeted her in all his handsome, despicable glory, having already taken up a place on the forward facing seat. There was nothing to do but sit beside him, like a true, happily married couple headed to their country honeymoon.

"Good morning," he said, as she settled beside him, not quite touching him.

"Good morning, my lord."

"Still 'my lording' me?"

She had the distinct impression he might have rolled his eyes.

"Pardon me," she said. "I was attempting to be polite."

He thumped the carriage's roof, signaling the groomsmen they were ready to set off. It would take hours to reach the Abbey, as it was situated beyond the Arlington country estate in Oxfordshire, hours to be alone together in strained companionship. At least Lord Wescott's carriage was comfortable. This was not the one they'd ridden home in yesterday, after the wedding. The seats were plusher, and the light-colored interior gave an expansive feel to the enclosed space. The windows were large enough to provide distraction.

"Do you like it?" he said, waving an arm at the compartment.

"It's a fine carriage. Very modern and new."

"Just delivered this morning, to replace the one I lost in the fire. I'm quite pleased with it."

She squeezed her gloved hands together in her lap and withheld a sigh.

"It barely jostles," he said in the silence. "It's got the newest suspension system, and larger wheels for rutted country roads."

"How lovely."

"Do you enjoy the country, Ophelia?"

Would he persist in this stilted chatter the entire trip?

"I haven't spent much time in the country," she said, turning to the window. "When I was home from school, we stayed in town. My mother preferred it." She inched another fraction away from him. He was so large, and felt even larger in the closed compartment.

In answer, he crossed one of his long legs over the other and heaved a sigh, not having the manners to withhold it as she had.

"What else shall we converse about?" he asked. "We've a long way to travel. Perhaps we can get to know one another better."

"Like a courting couple?" She twisted the wedding ring on her finger. "A bit late for that."

He sighed again, even more loudly. "Will you hold it against me forever?"

"Hold what against you?" *The despoilment at the inn? The marriage? The spanking last night?* "Of what do you speak? You've wronged me in so many ways."

He gave a tight, pointed laugh. "I saved your life, if you'll be so kind to remember it."

"Someone else would have, if you hadn't." She liked to believe that, anyway.

"And I'm sure you would have shown an equal lack of gratitude to whoever that poor fool was," he said.

"I would show more gratitude to you for saving me if you hadn't ruined me at the same time."

"For God's sake!" His loud exclamation startled her, as did his expression as he uncrossed his legs and fixed her with a glare. "If you had said one word to stop me, one word of caution or hesitation, none of this would have happened. If you'd uttered one word of who you were, one word imploring me to leave you alone—"

"I have told you, I did not realize what you intended." She matched his strident voice, so much that it hurt her throat. "I knew nothing that night of loveplay and seduction, and you—" She drew a sharp breath. "From your talents, it's clear you knew too much."

"You disparage my 'talents,' wife? You took such pleasure in them."

"As have many women, from what I understand. I suppose it's difficult to move from London and leave all your bachelor conquests behind."

"If you mean Lady June, the woman I intended to marry, she's already moved on to someone else. She's to wed Lord Braxton within the month."

"I mean those other women, who are not ladies. The type of woman you thought I was." His eyes darkened as she spoke. She should have stopped, but her high emotions carried her past reason. "I overheard my brother talking to my father after we were engaged, about your many assignations and adventures in brothels."

"First of all, your brother doesn't know me, not as a friend or acquaintance. We've greeted one another in passing, nothing more."

"But people talk—"

"Second of all, it demeans you to speak of brothels, and to listen at doors to other peoples' conversations."

"Do you deny what they said about you?"

"I'm a twenty-seven-year-old man, Ophelia. I haven't lived like a monk, no, but I haven't been indiscriminate either. I've no bastards, no mistresses set up in apartments. Women gossip about me out of fascination, or jealousy, and half of what's been said about me is made up." He gritted his teeth, his lips in a tense line. "Do you want to know the true details, or have you come to understand that my past 'assignations' are none of your affair? A proper wife shouldn't wish to discuss such things. Although, from your behavior last night, I don't think you know much of being a proper wife."

She would not let him upset her. She would not give in to tears, even if his gruff voice hurt her feelings. "If you're speaking of my preference for sleeping alone, how would you feel in my position?"

He made a sound suspiciously near to a snort. "I don't think you want to know that answer."

"You behave as if I'm prudish, but you're a stranger to me, and not a very kind one."

"I was more a stranger the night of the fire, dear wife, and you were pleased enough to spread your thighs for me then."

She turned her face, grateful to hide behind her bonnet's brim. "You enjoy shaming me with that fact at every opportunity."

"You admit it's a fact, then. I remember, Ophelia. I recall everything you said and everything you did, and that you enjoyed yourself very much."

His crassness could hardly be borne. Tears rose in her eyes, but she would not shed them. No, she was too angry. "You'll shame me forever, won't you?" she cried, turning back to him. "Our entire marriage?"

"As you will do to me, at every opportunity." His gaze held hers, his eyes green and flinty. "You should know that we will not go on like this together. I will not allow this sullen, sharp-tongued nonsense every time we converse. I tried to spank it out of you last night. The next time, I'll not be so gentle."

"What, sir?" She fumed. "Will you abuse me?"

Now his gaze flashed with a dangerous edge. "I'll discipline you as I must, until you learn to govern your tongue. It's not proper for wives to be shrill and off-putting with their husbands. Perhaps you don't realize it, having spent so much time among the Viennese."

He said the last bit as if mocking her, as if her years at the music academy had been her folly, her egotistical whimsy. While she sat shaking in fury, he looked away, plucking at his coat's cuffs and flicking invisible dust.

"You'll make me despise you," she muttered beneath her breath.

"What?"

She didn't know what possessed her to shout it aloud. "You shall make me despise you, Lord Wescott. You'll make me hate you. Honestly, I haven't that far to go."

"Good God. Very well, then."

Before she knew what was happening, he'd lifted her from her place and turned her over his lap. Her bonnet went flying, as did one of her slippers, but that was the least of her worries as he flipped up her skirts. He left only her thin chemise to cover her bare bottom. It offered no protection as he brought his hand down upon her arse.

"Ow. Oww!" The smacking sounded too loud in the compartment, and the pain of his giant hand was uncalled for and unfair. "How dare you? Let me go at once. Oww! Why are you doing this?"

"I'm doing this because you lack the most basic respect a wife owes her husband."

"That's because I don't want to be your wife. I never wanted to be your wife!"

Her cries didn't do anything to stop him from attacking her already-tender cheeks. She clenched and squirmed, but each blow fell squarely and left behind an awful, stinging fire.

"We've not yet left London," she pleaded. "Someone will look in the window and see me—and you—"

"You ought to have thought of that before now, my little crosspatch," he said, cinching her restless legs between his larger ones.

"Don't call me a crosspatch." She squirmed to break free. "No, you mustn't spank me again, please. I'm still sore from yesterday."

"That, too, you ought to have considered before now."

Smack, smack, smack. He pummeled her bottom cheeks with no respite in between spanks, no time to breathe and process the pain. She didn't deserve to be punished so harshly, did she? For uttering a few frustrated words?

"I don't think you understand how much this hurts." Her voice quavered on the edge of a cry. "It hurts. Please, it hurts!"

"There's a reason it hurts," he said, tightening his arm around her waist. "You're going to learn to speak to me civilly, or the spankings will continue, and next time I'll use a birch rod or cane."

"I won't speak at all, then. I'll never speak to you again."

She clamped her lips shut against the whines and cries that escaped with each smack upon her bottom. She would not admit that she'd earned this punishment. No one deserved such treatment, even if they'd turned their husband from their bed on his wedding night, and berated him the morning after with ill-spoken words. She would never speak again, then, just as she'd decided not to sing. She would go completely silent. How would he enjoy being married to a silent, soundless creature, with no words or personality at all?

It was hard to be silent, though. She gritted her teeth at the end, to stop herself from begging for mercy. When his cursed hand finally stopped spanking her, he refused to let her up.

"You've had your second spanking now, wife," he said in a lofty, bullying tone, "and we've only been married two days. Now, you'll apologize for your disrespectful behavior, and pledge that you won't behave like a shrew again."

She bowed her head and kept her lips shut. She wouldn't talk to him. She'd never speak again to spite him.

"I'm waiting," he said, and she knew without looking that his hand was poised over her bottom, ready to resume the spanking if she didn't comply. But she was afraid if she spoke, the only words she could manage would be *I hate you, I hate you, I hate you*, over and over.

"Very well," he said with a sigh. "Then your punishment will continue, but I shall have to switch hands. My right one is tired."

He stood her up and forced her down over his lap in the opposite direction. *I won't speak*, she told herself. *I'll never speak.*

But his left hand felt even more painful than his right, and by the tenth spank or so, her outrage was overtaken by the fear that he could spank her forever, that their standoff might never end. Her bottom felt so hot and sore, it might be red for days beneath her skirts. She stared down at the slipper she'd kicked off earlier and made herself say the words.

"I'm sorry, Lord Wescott. I'm sorry!"

His horrid hand stopped, the compartment going silent after the onslaught.

"And?" he prompted.

"And I should not have...have spoken so rudely to you."

She said the words tightly, with her lips half-clenched, because otherwise she'd start to cry.

"What shall happen, Ophelia, if you continue to be rude to me?" As he said this, his hand traced over her trembling bottom cheeks, squeezing each one, amplifying the pain.

"You will..." By God, she would not cry, would not give him the satisfaction of tears. "You'll give me a birching next time, or a caning, for not learning my lesson."

"Indeed." He released her legs from within his and let her rise from his lap. "As much as it hurts to be spanked, a birching or caning will hurt worse, so you had best conduct yourself as a polite wife from this moment forward."

She eased back onto the seat beside him, gingerly, as far from his large, intimidating figure as she could manage. Ow, it hurt just to sit, and to have to sit beside him all the way to Wescott Abbey? She wasn't sure she could bear it. As she bent to put her slipper back on, the carriage bumped over a cobblestone. She bounced on the seat and hissed at the resulting pain. He had done this to her, this awful man she was forced to marry. What a miserable life she would have, bowing to his disciplinary whims.

She looked out the window, and found they were already on the outskirts of London. How long had he spanked her? Too long. She smoothed her dress over her knees, trying not to look at Lord Wescott's long, muscled thigh beside hers. She needed no reminder that he was bigger, stronger, and more powerful than her, not just in their godforsaken marriage, but in every way. Her mind went unbidden to their time at the inn, when he'd pushed his shaft inside her. *I know I'm a lusty size, and you so small.* Even so, it had come to feel better, almost shockingly lovely to have him inside her there...

She shook off such thoughts. He did not arouse her anymore. She could not imagine him ever arousing her again, now that she understood his true character. Not only was he a rogue and a rake, but he was so haughty and overbearing a husband it could hardly be believed. She put her hands to the pins in her hair, to the neat coif that Rochelle had worked so hard to create. It was all mussed now, but she had no mirror to put it to rights.

"Give me my bonnet," she told him. "It's there by your feet."

"Ask me with a civil tongue, so help me, Ophelia, or I'll stop the carriage and find a birch tree to cut a switch right now."

She thought she'd explode from the indignity of it. How many more hours to Oxfordshire? She would lose her mind. "Please, Lord Wescott, will you hand me my bonnet?"

"No, I will not. I can't see your face at all when you're wearing that blasted thing. You may have it back when we stop to rest and stretch our legs."

He would not even hand her her bonnet. Why, by God, must he wield power over her in all things? It was the extent of what she could bear and still keep her composure. Her tears overflowed her will and rolled down her cheeks, silent, but so copious he could not help but notice. She turned as far from him as she could, staring out the window, seeing nothing as she wiped at the tears with her second-best pair of gloves. Hateful. So hateful. She hated him beyond reason. He was so utterly cruel and unfeeling. She had let him touch her once, caress and kiss her, and get so close to her it felt like magic, but now, it was all she could do not to throw herself from the carriage to be away from him.

I despise you. How she wanted to scream it at him, but she couldn't. Over the past week, she'd lost three things that mattered: her voice, her virginity, and her freedom. She feared she would never be happy again, that she had lost that ability along with her vaunted voice.

She put a hand to her throat and tried to stop crying, for it would solve nothing. A man as hard and unkind as the Marquess of Wescott would not be moved by tears, and they were not helping her at all, aside from giving her a headache. In time her lids grew heavy, and she closed her eyes and rested her head against the bolster at her side.

It seemed only minutes later that Lord Wescott nudged her awake. "We're here," he said.

"Here?" She blinked up at him, wondering why her head rested on his shoulder. "At the coaching inn?"

"At Wescott Abbey. You were sleeping so soundly, I let you be when they changed the horses."

How had she ended up sleeping against her husband, rather than the bolster? She could hardly believe she'd done so the whole way to Oxfordshire. She felt groggy as she sat up and put her gown to rights. He handed over her bonnet and she arranged it atop her sleep-disordered hairstyle as well as she could. Only then did she look out the window to see the country house belonging to the marquess.

House? No, it was hardly a house. It looked more like a sprawling, ancient castle, the thick stone walls rising three stories high, washed by time and sunlight. There were great, round towers at each corner of the house, with high windows and sloping peaks, and massive, carved battlements along the roof line. A vast lawn and manicured gardens surrounded the structure, bringing modern order to its archaic wildness. Her family's country retreat was grand, but not on this scale.

She gawked at the stone edifice, half expecting a parade of knights to issue from the wide front doors. Instead, lines of servants appeared, walking down the imposing staircase and taking up places alongside the entrance. All of them were dressed in Wescott livery, like the servants at his grand home in town.

"Let me help you down," he said, alighting before her. He held her hand as she emerged from the carriage, the polite and doting prince now that everyone could see. She didn't feel like much of a princess, with her wrinkled skirts and aching bottom. She tried to walk normally as he led her to the castle's entrance, where a stern-faced butler bowed to welcome them.

"Good afternoon, Dorset," said her husband. "This is my new wife, Lady Wescott."

"My lady," said the butler, bowing low again. "And my Lord Wescott. We congratulate you and the marchioness, and wish you a warm welcome home."

Ophelia wondered if the servants knew why they'd married. It had happened so quickly, they must have an idea it was somehow improper. She tried to smile as Lord Wescott led her past them, but could not achieve a natural effect, so she looked down at the stairs instead. Bewigged footmen pushed open the huge double doors at the top, and Wescott ushered her inside.

The home looked as ageless within as without, with a soaring stone entry hall lit by a massive hammered-iron chandelier. She wondered how many centuries old it was. Directly ahead, a wide staircase led to the second floor, where high, leaded windows let in filtered light. The whitewashed walls displayed large velvet tapestries, and the wood furniture was imposingly sturdy and plain.

"It's quite an ancient place," he said in a conversational, almost blasé tone. "Monks lived here ages ago, before this was Arlington land. The Abbey predates the main house by centuries, being an outbuilding of the original Arlington keep."

He spoke so casually of centuries, as if he'd truly come to England with the Vikings. She could so easily imagine it, with his long blond hair and light eyes, and his natural propensity for cruelty.

"It's been worked on over the years," he said, looking around, "so it's no shack, but it's not a palace like my parents' house, either. I'll give you a tour of the place when you're in the mood for it."

She'd been committed to disliking Wescott Abbey, since anything to do with her husband must be a bad thing, but she found herself fascinated instead. "This is a nice house," she said, in sullen understatement.

He gave her a look that brought to mind the spanking she'd gotten earlier, as well as the one she'd suffered last night. What could he do, turn her over his knee now, in front of all the servants?

"Mrs. Samuelson will show you to your rooms so you can rest and collect yourself," he said, indicating the housekeeper at her side. "Her staff is doubtless upstairs already, unpacking your trunks. Dinner is served at eight o'clock here. If necessary, one of the footmen will show you to the dining room. You need only ask."

There were haughty looking footmen everywhere. Such wealth he must have, to maintain this staff year-round.

No, she would not be impressed, for that would please Lord Wescott. She straightened her bonnet again and set up the stairs after Mrs. Samuelson, feeling his eyes on her backside the entire way.

Chapter Eight:
A Honeyed Moon

Wescott ate dinner alone in the Abbey's echoing dining room. His wife claimed to be too exhausted from the trip, and he let her hide behind this predictable fiction while the servants pretended nothing was amiss. He could have taken a tray upstairs and eaten with her, and spent the remaining evening hours alone with her, giving her pleasure and finding his own, but she wouldn't welcome that, especially after he'd punished her in the carriage for her poor wifely manners.

Well, she would have to learn.

After dinner, he went directly to his room. She was set up next door to him, in a grand suite recently refurbished for his eventual wife. He could have taken the few short steps to wish her good evening, but he feared receiving a cold reception. He'd try again tomorrow, or the next day. By God, Ophelia had not endeared herself to him so far. They'd have to find some way to present a united front in public, and raise children together when she finally uncrossed her stubborn thighs and let him inside her again.

Ah, he would like to be inside her again. He lay in bed in the dark, palming his cock, stroking its length and remembering how trusting and open she'd been at the inn. He'd experienced how sensual, how abandoned his prim Lady Wescott could be, and now that he couldn't have her, he seemed to be taking out his annoyance on her backside. Too bad for her.

As for him, it was not such a hardship. He enjoyed the disciplinary arts, and her lovely, round arse had colored beautifully under his hand. He stroked himself faster, imagining more creative ways to punish his new wife. Sodomy, perhaps. A bit of bondage. He imagined her tied face-down on his bed, squirming and pleading for mercy as he oiled her arsehole for a little buggery. There was no more pleasurable or effective way to discipline a naughty woman, and he brought himself off with breathless intensity, relieving the tension that had churned within him since she'd refused him last night.

He fell asleep soon after, relaxing into the clean, crisp sheets. The scents and sounds of this house were familiar enough that he drifted peacefully into dreams. Then, a terrified scream roused him from bed.

"My lord." His valet bent over him, shaking him to wakefulness. "My lord, it's Lady Wescott."

He was on his feet moving to the door as another scream rent the silent night.

"Would you like to dress first, my lord?" his man asked.

Wescott cursed under his breath and threw on the shirt he handed him. By the time he got across the hall, Rochelle was trembling in her night clothes and cap outside his wife's room.

"My lord, I tried to calm her, but she pushed me away and screamed in fear. Whatever is the matter?"

"Damned if I know. Come with me."

Ophelia screamed again as they entered, a sustained, ear-piercing wail that would almost have been musical, if it wasn't so awful. There was no one in the room with her, no specter or marauder, no villain making her scream for her life. She was asleep, caught in the throes of a nightmare.

He'd seen her this way before.

"Shall I call the physician?" Rochelle asked.

"No. She's dreaming of the fire again. Bring some cool water and a cloth."

While the maid hurried to comply, he strode to Ophelia's side and tried to wake her, but she was seized hard in the nightmare's grasp. It was frightening, and frustrating, to see her suffer so. He sat on the bed and pulled her against him, settling her tossing head upon his shoulder.

"You're dreaming," he said, repeating it as if she could hear him. "You're dreaming, you're dreaming. You're dreaming, little crosspatch. You must wake."

Rochelle bathed her forehead and cheeks with a cool cloth, though Ophelia struggled against the contact as if it were fire itself. She let out another scream, trembling in terrified spasms. The depth of her fear took Wescott's breath away.

"Why won't she wake, my lord?" the maid asked.

"She's a deep dreamer." He held her so she wouldn't throw herself from the bed. Finally, when he called her name loudly, she shook off the nightmare and regained her waking faculties. She was still afraid though, still gasping for breath.

"There's a fire," she said, struggling to get away from him. "A fire. We must go, quickly!"

"There's no fire. You're safe in bed, in your room at Wescott Abbey."

"I made the fire. It shot from my fingers and everyone is angry with me." She grasped his arms hard, willing him to believe. "I didn't mean to, but I couldn't help it. It burned me too." She drew her hands forward to show him, then turned them over, staring in confusion. "The fire burned me and I lost control of it. It chased me when I tried to push it away."

"You haven't started any fires. Nothing's chasing you, love. You had a dream."

Rochelle produced a cool glass of water and he held it to Ophelia's lips. She could barely drink from shivering.

"Is she ill, my lord?" asked the maid fretfully. "Perhaps she caught an ague on the trip, at one of the staging inns."

"We didn't stop on the trip. She's got no fever, and she has energy enough to fight me. She's merely overtired." He was doing his best to present a facade of capability in front of the servants. "Are you awake now?" he asked his wife, looking into her eyes. Her gaze still darted about the room, fixing fearfully on the candles and the dying fire.

"Shall I bring more light, my lord?" asked Rochelle. "I can send a footman for lamps right away."

"No. In fact, extinguish the candles for now. There's enough light from the fire. Close the screen upon the hearth, if you would."

The maid pulled the sides of the fire screen together, blocking the flames from view. All they really needed was the heat.

"You may go," he told Rochelle when she finished. "Get some rest so you can care for your mistress tomorrow. I'll stay with her through the night."

"Yes, my lord."

As soon as he climbed into bed beside her, his wife protested. "No, please. I'm too afraid of that. I don't want you to—"

"I won't, if you don't wish it." A flush burned his cheeks. Humiliating, for the maid to hear this exchange. "I'll only lie next to you, Ophelia. Good night, Rochelle," he said pointedly, as the maid dawdled on her way to the door. The servant was clearly the loyal sort, which pleased him, although at the moment, he wanted her gone. Not because he intended to mistreat his wife, but because he didn't want servants gossiping about her disdain for him.

"You...you needn't stay," Ophelia repeated.

She wasn't happy for his company, but he slid beneath her covers anyway and pulled her into his arms, so her cheek rested against his chest.

"There, see now," he said soothingly. "We'll only talk together until you've forgotten your nightmare and start feeling better."

"I'm better now."

"Hush, little liar. You're trembling like a leaf in a storm."

"I'm not a liar."

"I say you are. Be still. Take some calming breaths."

He cradled her against him and stroked her arm, up and down, up and down. She began to settle in stages when it became obvious a seduction was not at play. Her trembling stopped, her breath slowed, and she finally allowed herself to go slack against him as she had earlier in the carriage.

This time, though, exhaustion would not carry her away. Her fingers worked nervously at his shirt's sleeves, and she kept glancing about the room.

"You must be so angry with me," she said.

"Why?"

"I didn't mean to start the fire. It came from my fingers. Wherever I touched, things burst into flame."

He looked down at her. "Are you still dreaming?"

She stared at her hands, bewildered. "I don't mean to be so awful. Oh, I wish I could be a proper lady. That's why everything caught fire, you know."

"Ophelia, my darling." He wasn't sure why he called her darling, or why he bent his head to kiss her. He told himself it was to jolt her from her confused daze, but it was her lips too, the way she pursed them when she was uncertain or troubled.

She didn't pull away at once. For a while she responded to his kiss, bracing her arms on his shoulders. His body came alive, blood rushing to his cock, but then she came awake, truly awake, and drew her lips from his.

"I don't want to do that," she said. "Please."

He sighed. "I know you don't want to. Are you with me now?"

"Where else would I be?"

He tightened his hold on her when she tried to move away. "No. Stay here and rest, and let me hold you. You had a screaming nightmare, and then you went on and on about lighting things on fire."

Ah, those lips. They pouted now, as if she didn't believe him. "That's preposterous," she said. "I've never lit anything on fire in my life."

"You were dreaming. And I promised your maid I'd stay with you, so you can't send me away even if you don't want to perform your marital duties. Which are duties, Ophelia. Someday you'll have to accept me whether you wish it or not."

"I don't want to talk about that." She avoided his gaze, looking down at her clasping hands. "It's just that I feel I'm not a proper lady when I... When we...do that...thing."

"The thing we've done only one time?" He took one of her hands, to still its unconscious movement. "It must have seemed very real," he said after a few quiet moments. "Your nightmare. The fire."

She shuddered and nodded. "I've dreamed about it every night since it happened. The fire starts small, and I can't put it out, and then it's everywhere, burning me and destroying everything, and it's all my fault."

"Why your fault? You didn't start it. You were performing in the theater."

"I know, but in my dreams, it's always me starting it somehow." She sighed. "I'm so tired. I've barely gotten any sleep the last few days."

"We'll have to fix that, so you don't become even more of a crosspatch. Here, lie down with me. I'll keep you safe from nightmares."

He said it with confidence, but he wasn't sure he'd be up to the challenge. Lack of sleep would explain her waspish moods, but how to take those nightmares away when the fire had changed both their lives so dramatically? Was he tied up in the horror of the fire too, in her mind and in her dreams? Was that why she held him at arm's length?

"I won't be able to sleep," she said, squirming against him, her head restless upon his shoulder. "I'll dream of fire again."

"We won't sleep, then. Sing for me instead. I'm married to a famous singer, and I've never heard a note."

"Not famous. And I can't sing anymore. It won't sound fine at all, so I'd rather not try." Her voice sounded tight, like she might start crying. His poor, miserable wife.

"Let's talk then," he said. "Tell me about your music school in Vienna."

She tensed in his arms, and he remembered he'd mocked her about it earlier.

"Did you enjoy your time there?" he asked, taking care that no mockery touched his voice. "It must have been difficult to get into such an exclusive school. I imagine you had excellent teachers."

"Excellent? Yes. The very best."

He waited for her to say more, but her expression turned brooding.

"Was there much time for leisure, outside of music?" he asked.

She shook her head. "There was only music. Good and bad music. Sometimes I was praised, but mostly I felt my efforts weren't enough. You can never really be the best at a school like that. There were pupils from everywhere, nearly every place in the world, and all of them were talented."

"Did you want to be the best?"

She was silent a moment. "My mother wished me to do well. She used to say my voice was a gift from God."

"Hmm. Do you think that's true? Do you feel God's presence when you sing?"

"There were times I felt quite happy at school, but there were other times I wanted to tear up my music folders and come home. My Mama would have been disappointed if I'd left, though. She wished me to have a career upon the stage. She said I used to sing even as I learned to talk. Did you know I'm named for a tragic Shakespearean character?"

"I suspected you were."

She gave another melancholy sigh. "On the way to the wedding, my father told my mother she finally got the tragedy she wanted. Mama cried and told him to be silent. He meant me, marrying you."

Wescott's temper bristled. "For God's sake, you could hardly do better than me. I don't mean that to sound rude, you know, but I'm the Duke of Arlington's heir. I was supposed to marry the Earl of Mayhew's daughter. Lady June was quite put out."

"I don't know who Lady June is. I'm sorry you weren't able to marry her."

"I'm sure you are."

He regretted his snide tone at once and rested his chin on top of her head, wondering why he wasn't inside her where he ought to be.

"Ophelia, why do you make me so cross? We're on our honeymoon and I think you'd rather be anywhere else."

She turned toward the window. The curtains had been tied open, revealing a bright autumn moon overlooking the gardens and fields. Her lids looked drowsy, and he wondered if she'd fall asleep right there in his arms.

"I used to think people were saying 'honeyed moon,'" she said a moment later. "I thought they meant the time the moon looks amber, as if it's covered in honey. Have you ever seen a moon like that?"

"I have, more than once. A honeyed moon? I like that. It's very poetic."

He could see his simple praise pleased her, which made him feel oddly pleased in turn. How sweet a wife she might be, if she put all her prim, shrewish nonsense aside. As he held her in his arms, images came unbidden to him, so vivid his heart thumped in his chest. Images of Ophelia as a mother, singing to a baby snuggled in her arms. Singing to *their* baby, her Vienna-trained voice echoing in the Abbey's spacious nursery where generations of his forebears had been raised.

His blood rose along with his imagination. His cock went hard, and he wanted to mate with her, to make her pregnant right away. He wanted to be inside her for pleasure, for legacy. He wanted her God-given voice to cry his name when she reached her satisfaction, clinging to his shoulders. She'd done that at the inn, clung to his shoulders and writhed beneath him in bliss.

When? he thought. *When can I have you again? I'm dying to be inside you.*

He wanted to part her legs wide and thrust inside her, fuck her, excite her as she was exciting him, but when he looked down to tell her so, she'd fallen asleep, and he knew that, no, he could not have told her such things. She would have reacted with horror and run from the bed.

She turned her head against his chest in sleep, and he knew he must let her sleep, and let her come to him in her own time even if he felt like he was about to die.

He eased her back on her pillows and stared out at the moon. It was not a honeyed moon tonight, not amber gold and sensuous, but cold, stark, and white.

If he kissed Ophelia's lips, would she wake? He kissed her forehead instead and lay back beside her. His body burned for her, like the fire in her screaming nightmare, but his fleeting kiss was a surrender.

I will wait, he thought, for he had no other option. *I will wait as long as I can before I go mad.*

Chapter Nine: Afraid

On Ophelia's fourth day at the Abbey, after luncheon, Rochelle brought her a walking gown and told her the marquess requested her company. Her first impulse was to plead exhaustion, as she had the three previous days, but she could not hide in her rooms forever.

Instead she rose and put on the silver-gray gown Rochelle brought her, and let the maid fuss and putter over her hair. When she finished, Ophelia looked at herself in the vanity mirror. She looked awfully pale, although the gossamer silver gown flattered her eye color. She pinched her cheeks, then wondered why she bothered. The last thing she wanted was for her husband to develop a deeper attraction to her.

"Your bonnet, my lady," said Rochelle, handing her the pale gray hat that matched her gown. "I've a feeling Lord Wescott wants to get you out in the sun."

"Is it a nice day?"

"I believe so, my lady."

Ophelia had been inside so long she didn't know. She let Rochelle arrange the bonnet atop her loose chignon and went to meet Lord Wescott at the bottom of the sweeping staircase. He looked every inch the country peer, from his fitted navy coat to his spotless buff trousers. He'd pulled his hair back in what she'd come to think of as his "civilized" look, and held a hat between his fingers. His eyes raked over her, and she felt heat rise in her cheeks. Did he find her pretty, attired for a walk in the garden?

Did she wish him to find her pretty?

She lifted her chin as she came face to face with him, waiting on the second stair.

"Good afternoon," he said. "How are you today?"

"Tired, my lord."

Of course, he knew that, for he spent each night drawing her from repeated fiery nightmares. The first night, she dreamed she started the fires herself, that her hands burned everything they touched. Another night the fire came to her onstage, a flaming ball from the wings. She ran to the stage door to escape it, but this time the marquess didn't come, or her parents, or anyone to save her. The dreams felt so real, she'd choke and gasp for air, and then the flames would envelop her, bringing unbearable pain that made her scream.

Each night, he came to her and shook her awake, and chased the flames away. *Where were you?* she asked the night the fire billowed from the wings. *You didn't come for me.* He'd looked at her with a combination of worry and exasperation and said, *I'm here.*

In the mornings, she'd wake and find him still sleeping beside her. She'd study him for long moments, taking in his tawny skin and gold hair, and increasingly familiar features, fascinated, but also afraid he'd wake and demand she perform her marital duties before she got away.

Then she'd creep to her dressing room and wait for Rochelle, and by the time she washed and dressed for the day, he was always gone. Even now, in the afternoon, she could see a little of her exhaustion reflected in his eyes.

"I hope you slept well," she offered, ignoring the fact that neither of them had.

"I slept about as well as you did."

She bit back the apology she knew she ought to utter. It wasn't as if she could help her terrible dreams.

"I had an idea to walk with you about the Abbey's grounds, since it's such a gorgeous day," he said. "I'd like to show you a bit more of your new home. The property is famed for its old gardens and pathways, and wind-blown fields. I thought we might enjoy a picnic, if we could find a nice spot of sun."

The servants had prepared a basket, which he presented with a flourish. She supposed a picnic was a proper honeymoon activity, even if their honeymoon, thus far, was a failure.

"Of course, I'd enjoy seeing more of the Abbey," she said. That was not a lie. If this was to be her home, she might as well know the ins and outs of it, if only to know where she might go to avoid him when they were in rivalrous moods.

When she offered her hand, he helped her descend the remaining stair, then led her toward the back of the main floor, to the filigreed iron doors that let out to the gardens in the back. All the Abbey was imposing stone and iron until you went outside, then nature bloomed everywhere. Before she could stop herself, she drew in an audible breath.

It was a lovely, sunny day for autumn, with just a few clouds in the sky. As they walked on to the main path, a gentle wind ruffled her gown's sheer overlay, and the sun warmed her skin after the house's stony chill. This was the sort of pretty day that made her want to sing as she used to, with all her heart and breath. Was that what Wescott had meant, about feeling God's presence in her singing? The birdcalls, breezes, and sunshine summoned her voice to rise from her lungs and harmonize with nature, but she clenched her teeth against it. Why bother to sing now?

"This was my home away from home when I was a boy," he said. "My parents' country house is just on the other side of those woods, called Arlington Hall. It's much grander and modern, but one could never get into mischief there without someone finding out."

"So you got into mischief here?" She could certainly see it, if he'd been as brash and strapping when he was a lad. "Did you know the house would be yours when you were older?"

"I suppose, although it didn't mean much to me then. My friends and I preferred the gardens and woods for our childhood games. You met them at the wedding, if you'll remember, Lord Augustine and Lord Marlow? And Lord Townsend," he added in afterthought.

Lord Townsend was the gentleman who'd lost his head over her. She'd never forget their fight the day of her betrothal. "You grew up together?" she asked.

"We were closest in age, all the oldest sons." He chuckled. "But there were many more of us, all our younger brothers and sisters and their friends, tearing about the Oxfordshire countryside when our tutors would let us. We were usually granted freedom on pretty days."

"Your sisters too?"

"Oh yes, they followed us everywhere, even when we begged them to stay away."

He said this with good humor, but Ophelia was shocked by the idea of young girls roaming the countryside. She'd been strictly supervised her entire childhood and put to womanly pursuits when she was old enough. Embroidery, letter writing, dancing lessons. She'd been allowed to read the occasional novel, if approved by her Mama. And music lessons, of course.

"It is a beautiful property," she said. "Is that the pond I see from my window?"

"Yes. There are several in the area. Do you enjoy swimming?"

"Swimming? In a pond?" Was he teasing her? "I...I don't know. I've never tried it."

He said something under his breath, something like "Why am I not surprised?" She regarded the pond with suspicion, wondering how deep it was.

They skirted around the rippling shoreline and across another lawn surrounded by manicured hedgerows. He shortened his long stride so she could keep up, especially as she couldn't resist looking around at the expert gardening and stone follies, including a detailed replica of a Greek temple at the edge of the woods.

"Who created all this?" she asked. "The monks?"

"Oh, no. My mother planted many of these gardens when she ran out of space at the other house. You may change them around as you wish. She wouldn't mind."

Gardens, ponds, an old, medieval-looking house. She ought to be excited about such things. A proper woman would be honored to be Lord Wescott's wife, and mother to his children. One day she would be a duchess. It ought to make her happy, but she mostly felt lonely and lost.

"Shall we stop here?" he asked.

For a moment she thought he spoke of their marriage. *Yes, let's stop here. Then I could stop worrying.* But no, he spoke of their picnic lunch in the sun, so she helped him spread the blanket and take the food from the basket.

His servants had wrapped up cold roast beef and chicken, with fresh bread and pickled salads, as well as an assortment of cakes. It was the first meal they'd eaten together since their wedding breakfast, and that hardly counted, since so many other people had been milling around. She felt achingly self-conscious as she picked at the food on her plate.

"The fare isn't to your liking?" he asked, studying her.

"No, it's very good."

"You don't like the sun, then? I thought the fresh air and light might help you sleep more soundly when you retire."

"I'm sorry about the nightmares." She tucked her feet more closely beneath her. "If I could stop them, I would."

"I don't blame you for them, I only wish you'd feel better. My mother has always been a great believer in the power of sunshine. She's Welsh, you know, and believes in all sorts of whimsical things."

Ophelia blinked at him. Her own mother couldn't be farther from whimsical. Both her parents were the strait-laced sort.

"She seems a fine lady," she said. "Your mother."

"Oh, she's the best lady and everyone loves her, most of all my father." He looked away from her. Did he realize how his careless words stung?

"They married for love, then?" she asked.

"Goodness, no. They hardly knew one another when they wed, but they ended up suiting in the end." He shrugged. "I suppose it happens if you're lucky. Would you like to take off your bonnet?"

She touched the wide brim. "I'd better not. I might freckle."

"They never sunned you at your school?" He frowned. "All of you pale and wan, and musically talented."

Whenever he spoke of her school, he made it sound like a joke. Her whole life, her dreams, her voice, her goals, all of them were meaningless to him. She was nothing more than a woman he'd seduced—in error—and been forced to marry. Perhaps she ought to sing for him, to show what he'd taken away from her.

No. She would not sing for him, not ever. She wouldn't let him enjoy the voice he'd stifled.

They passed the rest of the picnic with small talk, and lengthy silences neither of them tried to fill. When they finished, they repacked the dishes, and she stood so he could fold the blanket. "Why is that temple here?" she asked, pointing at the Greek folly in the distance. "I thought this was an abbey before, a Christian place."

"It was an abbey, long, long ago. The gardens and follies were installed later, when this became a residence. My great-great-grandfather built that particular folly in the early 1700's, after he traveled to Athens and toured the Greek ruins. He was a historian of sorts." He set the basket on a nearby bench and gestured toward the temple. "Would you like to go see it?"

"I'm not sure." She eyed the marble structure. "It looks so desolate among the trees, as if it might harbor ghosts."

"It's not haunted. No, it's far more interesting than that."

His expression puzzled her, moving between gravity and laughter. She replaced her gloves and pursed her lips. "Are there snakes inside it? Rats and badgers?"

He did laugh then. "No, it's kept locked tight, so no animals can get in. It's a place for erotic punishment." He said these stunning words and continued on, even as Ophelia flushed in shock. "My parents forbade me from exploring it when I was a boy, but my friends and I broke our way in as soon as we were old enough to meddle the lock."

"What do you mean by...by that thing you said?" she asked. "Erotic punishment? Punishment of wh-whom?"

Wescott raised a brow. "In my great-great grandfather's case, I don't know. Perhaps it was fitted out later. I know my father made use of it, because he erected an exact copy in the gardens of his town house, and my parents visited it often when they thought we didn't know."

"Oh goodness. Your parents?"

"And their friends, sometimes. You look shocked, Ophelia. I'm certain they all enjoyed themselves. Shall I explain the particulars of erotic punishment?"

"I don't want to know." She put her hands to her eyes, then her ears, daunted by his smile. "Do you...have you...?" She couldn't finish the question.

"Have I engaged in erotic punishment in that temple?"

She nodded. "Whatever that is."

He was guiding her toward the folly, not that she wanted to go.

"I have, in the past," he said. "When my friends and I found this place, we didn't know what it was for. When I got a bit older and wiser, I made use of it during the wilder house parties of my bachelorhood. It's quite fun to imagine you're in ancient times, doing perverse sorts of things."

She couldn't picture these "perverse things," could hardly believe what he said was true. When they reached the temple, he looked behind a rock at the edge of the foundation and extracted a long, narrow key. This opened the lock handily.

"You see," he said, pushing open the door. "No snakes or badgers."

She could see at a glance that the room was indeed created for the business of punishment. There was an imposing pole in the center that made her draw in a breath. On closer inspection, she saw it was a polished whipping post with cuffs attached. She turned about and noticed a pair of shining chains hanging from a corner. There was a rack on the opposite side with more leather cuffs, and several platforms and benches arranged along the smooth, stone walls. The only light for the room issued from the doorway, as well as four small windows at each side.

She did not dare step inside to inspect anything more closely. What if he closed the door and rolled up his sleeves, and said *I believe I shall punish you right now, Lady Wescott*, in his lofty, lackadaisical way? What if he locked her in there and bound her into one of those sets of cuffs? And then he...

No. She couldn't imagine it. Erotic punishment? She didn't want to imagine it.

"Were they frightened?" she asked, backing away. "The women you brought here to punish, were they terrified?"

"Dear girl, they were willing. It was all in fun, for excitement and pleasure."

"Pleasure? I don't understand."

He sighed. "You wouldn't." He took a last look inside, a longing look that unsettled her, and shut the door.

"You shouldn't have married me," she said. "If these are the things you like, then I...I will never make you happy."

"I didn't have a choice, remember?"

She watched as he locked the secret room away. "I cannot imagine enjoying anything like..." She waved a hand at the door. "Like that."

"Nor can I, when you've such an attitude of aversion." He placed the key in its former hiding place and returned to her. "It doesn't matter. I'll only require one thing of you in our day to day life, and it will happen soon." His piercing eyes held hers. "I've given you time, Ophelia, but a honeymoon is a honeymoon. You can't push me away forever, especially when I'm sleeping next to you each night. It's not easy for me, you know. My control can only stretch so far."

Her chest constricted, her body quailing away from his, even though he didn't touch her. She must stop having the nightmares, so he wouldn't need to lie in her bed. It gave him the excuse to come to her, to touch her. Soon, he would take full possession of her body again, come inside her as he'd done the first night she met him. He'd had so much power over her then.

"I'm tired," she said, walking away from her husband and his profane Greek temple. "I think I ought to go inside."

"Yes, and rest, so you can come down and join me for a proper dinner tonight. Eight o'clock. The servants must see us dining together as husband and wife, or gossip will soon reach London."

"Good servants don't gossip."

"All servants gossip," he said. "I'll send a footman to fetch you, so you won't have any trouble finding the dining room."

He was giving her an order to join him for dinner, and as the temple reminded her, he was only too happy to dole out punishments for poor behavior, erotic or otherwise. He'd given her two spankings so far for displeasing him. She didn't care to receive another.

"As you wish," she said, walking with him back toward the manor. She kept her expression neutral beneath her bonnet's brim, but her blood beat in her veins, frenzied as her panicking heart.

* * * * *

When she met him at dinner, she was still unsettled, her mind turning on the alien concept of *pleasurable punishment*. She supposed she'd been too sheltered, for she could not imagine such a thing, but he admitted the vice with no embarrassment whatsoever.

She found herself watching his movements more closely, trying to imagine him in that temple doing scandalous things to ladies. Punishing them because they wanted it. She stared at his hands as they rested on his wineglass or slid along the table, and thought of all the perverse things he might do with them. He'd touched her with those hands, touched her very intimately.

And she'd been swept away by his touch, transported to earth-shaking ecstasies. She remembered that, even if she couldn't admit it out loud.

"You're quiet tonight," he said, as the servants removed the main courses. "What troubles you, Lady Wescott?"

She let out a breath. "I wonder if our walk exhausted me. Perhaps I should retire."

"You shall not retire, not until you've tried some of the cook's berry trifle."

A bowing footman offered a choice of blackberry or elderberry, the shiny fruit covered with toasted biscuit crumbles and cream. She selected the blackberry and stared at it. It was better than staring at his hands.

"Go on then," he said. "Take a bite, for God's sake. You'll enjoy it. This moping and withering of yours has got to stop."

"Moping and withering? My lord, I'm tired."

"You're not tired. You merely wish to discourage me from seeking your bed, as you do every night. Eat that blasted dessert before I feed it to you myself."

She stiffened her spine and tried a bite, and found she enjoyed it in spite of herself. The berries were the sweetest and juiciest she'd had in a while, not that she would tell him that.

"It's quite good," she said in a dull tone, hiding her delight. She knew she sounded shrewish. He would grow to hate her past the point of bearing, and then he'd leave her. Perhaps that was what she wanted.

No, she didn't want it.

She didn't know what she wanted anymore, or how to fix things when they'd gone so very wrong. The next bite stuck in her throat, as her eyes filled with tears. Crying over blackberries? She tried to will the tears away, but it was useless. She swallowed the berries and looked away from him. She'd been trying so hard to resist her roiling emotions that they exploded in a rather dramatic way, her tears soaking her cheeks.

When she looked for a napkin, he reached within his coat and produced a handkerchief instead. She took it and pressed it to her eyes, and realized that it smelled like him, like his earthy, spicy cologne. She knew his smell and his voice, and was coming to know his expressions. Why, she knew everything about him. Mostly, she knew how disappointed he was in their marriage.

"I wish I could go home." That was what she said aloud, but inside her mind the words tumbled, *I'm afraid, I'm afraid, I'm afraid. I'm afraid of you touching me. I'm afraid of you hating me. I'm afraid to be your wife.*

"You can't go home, Ophelia. Your home is here now." He took her plate away as she stabbed blindly at blackberries. "Come, leave that. I've something to show you."

He led her from the dining room into the hallway, then turned her toward the other side of the house. They passed the formal parlors and receiving rooms, him drawing her along so quickly that she didn't think to resist. She swabbed at her tears as he opened a door to a salon at the end of the hallway. A pair of footmen materialized with lamps to light the darkened room.

She looked about as the lamps illuminated luxuriously papered walls. They were in a gallery filled with dozens of grand family portraits, some with a single subject and others with a posed arrangement of parents, children, and pets. The sumptuous paintings drew the viewer back through time, the subjects' clothing and hairstyles recalling earlier eras. On the oldest, faded paintings, the eyes seemed to move as the lamplight guttered and rose.

"This is why you can't go home," he said. "These are generations of my family, dukes and marquesses, earls and knights and barons who've lived upon the land and the land around it." He watched her as she stood immobile, wringing her hands. "You've doubtless got family portraits as well, and a proud Halsey history. Now our families have joined together, through us."

"I know." She turned about, feeling judged by every face, every smile and staunch expression. Then she noticed a portrait of his parents, both of them smiling in marital bliss, and thought of the temple out in the garden. "I know that. I know I've not been a proper wife." She turned back to him. "I did not imagine my life going this way. I wanted to sing for a bit longer."

"You wanted to sing? You won't even sing for me."

"I wanted to do more than marry," she said in a burst of bravado. "I wanted to go beyond Vienna and music lessons. My mother promised I could see Italy and Spain, perhaps even Greece." Her voice trailed off. She wished she hadn't mentioned Greece, the place that had inspired the folly in the garden.

One of his brows rose. "I didn't realize you had such an affection for travel."

"I don't. I haven't. I mean, I haven't gone anywhere yet, and now..."

"Now you are married to me and imprisoned here in my pile of rocks in the country. I see how that could dampen a lady's mood."

"You mock me. Nothing in your life has changed, but I have lost... I've lost everything." Her tears came back, and she wiped them away angrily. "I'm very cross about it all, not that you care."

He came to stand beside her, his arm coming around her waist when she moved to evade him. "Come here, little crosspatch. Kiss me."

"I don't want to."

"Indeed, I see that. I've never had a young lady speak to me as you have, with such drama and emotion. You're not onstage anymore."

She pushed at him. "I don't want to be."

"You don't want anything, do you, except to flail and complain and bemoan this miserable marriage?"

It was true. She was flailing and making a scene, pushing him away, resisting everything she must submit to. His body felt hard against hers, and overwhelming. He took her face in his hands and made her look into his eyes. How green they were, how intent, like chips of jade.

"For all that you don't like me," he said in his fine, haughty voice, "I like you very much. I want to have children with you, children with your beauty and spirit, and your cursed stubbornness."

"I'm not stubborn."

He laughed. "Not when you get your way. But the rest of the time, you're a stubborn, annoying pain in my arse." She gasped at the insult, but he laughed. "No matter, little crosspatch. We're a pair now, a couple, whatever we wished for before."

He indicated his handsome, formal ancestors, looking at them from the portraits on the walls. "I know you don't want to be married into my august family, but you are. We're husband and wife forevermore, and we'll come to know each other and put up with one another's quirks, like your utter fear of intimacy. I'll break you of that eventually."

She would not cry. She would not give in to the crushing guilt she felt about her failure in this quarter.

"You are not natural," she said, the first excuse she could spout at him. "When it comes to intimacy, you want things no one else wants, things no proper gentleman should enjoy."

"I don't believe that's true, having more knowledge of sexuality than yourself." He tightened his embrace as she tried to squirm away from him. "Perhaps I've been amiss in my tutoring. I can't expect you to enjoy things you haven't been taught."

As he said this, he moved his hips against hers, so she could feel that hard, thick part of him that marked him as male. It sent her into a panic.

"Please, no," she said. "I don't want that. I'm still not ready."

"Very well. Then you must be punished for denying me my husbandly rights." His expression deepened, his fingers moving up her spine as she tried to escape his embrace. "A bit of erotic punishment seems just the thing, since you're curious about it."

She gaped at him. "I'm not at all curious. I'm not."

"You will be, by the time I'm finished with you."

With those frightening words, he swept her into his arms and carried her from the room, toward the great stone stairway in the outer hall.

Chapter Ten: Erotic Punishment

Wescott stopped at the door to his room to request some needed items from a footman. A cane, some fragrant oil, a stout ginger plug. The Abbey's kitchen staff was used to such requests. As for Ophelia, she trembled in his arms.

He would make it bearable for her, and yes, erotic, but there would be an element of punishment too. She must learn to submit to this marriage, and to him. If it took a certain amount of painful training to force her obedience, well, that was her choice.

He set her down in the middle of his bedroom, hoping she wouldn't make a scene and try to escape by banging on the door or some such nonsense. To his relief, she did nothing more than back away a few steps.

"I don't know what you mean to do with me, my lord, but I don't...I don't want it."

"You've made that clear." He gave a show of casual control, but her pouting lips had him aroused nearly to a boiling point. "You'll need to remove your clothes now, Ophelia, all of them. You may do it yourself, or I can call a maid to help you."

She waited, still trembling. "Why must I remove my clothes?"

"Because it will make it easier to place the ginger fig in your bottom and cane you, as I have planned."

Her mouth fell open. "But you can't do such things! What are you speaking of? You can't mean to—"

"Shall I call Rochelle?"

He moved toward the bell pull and saw the choices flash across his wife's expression. If Rochelle came, Ophelia might plead for her help, but that would only put Rochelle in an awkward position. Worse, the servant would know her mistress was being punished.

"Very well," she said, half in tears. "I'll remove my gown. But I cannot undo the buttons."

He moved behind her to assist, easing her tiny pearl buttons from their loops. He felt a pang of guilt. She was so young compared to him, so small and afraid and inexperienced. He would not hurt her, not really. He was only showing her what intimacy meant to him, and therefore, must mean to her.

"You may lay your gown across the divan," he said.

She obeyed, crossing to the dark furniture in her underthings. Her frilly froth of a dress looked out of place in his bedroom, which was hard and dark and masculine. How gracefully she moved, perhaps because of her stage training.

"Remove the rest," he said when she turned back to him. "I'm your husband now. You must learn not to hide your body from me during intimate times."

She didn't want to follow his instructions, but she did, stripping off her stays, chemise, and stockings while sniffing back theatrical tears. Poor thing. She was right about one thing...her life would have been very different if she hadn't married him. But she had.

He removed his coat and rolled up his shirtsleeves, going over his plans in his head. He might not seduce his way inside her tonight, but he would teach her the power he wielded over her. A quiet knock at the door told him the tools he needed were at hand.

"You may stand behind the bed," he said, "so the servants do not see you."

She scurried over to the head of his bed, to the long, obscuring velvet curtains, and waited there as a pair of maidservants laid the cane upon a table, as well as the tray containing the oil and an already trimmed and feathered ginger plug. When the maids left, pink flushes upon their cheeks, Ophelia stayed hiding behind the curtain.

He moved a chair over beside the table and seated himself, patting his lap. "Come, little crosspatch."

"I don't want to." Her voice was muffled in the corner. "What are you going to do?"

"I'm going to put a ginger fig in your bottom to make you feel naughty and punished, and then I plan to stand you against the bed and subject you to the cane." He picked it up and showed it to her. "Have you ever been caned, Ophelia?"

"No," she cried. "And I don't wish to be."

"Hmm. But I think you need it. Come here and lie across my lap, so you can see how it feels to be gingered like a bad girl."

"I don't want to," she pleaded.

He gave her his sternest Arlington glare. "Shall I drag you, then, and throw you over my knees? Either way, this is happening. If I must force you, you'll receive twice the cane strokes. That's an ongoing rule in this house. Refusal doubles the punishment."

"You are a despicable man." She approached him with a quick, panicked gait, covering her breasts and her mons with her hands as well as she could. He drew them away as soon as she reached him and arranged her across his knees. She was so tense she could barely bend. "Easy," he said. "If you fight me, it will go worse."

"But I don't want this."

"Indeed, but wanting and needing are two different things."

He held her protesting form still with one hand upon her waist and reached for the ginger with the other. If she was one of Pearl's wanton courtesans, he would have made a point of shaming her, spreading her cheeks and teasing her small hole before he thrust in the ginger, but this was his wife, and she was shy and afraid. He felt a perverse spark of lust, as well as protectiveness.

"This will feel cold and uncomfortable," he warned. "As it's meant to. If you fuss and toss around as I punish you, it will become more uncomfortable still, so behave, and resign yourself."

She stiffened as he prodded the narrowed tip of the fresh ginger against her tiny arse hole. When he began to slide it in, she made frantic sounds of dismay. It was slim, too slim to really hurt her, but her embarrassment was evident. She trembled violently as he pushed it home, so it rested just inside her rectum, with a flange outside her bottom to keep it seated.

"There," he said, holding her steady across his lap. "Now, you may feel it tingle and burn. This is to remind you how naughty and stubborn you've been."

"It hurts," she said weakly. "Please, take it out."

"It doesn't hurt. You haven't felt hurt yet."

He could see the ginger's burn take effect in the moments that followed, because her pale, heart-shaped bottom cheeks began to twitch and tense. She reached back, but he caught her hand. "No, my dear. You're not to interfere when you're being punished. Keep your hands in front of you, placed right against the floor."

She obeyed with a moan, but it was, perhaps, a slightly confused sounding moan. As ginger burned and tingled, it also stimulated carnal feelings. He made as if to settle her more firmly in his lap, and brushed his fingers twice across the small, sensitive spot between her pussy lips. To his amusement, she trembled in response, moving her hips. Of course, as she squirmed, her arse squeezed the ginger, intensifying its sting. She let out a chastened gasp.

"Please, my lord, how long will it...will it stay in?"

"Call me Wescott."

"Please, Wescott, how long must it stay in? It burns so."

"That depends on your own behavior. Stand up now. Go to the bed and brace your hands upon it."

She moved where he guided her, with much less resistance than before. It never failed to amaze him, how punishing a woman's arsehole made her so much more submissive. He'd have to remember that for Ophelia's more ornery days.

"Don't shrink away," he said, as she cowered against the bed. "You must present your bottom for caning, or the strokes won't count." He took up the solid rattan implement and gave her a couple soft taps with the tip. "You'll receive only five strokes since this is your first time. If you don't stand perfectly still and submit to each stroke, that number will increase to ten, then fifteen, and so on."

He thought he heard her utter a whispered prayer. How he wanted to fall on his wife as she held the edge of his bed, her bottom tense and trembling, her feet restless upon the floor. He wished to strip off his clothes and thrust inside her pussy while the ginger burned and tormented her arse, and ride her that way until the fierce desire inside him was released. But no, she would be afraid of him in truth then, afraid of how passionate he could be.

Instead, he drew his arm back and delivered a short, crisp stroke of the cane. It was barely a tap, but on a virgin bottom like Ophelia's, it doubtless felt awful. Her legs buckled and she let out a shocked cry.

"Oh, no. No." She fell to her knees and turned to him. "Please."

He'd left a faint stripe across the perfect center of her cheeks. How lovely it looked with the ginger peeking out in the midst of it, but her gaze was awash in pain.

"Stand up," he said. "You've four more to go. Nine more, if you won't cooperate."

"I can't. I couldn't." Her voice shook. "Please, my lord. I mean, Wescott."

When he did not relent, she got to her feet and stood against his bed again, a cowering ball of reluctance. The second stroke connected, leaving another pretty mark across her bottom. Her reaction was the same, a collapse, pleas, and tears shimmering in her eyes.

"You've only had two strokes," he scolded. "Five isn't so very many to bear."

"Please, I can't. The ginger burns so, and my bottom feels as if it's on fire."

She covered her striped cheeks, begging him not to continue. He pretended disappointment, tapping the cane against his leg.

"If you will not submit to your punishment, you will have to placate me in some other way." He placed the cane on the bed in front of her, as a reminder and threat, and sat to her side, sliding his hand down against her mons. She was hot and wet, perhaps from angst, or perhaps from some burgeoning sense of the erotic. When she moved her hips away, he made a sound in his throat.

"No, this is your only other choice besides the cane. Stand still. Let me do as I wish."

She still held onto the bed's edge, and looked straight ahead, avoiding his eyes as he slid his hand lower, parting her with his fingers. He found her hidden button and massaged it slowly, drawing moisture from her quim to slicken his touch.

She shifted, trying not to be affected. Her breath quickened, but she said nothing, just held tight to the bed. He rubbed her buttocks with his other hand, tracing over the pink cane welts that must still hurt. She gritted her teeth as he massaged her both places, giving her pain and pleasure in equal measure. His cock strained against his trousers. This was as excruciating for him as for her. It was also wonderful.

"Unbutton my shirt," he ordered, giving her a quick spank when she hesitated. She set to the buttons, trying to concentrate on the task as he continued to tease and caress her hidden pearl. "Now take it off me," he said when she finished.

He ceased caressing her so she could remove his shirt. As she stared at his chest, he eased closer to her. The poor thing didn't know what to do with her hands. "Unbutton my trousers now," he said.

She met his eyes, because looking at his trousers seemed too much for her sensibilities. He'd gone rigid beneath the buff fabric, his cock a bulging, obscene outline. He smothered the impulse to laugh as her fingers skirted the obvious protuberance. Ignoring it would not make it go away. As she unbuttoned his falls, his cock emerged, quite in his wife's face. Well, let her see what she did to him.

"Touch it," he said in a low voice. "Stroke it with your hand."

"I don't know how."

"Do it." He took her hands and placed them on his length. "You know how to touch things."

She gave in and moved her hands beneath his, with the softest, most teasing glide of her fingers. "It's too big," she whispered. "I don't like it."

"You are honest to a fault." He huffed out a breath. "Stay where you are, crosspatch. Don't move. I'm not finished with you, or this erotic punishment of yours."

He went to the tray to fetch the vial of slick oil. He smoothed some onto his fingers, and over his straining member. "There," he said. "You must rub it into me now."

She stared at him, her small fingers clasped before her chest. Her upturned nipples taunted him. She was so much more lovely than she knew, so much more lovely than a prudish woman like her had a right to be.

"Why must I do that?" she asked.

"Because I've said so. Here." He poured more oil into his hands and then onto hers, coating her fingers. The oil's perfume was subtly exotic, flowery but musky, the scent rising between them. His balls ached, and his shaft was near to exploding. "Stroke me," he insisted. "And don't stop until I tell you to."

As she anxiously handled his length, he put his hands back on her, sliding his fingers to her mons and lower. While the ginger continued to tingle in her arse, he fingered her quim, shoving a finger up inside her. She rose on her toes and tried to twist away. With a patient sigh, he put her hands back on his cock, showing her how to stimulate him. Whenever she stopped, he gave her a spank or two until she started again.

Meanwhile, he played between her pussy lips, trying to draw her attention to the pleasure within herself. She caressed his granite-hard shaft in fits and starts, but he gave her no respite from his own skilled touch. Soon, her hips rocked in conjunction with his movements. Her breath shortened, coming out in little gasps.

"Yes," he said. "This is your penalty, if you won't take your caning. You must show me how naughty you are."

"I'm not naughty." Her words were a plea, a whimper. She pressed her forehead into his chest as he redoubled his assault.

"You're very naughty, I fear."

She didn't stroke him anymore, but he didn't mind in the moment. He pinched one of her nipples, and was rewarded with a harried sigh, and another lovely jerk of her hips. He pinched it harder when she tried to squirm away. He could have lifted her onto his cock now. She could not have resisted, but he decided to play with her instead, to show her what he could do even if she wouldn't let him bed her.

"Do you like that?" he asked. "Shall I continue?"

"Oh, no." She shook her head. "You shouldn't."

Even as she said it, she bucked her mons against his hand. His middle finger slid over her center, wet and slick with her own juices in addition to the oil, and his other hand molested her without quarter, even pressing the ginger more deeply into her arse. She could barely stand, but he made her. This was a punishment of sorts, after all.

You see, he thought, drawing her ever closer to release. *You see what I can make you do, little crosspatch? You see that you will be mine? You'll be mine if I wish it.*

Her trembling reached an apex. She let go of the bed and braced herself against his chest, moaning as his fingers pushed her over the edge. When she came off, it was as if she frightened herself. She hid her face, muffling cries of erotic agony against his chest. A lovely punishment, this. He thought so, if she did not. When she pulled away from him, her crisis ended, his cock still rose between them, straining even more.

"Stroke me now. Don't stop." He added more oil and forced her to move her hands along with him, their fingers tangling upon his shaft. He could see in her gaze that she thought his cock was great and imposing, some fearful, curious thing. Again, his carnal side wished to lift her and impale her immediately, to come inside her and spend his seed. But he wouldn't. *I will be inside you,* he thought, *but not until you welcome me. Not until you crave me. I won't force myself in.*

He held his wife's hands upon his cock and shoved into them, letting her feel his member pulsing as he reached his satisfaction. His seed spurted with great force, falling on his stomach and chest, and on her hands. Some landed on the bed. Every nerve fired with pleasure, until he felt wrung out. He'd been too long without release, and his prickly, prudish wife fired his blood to hell for some inexplicable reason.

But he did not do much for her. She regarded him with barely veiled disgust, as if she'd received no pleasure at all a few minutes earlier.

"It's a perfectly natural biological function," he said in his defense. "Your satisfaction, too."

She stood beside him, so close and yet so far away. Ah well, it would take more than sensual satisfaction to cure what was wrong between them. At least they'd shared a few moments of bliss.

He relieved her of the ginger in her bottom and sent her to his washroom to clean up. Afterward, he made her climb naked into his bed. Did she consider that a punishment? Probably, but he chose not to ask. He wanted her near him after they'd shared such heady, perverse acts. If she had nightmares—of the fire, or of his "awful" cock rising up before her—he might as well be right there next to her to soothe her terrors away.

"I like you," he said again as they lay together in the dark. She curled as far from him as she was able, but in sleep, she always ended up in his arms. "I like you even if you don't like me."

"It's hard to like you when you're always punishing me," she said. "Especially when it's not deserved."

"I decide when it's deserved. Perhaps I'll take you to the Greek temple next time."

She made no answer to that, only lay very still as if to discourage that line of thought, or escape his notice altogether. He was probably making a mess of things in their new marriage, but he'd always been one to act up and do as he pleased. His father called it boldness and thought it was good. His mother called it mischief and chided him to be civil. His wife...

Well, she had two stripes across her bottom, and a lingering bit of sting in her arsehole for good measure. She would lie still and pretend surrender for now, but it was temporary, which pleased him. If they must be rivals, he would turn it to his purposes time and again, until she realized her resistance was pointless.

When she began to murmur in her restless dreams, he drew her naked limbs close and cradled her until the tension ebbed and eased away. "Sweet songbird," he whispered. "This isn't a cage, you know. I'll hear you sing again one day."

He didn't stir again until late the next morning, when he heard his valet tap softly from the dressing room.

"What is it?" he asked, blinking to wakefulness. His wife came from a heavy sleep, stirring against his side. She looked tired in the late morning light, rumpled in the most alluring way.

"My lord," he said through the door. "You have visitors: your parents the Duke and Duchess have arrived with Lady Hazel and Lady Elizabeth, and a pair of your gentleman friends."

He rubbed a hand through his hair, stifling a groan. Visitors? It hadn't been a week yet since they'd married.

"Marlow and Augustine?" he asked.

"Indeed, my lord. They've apologized that it's not winter yet."

Marlow and Augustine would have come to the country with their families to spend a few days. He supposed he was lucky the entire Oxfordshire circle hadn't arrived on his doorstep. Here he was in his honeymoon bed with a morning cock as stiff as petrified wood, and a drawing room full of visitors.

"We've offered them luncheon in the larger parlor," his valet added when he didn't stir or reply.

"Very well," he called toward the door. "I'll get up to dress in a moment."

"I await your pleasure, my lord."

As Wescott stretched beside his bride, memories of the previous night returned, making his cock ache even more. She remembered too, if her sudden blush and frown was any indication.

"Some family and friends have come to visit," he told her. "That's the only thing about the Abbey. It's situated far too close to everyone else's home." He reached to touch a lock of her hair, so blonde and fine. "As much as you love lying abed with me, we must awaken and dress."

She needed no further invitation to escape his company, and made as if to rise at once, but he pulled her back and surprised her with a kiss. Perhaps it surprised both of them. She responded at first, moving her lips against his, but as soon as he pulled her closer, the mood was broken and she scooted back.

"It would be rude to keep our visitors waiting," she said.

His only answer was a frustrated sigh as she went for her dress and stockings, and wrapped them about her waist to hide her naked, cane-marked bottom as she left.

Chapter Eleven:
Visitors

Ophelia shifted in her wing chair, her bottom still sore from last night's "erotic punishment." Worse, her husband kept catching her eye amidst the company's merry conversations. She suspected he enjoyed watching her discomfort from across the drawing room, where he sat with his friends. That was the sort of perverse person he was.

Their guests kept the tone light at the after-dinner gathering, and she tried to fit in, playing the contented wife as far as she was able.

Which wasn't very far.

Oh, she knew enough to play a gracious hostess. She'd learned it from her mother, in between embroidery and music lessons. She directed the seating at dinner and conferred with the cook on a pleasing menu, and had the servants make up comfortable rooms when it seemed their guests might be staying for a few days.

It frustrated Wescott, but what did it matter if they had visitors? Their honeymoon had been over before it began.

She was also capable of making polite conversation with her husband's parents, who were not haughty at all, despite their ducal titles and wealth. His mother spoke kindly to her, asking how she liked Wescott Abbey. What she meant was, *how do you like being married to my son?* Ophelia had answered that it was a lovely place, not mentioning that she'd barely roamed beyond her own suite of rooms, at least inside the house.

"Ophelia, you look so far away."

Elizabeth's voice at her shoulder startled her from her darkening thoughts. Wescott's youngest sister was sixteen, only a couple years younger than her, but she was so innocent, bright, and pure that Ophelia barely knew what to say to her. The ebony-haired young woman had played the piano when they first retired after dinner, and encouraged Ophelia to sing. Instead, she'd sat by the fire, blushing and refusing to share her talent. *I still cannot sing,* she'd lied. *I'm sorry. The fire...*

"I'm not so far away," she said, smiling at Elizabeth. "Just thinking of your skill at the piano. You must practice a great deal."

"I don't practice as much as I should. August is better, and you ought to hear his father play. Do you remember Lord Barrymore from the wedding? He looks exactly like August, but for a few strands of silver in his hair."

"Indeed, I remember meeting Lord Barrymore, as well as his wife. You are all very close," Ophelia observed.

"Family friends." Elizabeth rolled her green eyes, so like to her brother's. "Which is well enough until you must go to this party or that because Mama's friends are planning it, or dance with this or that son at a ball because you haven't enough names on your dance card. That didn't happen to me," she added. "I'm not old enough for balls yet, not really, but Mama allowed me to attend a few given by the Warrens, as long as I didn't dance."

"I haven't been to many balls." Ophelia's own foray into society had been so brief, and so fraught with worry about her reputation, that she hadn't been able to enjoy much dancing, flirtation, and courtship. "I was studying music in Vienna for the last several years."

"How interesting, that you lived in Vienna. I've never been there. I haven't done a great deal at all, although I will when I'm older. At least I hope so."

She made a small frown, and Ophelia thought again how very innocent she was. The girl would have less opportunity to do things in the future, if she married. Even a duke's daughter would find her world shrunk down to a respectable, confining box within society.

"Will you tell me what it was like at your music school?" she asked. "Did you have daily lessons? Were any of your teachers famous? Did you sing in many operas? How often did you perform?"

Ophelia smiled at Elizabeth's curiosity and glanced about the room, saw that Wescott's parents and his other sister had taken up a game of cards with Lord Marlow, and that her husband was deep in conversation with Lord Augustine. "I did have daily lessons, and we performed quite a lot as part of our studies. We were graded on our performances, even ranked against one another. I suppose some of my teachers were famous. At times, great masters would spend a few days in our classes to instruct and inspire us."

"And were you inspired?"

"Some of the time."

"Do you like being married to my brother?"

Elizabeth's abrupt change of topic took her aback. She could be very direct, her light eyes piercing beneath her deep black hair.

"Of...of course I like being married to Wescott. He is a very...good husband."

"A good husband." She smothered a laugh behind a small, gloved hand. "What a perfectly polite thing to say. Now tell me the truth, Ophelia, because I'd always pictured Jack being a bang-up husband when he finally got married, but the two of you are chilly as anything together."

"Chilly?"

"Chilly," Elizabeth repeated, not taking any of the bluntness off the word. "Like you don't care for each other very much."

Ophelia blinked, wondering how to explain the direction of their marriage so far. Chilly, yes, and a disaster too, especially in the bedroom.

And that, Ophelia, is entirely your stubborn fault.

"We are still getting to know each other, I suppose," she said aloud.

Wescott's sister had an uncanny habit of studying people's faces, and whenever she turned those eyes on Ophelia, she felt she could read every emotion there—even the ones she hid.

"You know, we have hardly been married," she went on. "It's only been a few days. Things can't be perfect all at once."

"No," Elizabeth agreed. "Things will improve when you know Wescott better." Her sincerity was endearing, as was her adoration for her big brother. "He's the best sort of man. He can tease and be sweet, but be strong and protective too. He knows how to fight with swords, did you know that?"

Ophelia shook her head, glancing over at her husband, deep in conversation with his friend. What was he telling him? How awful she was as a wife? How many times he'd had to punish her thus far?

"He learned to wield swords because he was too restless to succeed at piano," Elizabeth went on. "My brother Gareth and he used to practice with swords for hours, and pretend they were knights rescuing damsels. Gareth grew out of it, he's off now at university, but Wescott stayed with it. When he's in London, he practices at a club with other swordsmen, not that gentlemen fight with swords anymore like they did in the old days. But he looks so dashing when he does."

Ophelia sat quietly, listening to all this. Wescott, adept at swordplay? What an interesting hobby, and she hadn't heard a word about it from him.

"He has an armor room here at the Abbey," Elizabeth said, her voice dropping to a whisper. "I don't know where it is. I've never been allowed in."

"Why not?"

She giggled. "Because I'm his annoying little sister and he doesn't trust me with the knowledge. It's hidden away. There's a secret passage or something to get there. I suppose it's down underground, so I don't want to go there, but isn't it interesting? I'm sure he'll show it to you some day."

Ophelia wasn't so sure, but she held her tongue.

"There are ghosts too, I think," Elizabeth went on. "Perhaps they take up the swords in Wescott's secret armory and have battles while we all sleep."

Goodness, his sister was imaginative. "I'm looking forward to meeting all the ghosts here, and finding Wescott's secret hideaways."

Elizabeth looked pleased, her pretty face lighting up. "Oh, I hope you do. It's the perfect continuation of your love story."

"I don't know that we have a love story yet," said Ophelia, not quite suppressing a sigh.

"Oh, but you do. He rescued you the night of that awful fire, like a knight in shining armor." Elizabeth clasped her hands, her voice going soft and dreamy. "You were a real-life damsel in distress."

"That was a terrible night, though, not a fantasy in any way."

"But he saved you, and look at you both now, married, setting up a home in this fascinating, mysterious old place."

Ophelia couldn't imagine how Elizabeth thought any of those were good things, or romantic things. She'd had so many nightmares about the fire, and now his sister was stirring up the idea of ghosts...

Wescott turned at that moment to look at her, and in his gaze she saw a protectiveness she didn't expect. He appeared quickly enough each time she had a nightmare, and beat away the fiery demons that tormented her. It wasn't difficult to imagine him brandishing a sword, and probably besting all the other gentlemen at his London sports club.

"The swords have blunt edges," Elizabeth said, as if she'd heard Ophelia's thoughts. "So they can't stab each other, although they do get hurt sometimes. Wescott came home with such a bruise one day when he was younger. It ran all along his side and up his right arm. Mama didn't like it at all, but Papa said he could be brash if he liked it, for he was to be the duke one day."

"He's good at being brash," Ophelia said, turning from her husband's gaze.

"How was it when he rescued you?" asked Elizabeth wistfully. "Was it as romantic as I imagine? I'd like to be rescued someday. It must be a lovely feeling, to be whisked away from danger by someone caring and strong."

How naive the young woman was. Her rescue hadn't been lovely at all. "That night was more frightening than romantic," she said, looking down at her hands. "Of course, I would have hated to succumb to the fire, but it was also scary to be rescued by your brother. I didn't know him when he swept me up onto his horse."

"Ah, he swept you up." A soft blush pinkened Elizabeth's cheeks. "My head is full of silly dreams, everyone says so. Forgive me. Of course the fire was frightening and not romantic at all. I'm glad you're here now, and safe. Wescott will always keep you safe and help chase away your fears."

Ophelia glanced again at her husband, wondering if he'd told his family about her nightmares. "I'm sure he wants me to be happy." By some miracle, she kept the doubt from her voice.

"Oh, yes, of course he does," Elizabeth said with no doubt at all. "He was the best big brother to me and my sisters, the very best. I know a great many things about him even though we're the farthest apart in age. I shall tell you some things right now, so you can know him better. Where to start?" She laughed. "Well, he can be a bit high and mighty at times. You've probably already realized that."

Ophelia shifted on her bottom without thinking. "I did realize that early on."

"Let's see, what else? He enjoys gambling at cards, but he's not a problem gambler. He mainly plays at parties so he can win small prizes and gloat."

"I can see him doing that." Elizabeth's comical tidbits about her brother were starting to mellow Ophelia's dark mood.

"He also likes the theater. Oh, I hope your voice recovers, because he'd love to hear you sing. As far as what he likes to eat, it's pretty much anything and everything, although he's especially fond of Welsh shortbread."

"Welsh shortbread?" Ophelia tilted her head in question. "How is that different from Scottish shortbread?"

"It's not different at all," said Elizabeth with a grin. "But Mama told us it was Welsh whenever the cook made it for us, because that's where she was from. We're all half-Welsh, which is where I got this dark hair. It runs in her family. I wonder if your children will have dark, Welsh hair. Probably not, since Wescott got my father's blond hair, and you're blonder still. Are you half-anything?"

Ophelia thought a moment. "I'm...well. Perhaps I'm half used to being married to your brother." She might as well tell her the truth. "I'm half worried, and half pleased. Sometimes I look at him and find him very handsome and interesting, and the other half of the time, I wish I was back at my parents' house in my childhood bed."

Elizabeth's easy smile dimmed a little at those words. "Oh, Ophelia, I suppose that's how things naturally go, if you don't marry for love. I'm sad things aren't falling right into place for both of you, but they will. You must believe that."

Whether they do or not, I'm stuck for life. She didn't say the words to Elizabeth. His sister was so kind, and so fond of Wescott, she couldn't say anything rude.

"You must come visit me at Arlington Hall this fall and winter," she said. "Whenever you're frustrated or lonely, ride over to see me and we'll pretend to be real sisters, and tell each other all the secrets we wish. I can help you solve any problems that come up, and you can help me prepare for my first season, since you'll be a wise married lady and I've not even danced at any balls." She clapped her hands. "Oh, and we can use familiar names with one another. Sometimes my family calls me Lisbet, and you...perhaps I can call you Fifi. Isn't that a pet name for Ophelia?"

She hid a grimace. "You can call me Fifi if you like."

"Perfect. Come, would you like to talk to Hazel? I believe their card game is at an end. Look how my sister pouts, she must have lost badly. By the by, Hazel thinks your fine, pale hair is ever so pretty and elegant. She's jealous but she wouldn't admit it. She's just your age, and she can't wait to be married. Our other sister Charlotte just married last year, and she and her husband are expecting a baby soon, and my oldest sister Louisa, well, she's been married forever." Elizabeth paused to laugh. "Louisa gives all of us advice about husbands and children whenever we see her, whether we ask for it or not."

"My sister recently married too," Ophelia offered, trying to get in a word edgewise. "Her name is Nanette."

"I imagine Charlotte and Hazel might know her. Let's go ask."

Elizabeth took her hand and led her over to Hazel, rattling off the primary men her sister was interested in, as well as the hopefuls who didn't stand a chance. Ophelia didn't know who any of them were, but the sisters' chatter was so amusing, she could almost picture the hapless men trying to keep up.

Like Elizabeth, Hazel was well-spoken and warm, and indeed eager to marry and have children. Why couldn't Ophelia be happy with such traditions? Why had she pined for a more adventurous life, only to lose any chance of it?

Worst of all, why couldn't she situate herself with Lord Wescott, when those around him esteemed him so greatly? In this room of his family and friends, she felt lonelier than ever. She felt like the very worst wife.

* * * * *

August nudged Wescott with a grin. "Look at your poor wife," he said. "Hazel and Elizabeth are chattering her ears off."

"Good, it's been too quiet here for her." He leaned back in his chair, crossing one leg over the other. "It's good that they're getting along."

"How are you getting along?" he asked when Wescott fell silent.

He met the query with a shrug. "As well as any strangers who were recently forced to be married. Lady Wescott holds the whole situation in disdain, not that it matters at this point. You know me. I'm one to make the best of things and move on."

"Indeed."

They watched the women talking, as August shared news of his twin sisters Isabella and Constance, their husbands, and their ever-growing brood of chatty little girls. His sisters adored their impish "cousins," even though they weren't real cousins. In their circle of friends, everyone was family.

Wescott appreciated that Hazel and Elizabeth were doing their best to draw Ophelia into the familial group. He could also see his wife was not as comfortable as she pretended to be. He wondered how often she'd had time to sit about and gossip with friends at her blasted Viennese school.

"I don't think she likes me," he finally admitted out loud. "Not even a little. She wants to be somewhere else and lets me know it with daunting regularity. Back at home. Onstage. Traveling the world, she told me, as if her parents would have allowed it. She's a silly ninny most of the time."

Augustine studied Ophelia, his features creased in question. He tended to be quiet and clumsy, and was often the butt of their jokes, but he was probably, also, the most thoughtful of the four of them.

"Do you have advice?" Wescott asked.

"I can't say I do. Haven't been married, my friend. The most experience I have with women is jollying up the tarts at Pearl's, and I can't even do that now, until the madam rebuilds from the fire."

137

"Wives are nothing like the tarts at Pearl's," he said drily. "They're far more sensitive, in all the worst ways."

"Sorry to hear it, Wes. You know, we would have waited longer to intrude upon your solitude, but Elizabeth was bound and determined we must come at once." August turned his thoughtful gaze to Wescott's sister. "We told her you needed more time alone together, but you know how she is with her..." He gestured into the air. "Her mysterious intuitions."

"My parents should not indulge her intuitions. If she doesn't take care, she'll get a reputation as some sort of spiritualist."

"You must admit, her instincts are often true."

Wescott shrugged again. From an early age, Elizabeth had exhibited the strangest talent at reading people's faces, and often, eerily, their unspoken thoughts. He'd flattened a man once for calling his sister the "Arlington witch."

"She must learn to keep her instincts to herself," Wescott said, as Marlow joined them. "Although I'm grateful for my family's company, and yours. How was the game?" he asked Marlow.

"Convivial as always. Your father trounced us soundly, and Hazel came dead last. She has no talent for cards."

"Or very much interest," Wescott said with a laugh. "She'd rather be dancing or playing the piano, or buying new gowns."

"She'll be breaking hearts next year on the marriage mart," said August. "I know at least fifteen men who want to court her, and only five or six are in it for the family connections. She'll have her choice of the best."

"I hope neither of you are on that list."

Marlow huffed out a laugh. "I'd just as well court my sister. I'm afraid our families are too close. I played with Hazel when she was in diapers, and Elizabeth too."

August made a lackluster sound of agreement, and Wescott wished he hadn't made the thoughtless joke. They all sometimes forgot how much the young Lord Augustine had pined for Townsend's oldest sister, Felicity. August had worshipped the ground she walked on, even as she kindly pushed him away, wanting nothing to do with such a young, awkward boy. She was long wed now, to a dashing Italian prince who'd swept her off her feet as August looked on helplessly.

"My advice to both of you is not to marry at all, for as long as you can hold out," he said, to change the subject. "It's a terrible disruption to the bachelor life."

His friends laughed. "Thanks for warning us," said Marlow. "We wouldn't have known."

Wescott had felt at ease with the other two gentlemen for as long as he could remember, but something was missing. They all felt it. Townsend had always rounded out their conversations with his pithy remarks. "What do you think Towns is up to?" he asked, trying to sound casual. "Have his parents had any letters?"

"You ought to ask Hazel," August said. "She and his sister Rosalind are close in age. The two of them ought to scheme to get him interested in some other lady..." His voice trailed off.

"Some other lady than my wife?" finished Wescott wryly. "That would probably be best. I'm not certain he won't slap a glove in my face when we all return to London."

"By Christmastide, he'll have mellowed," said Marlow. "We'll drag him along for our winter visit here at the Abbey and force him to come around with country dances and sherry."

"We'll put mistletoe everywhere," agreed August. "And keep your pretty wife away from it. She is pretty as blazes, Wes. That must make you happy."

"We're happy enough." He frowned. "For people so recently wed."

Marlow shook his head. "That doesn't sound very enthusiastic."

"He says she doesn't like him at all," said August. "Bit of a shame."

Marlow's eyes lit with mischief. "You must step up your powers of seduction, then. I can offer some tips if you like."

"Obnoxious," murmured August. "Just because you're the ladykiller of our group."

"I've never killed any lady, except with pleasure."

"Gentlemen," said Wescott. "We're not drunk enough for this conversation, and not alone enough." He swept his glance about the warm, bright parlor, and lowered his voice. "Although I'll say things are just fine in *that* area of our marriage. It's the one time she goes quiet, if you know what I mean."

August shook his head. "I'd rather not know what you mean."

And I'd rather not admit the truth, that I haven't been inside her once since we've been married. How they would mock him forever afterward about it, even if he managed to bed her tonight. He was relieved when Elizabeth and Hazel came to join them, along with Ophelia. She stood awkwardly, not knowing how to greet him in front of the others, so he took her hand and brought it to his lips.

"She says we may call her 'Fifi,'" Elizabeth said, eyes shining. "And we've told her all about you, all the things you should have told her yourself."

"Such as?" He raised a brow.

"Why, how adept you are at swordplay, for one thing."

His ignored his friends' guffaws, sending them warning looks. Ophelia smiled uneasily. He wasn't sure she got the joke, but having seen his "sword" on a few occasions now, she might have. He was proud of his swordplay in both the literal and provocative sense. If only she'd let him show her what else he could do to bring her pleasure.

"It grows late," he told her softly. "When you see fit as hostess, you are free to invite our houseguests off to bed."

Chapter Twelve:
Trying to Understand

Wescott came to her room before she'd even finished her evening ablutions, dressed in his bed robe. Rochelle helped her don her night shift, then bobbed a curtsey, excusing herself. Ophelia rather wished she'd stay, because her husband seemed in an amorous mood.

He was a different man around his friends: happier, bolder, more at ease. He lounged on her bed with an air of carnality. *It will happen eventually. He will demand it, eventually.*

She didn't know why she continued to resist. She had found pleasure in their first joining, dread and confusion notwithstanding. In moments of reverie, as she looked at him, she admitted to herself that he had thrilled her that night at the inn, even if the morning after covered all of it with a veil of shame.

It would be better, more wifely, to give herself to him, but some stubborn part of her held to reservations. Once he had her, she would never be herself again. She'd be changed into his wife in truth, her past self no longer relevant at all.

A line played in her head from a duet she'd performed in Vienna on the topic of marriage, part of Mozart's *The Magic Flute*. The

German lyrics, roughly translated: nothing is more noble than man and wife. *Mann und Weib, und Weib und Mann.* Man and wife, and wife and man. She'd sung it over and over as the character Pamina, enjoying each note as she harmonized with the young baritone who'd played Papageno. It had only been a year ago, but how innocent and ignorant she'd been.

Man and wife, and wife and man. She wished the voice in her head would be silent. She'd never be able to sing that again with the same light, easy sense of romance.

"What are you thinking about?" he asked.

She realized she'd been rearranging the perfume jars beside her mirror for over a minute. She turned to him, taken aback by his haughty beauty, the ease with which he sprawled before her.

"I was thinking of something I used to sing," she said. "A trifle of a duet, but with lovely notes, the type I enjoyed performing. Mozart had a talent for that."

"*Così fan tutte?*"

"No, *The Magic Flute.* It was part of our winter performances last year."

He leaned forward on the bed, resting his head on his hand. "Sing it for me, Ophelia. Whatever song you're talking about."

"I can't."

He snorted, his gaze darkening. "You mean you won't. Come lie with me, at least, if you're going to be cross."

"I'm not cross," she said, although she knew she was acting cross as anything. She gathered her courage and joined him, sitting on the edge of the bed, her knees pressed firmly together.

"I suppose it doesn't matter that everyone's descended upon our honeymoon," he said. "We're like an old married couple already, arguing and frowning at one another."

Ophelia softened her frown, hating that he'd called her out on it. "The problem is, my voice is out of practice. Also, the song was in German. I doubt I'd remember all the words correctly."

"You could at least hum the melody for me." He moved to sit beside her, meeting her eyes. It felt intimate just being close to him. Too intimate.

"I enjoyed spending the evening with your family," she said, to change the subject. "How interesting they all are. And your friends."

"Interesting is one word to describe them," he said with a laugh. "Marlow and Augustine will move into their own ancestral holdings out here when they're married. For now, they hang about London, if they aren't with their families, or at some house party being set up with this young lady or that. They try to avoid that."

"Don't they want to marry?"

He made a face. "It's complicated. August wanted to marry Townsend's older sister, but she wed an Italian prince years ago. Marlow isn't ready to marry anyone, and Townsend..." He paused. "Well, he couldn't marry who he liked. He's run off to the continent to lick his wounds. How cruel you were to him."

"What?" She turned on him, aghast. "I didn't know him well enough to be cruel to him."

He took her arms and caught her in an embrace. "I was teasing you, crosspatch. Why must you snap at me? I'll have to spank you again."

He was in a jolly mood, but she wasn't. "Please let go of me."

She pulled away but he pulled her back. "You didn't dream of the fire last night, did you?" he pointed out. "It was the first peaceful sleep you've had in a while."

"I don't know if it was peaceful. I dreamed of ginger and canes."

"But you slept. I think the punishment was good for you. For both of us." He grinned. "Come, Ophelia. Let me see how things look the day after."

"How things look?"

He meant to inspect her bottom? She stiffened as he strong-armed her over his lap.

"Come now. No protests. Just do as I ask."

He didn't give her much choice. No matter how she resisted, she couldn't escape his grip, so she let him have his way and lay over his knees, across the bed. How cruel he was, amusing himself by exposing her this way. He pushed up her robe and night shift, baring her bottom. She knew the two cane welts were still there; she'd felt them all day.

"I should give you a couple of cane strokes each night," he said, his fingertips tracing over the welts. "That'll keep you properly in line. I can add more for poor behavior, or take a stroke away if you've been especially good."

She pressed her lips shut, refusing to dignify such a horrid idea with an answer. When would he let her up?

"What do you think?" He goaded her, pinching one of the sore stripes. "It might improve our marriage."

"It will make our marriage worse," she said through gritted teeth. "You shouldn't treat me this way. A proper husband wouldn't embarrass his wife in this fashion."

"Why should I act like a proper husband, when you refuse to be a proper wife and perform your marital duties?"

It always came back to that. Stupid, lecherous man. Why, she would never please his perverse appetites, even if she gave in and welcomed him in her bed. She tried to keep her temper as he traced the cane stripes again, for he would spank her for any reason. If she gave a snide answer about "marital duties," she was in the perfect position for reprisal, so she held her tongue, even as his caresses grew bolder.

He kneaded her hips, stroked the small of her back, even dipped a few fingers between her thighs. She lay still, wishing he'd release her. Instead he pushed her back on the bed, coming over her. She froze, praying his robe wouldn't fall open any more.

"Look at your frown, silly thing. Won't you let me have you? Because I want you very much, Ophelia. You're mine, you know, no matter how you resist." He caressed her cheek. "I like that you belong to me."

She reeled back from him, edging toward the headboard. "I don't belong to you. I'm not 'yours,' Wescott. I am my own person, and I don't like being played with and tossed about like a doll."

She knew she would anger him with such talk, but her own anger had been bubbling all evening, trapped beneath the pretty smile she'd put on for his visitors.

"How do you think I feel when you paw at me and brag about your 'ownership,' as if I'm a plaything for you to grope at your whim? It's not gentlemanly."

"Gentlemanly?" His antagonistic tone matched hers. "You're my wife. Men touch their wives."

"Yes, in polite, respectful ways, but I don't think you know anything about that. Do you think I enjoy being thrown over your lap to have my bottom 'inspected'? Do you think I'm happy that I've been sitting uncomfortably all evening because you caned me?"

He sat up, his green eyes glinting in the dim light. "Here, now. What is this attack about? If you were not such an ornery grump, you wouldn't have been caned in the first place."

"And if you were not such a perverted lecher, you would not have taken my virginity that night at the inn, and I wouldn't be here in this room with you being ornery and grumpy. I'd still be the person I used to be."

"The person you used to be? The actress? The stage performer?" He snorted. "What a great lady you were then."

Oh, he made her livid. "I *was* a great lady," she cried. "I was talented. I tried hard, and it wasn't all from God. It was my work, too." She backed away from him until she was trapped, her spine against the tall headboard. "I wanted to do things in the world, and see things, and then you ruined everything because of your base urges." She knew she ought to stop, but she seemed to have lost control of her temper. "Do you understand how much I despise this life and this marriage, and this miserable pile of rocks you've brought me to? I don't care if you're a duke's son, or that other ladies wanted you. I don't want you."

"Lower your voice," he said. "It's bad enough that you scream at me so, but if my friends hear—"

"I don't care what your friends hear, just as you don't care about me."

"Ophelia—"

"You think of me as some possession because we've married, but you care nothing for my feelings, nothing at all for what I've lost."

"What you've lost?" He raised his voice now, just moments after he'd told her to speak more softly. "What about what I've lost, you shrieking child? Do you think I wanted to marry you? Because I didn't, not at all." He grasped her forearm when she tried to avoid his fierce gaze. "You were dead last on my list of marriage prospects, because until that damned night, I didn't know you existed. I married you out of duty, when I could have had a dozen ladies, prettier, richer, and better situated than you."

"I wish you had had any of them," she yelled back. "Any of them but me."

"I wish it too, by God, every hour of every day, every time you throw your sadness and regrets in my face, as if all of this is my fault."

"It is your fault. You shouldn't have touched me! You shouldn't have made me do the things I did that night."

"That night." He groaned, releasing her arm. "That night, that night. It will always be that night, and you condemning me in your goddamned righteous tone, like you didn't beg me every moment to keep going with your sensuous movements, and your breathless moans."

She shook her head, jumping off the bed. "I didn't do anything sensual. I wouldn't have. I did not moan."

"You did," he said coldly. "I remember it. I hear it in my head every time you recoil from me now, and it reminds me that you're just as guilty as me. It sounded like this."

He made a soft, high, womanly moan, so real to what she might have sounded like that she brought her hands to her ears to block it out. "I didn't mean to act that way," she said. "If I did, it's because you made me."

"You may tell that lie to yourself as often as you like, but we both know it's not true. As for your loss, your sadness, know this, Lady Wescott. If I could go back in time by some magic, I would have left you where you stood in your damned wig and dress and given you up to that fire."

His words were so curt, so cold and cruel that she couldn't think of a retort. She burst into tears instead, into loud, awful sobs. "I wish I'd died too," she cried. "It would have been better, wouldn't it?"

He stared at her, his lips tight and trembling. "Damn it, Ophelia. I didn't mean what I just said."

"You're saying that to be polite. You did mean it."

"Of course I didn't."

His voice was strained, and his eyes wide. She couldn't bear to look at him through her tears. He hated her. Why wouldn't he? She was so terrible and disappointing, and so bad a wife. Everything she touched was ruined, just like her dreams where she lit everything on fire.

God help her. She needed air. She couldn't breathe. She pulled her robe tight around her waist and ran for the door. She heard him call behind her, but she didn't stop. She couldn't be near him now, couldn't be near someone who hated her so much.

You hated him first, her mind whispered. *You started the argument tonight. Look where it ended up.*

She ran blindly down the hallway, past still, quiet rooms, until she got to one of the tower doors. She flung it open and started climbing, only to expend the emotions roiling inside her. The ancient stairs rose in a twisting circle, the stones worn by generations of treading feet. She heard Wescott call behind her, but she couldn't stop fleeing now that she'd begun. She wouldn't stop until she was out of this cursed manor house, out on the parapets beneath the chilly night sky.

"Do not follow me," she called back to him. "I want to be alone."

He was just behind her, reaching to catch her robe. "What are you going to do up there?"

She paused on the stair. "Do you think I'll throw myself from the battlements? I despise you, but not enough to take my own life. Leave me alone. Pretend for a while that I did die in that fire, so you can feel some joy for precious moments."

"Ophelia—"

She reached the top of the stairs, all out of breath, pushed the door open, and hurried through to get away from him and his gruff, exasperated voice. It was colder up on the roof than she'd imagined, but not too dark. The night was lit by a full moon.

She ran to the roof's edge, which wasn't really an edge. Battlements lined the perimeter, rectangular barriers that looked small from below, but were as tall as she was. She leaned against one and looked up at the sky. *O Moon, silver Moon, in the deep, dark sky.* Another song, another opera. The words had been in Latin, although she'd learned them in English too. *O Luna, Luna, Luna...*

It had been a song about a maiden's lost love, and she had pretended to weep as she implored the moon to shine on the earth and find him. She'd been so young when she sang that song, not realizing how destructive and confusing real relationships could be. She leaned back into the solid stone and let it hold her as she looked up at the night sky. What had she done? What had she shouted at Wescott in her impassioned hysteria? The same sort of awful things he'd shouted back to her.

Oh, she wished she could be anywhere else.

She heard Wescott to her right, just as she realized her feet were freezing in her slippers.

"Come inside," he said. "Don't punish yourself because we argued."

"I'm not punishing myself. I need to be up here. I can't breathe."

He took a step closer, tightening his robe across his chest. "You can't breathe because it's cold. You can come up here during the day, when the sun's out."

She shook her head, holding him off. "During the day, I won't be able to see the stars."

She heard his quiet sigh, then only silence. He didn't leave, not even when she turned her back to him. Now and again, she wiggled her stiffening toes.

"I'm trying to understand you," he finally said. "I'm *trying*, Ophelia. I didn't think things would be so bad between us."

She hugged herself tighter. "They'll always be bad, because of how...how we began."

"We need to let go of that. We need to move forward as husband and wife—"

"But this isn't what I wanted." She pressed her palm against her heart. "Now I can't go back."

"What is it you want? What is it you think you've lost, that I've taken from you?"

"What might have been," she said wearily.

"You wanted to travel? Fine, we can travel. You can still sing, although you don't seem to want to." He sounded tired. "You could stay safe and easy here. Most English women are happy enough with a life of leisure, with tea parties and dances, and trips to the theater, and pretty gowns and jewels."

She turned back around to face him. "I suppose you think something's wrong with me. Maybe there is."

He stared back at her with an unfathomable expression. She wasn't sure if he wanted to embrace her or throw her from the battlements.

"I'm not giving up on this marriage," he finally said. "And there's nothing wrong with you except for your penchant for emotional tirades. You ought to be spanked for dragging me up here, with both of us in our damned night clothes. It's too late tonight, but at some point in the future, a reckoning shall be made."

She lifted her chin. "I'll run away, then."

"Yes, Lady Drama, I don't doubt you will, but as I said, it is too late tonight. Let's go down and go to bed."

She hugged herself against a sudden breeze. "I'd rather not. I want to sleep up here."

"Of course you do, but it's not possible."

She sank down against the wall, finding a smooth expanse of rock to support her back. She pulled her feet beneath her and held her robe closed. "Perhaps the fresh air will be good for my *emotional tirades*," she said with a sniff.

"Such a spanking," he replied, so quietly she could hardly hear.

She wouldn't go down with him now, not with that hanging over her head, even though she probably deserved to be punished. "I wish to sleep up here," she said again. "You may go down."

"Oh, may I?" His voice dripped with forbearance. "I don't know what I did to deserve you in my life. Fine, I'll go for some blankets and pillows."

She hugged her knees and waited for him to return, looking forward to getting her cold toes warm again. When he came back, he had armfuls of blankets. A baffled footman followed behind with pillows.

"You can't sleep so close to the edge," he said, putting the blankets down near the stairwell door. "Come over here."

She was too drained to argue with him any longer. She went where he pointed and curled up in the blankets. Now she could look up at the sky all night, at the twinkling, bright stars. "You don't have to stay," she said, when he laid down next to her.

"I plan to stay."

She wondered if the sky over Wescott Abbey always looked so clear and cloudless, or if tonight was a special case. When her eyes started to close, she wrenched them open again. She wanted to stay up in the bracing night air, but the blankets were warming her tense muscles, and her husband had gone silent and still beside her. She stole a glance at him, to find him staring back at her, his expression pensive.

"Go to sleep," he said, his head propped on his hand. "You wanted to sleep up here, so sleep."

* * * * *

Ophelia woke in her bed, and for a moment, she thought the previous night's events might have been an especially vivid dream. She hadn't shouted at Wescott, had she? And run up to the roof, and demanded to sleep there? Because she was here now, under her own covers.

No, not her own covers. She was still wrapped in the thick down blankets Wescott had carried up to the roof. He must have carried her back down and deposited her here once she slept, or worse, asked a footman to do it. How embarrassing.

Well, it was her fault. She threw off the heavy blankets and found she was still in her night robe also. So yes, all of it had happened. The memories came back to her, the fighting and accusing and running away. Why, she'd gone so far beyond the pale of proper wifely behavior that Wescott hadn't even stayed after he brought her here.

Not that she was disappointed. It just wasn't like him.

She turned toward the sun streaming in the window, and noticed a note propped against her pillow. She dreaded to reach for it. Was it a lecture by pen? A summons for a punishment as soon as she awakened? She picked it up and angled it toward the light.

Dear Ophelia,

I'm sorry, but it was too cold to let you stay the entire night on the roof. I brought you down just after you fell asleep.

By the time you awaken, I will have left for London with Augustine and Marlow, as I have some business to attend to there. My parents and sisters will stay with you until I return. My mother will listen for any nightmares, so you needn't suffer your fiery terrors without help.

I've left word with the staff that you're forbidden from sleeping on the roof while I'm away. I advise you to obey me in this, as I still haven't decided on a consequence for your behavior last night.

Regards,
Wescott

She read it again, then again. That was that, then. He'd left her to run off to London with his friends, leaving her under his family's care for added humiliation. He claimed to have some business to attend to there. She'd heard nothing about such business until now. She imagined instead he would do whatever his bachelor friends did—drinking, gambling, and socializing with immoral women.

It was what she wanted, wasn't it? To be free of his company?

She tossed the note aside and turned over in bed, hugging herself and willing away tears. She would not cry again, even if she felt embarrassed and rebuked by his sudden departure. Well, perhaps she'd cry a little, since she was alone, and she'd have to put on a brave expression soon to face the servants and Wescott's family.

Which would be difficult, for she felt unaccountably hurt. She'd pushed him away and denied his advances, and been an unpleasant wife in every way, but she hadn't expected him to desert their marriage so quickly and go to visit...visit...well, that awful word. Whores.

She tried to cry quietly, muffling her sobs in her pillow, but soon she was weeping in earnest, so her eyes and her head hurt. He'd said he wouldn't give up on their marriage, but maybe, as he carried her down the stairs to put her in bed, he'd changed his mind. She'd been such a trial, such an *ornery grump*, as he said. She wouldn't have fought with him if she'd known how close he was to abandoning her.

Now she'd broken everything, set everything on fire in a way that might never be fixed.

Chapter Thirteen:
Doomed

"For God's sake, look at him go."

August's wry words carried across the echoing studio, as Wescott hacked away at a practice dummy that had long since lost its head and arms.

"Perhaps settling down to married life in the countryside disagrees with him," said Marlow. "I sense a great deal of pent up angst."

"Pent up something, that's certain," August agreed.

Wescott spun on his friends, pointing with his sword. "You said you would be quiet. Get out."

"We're not leaving you alone with that poor clump of straw and canvas." Marlow crossed his arms over his chest. "Next you'll be attacking the bloody walls. It's been three days, friend. When are we going to do something fun?"

"Yes, something fun. Wine and women." August glanced at the tattered dummy. "It would be good for you. Might help you cool your head."

"And your temper," Marlow added.

Wescott frowned and turned his back to them, his mind churning on many frustrations, first and foremost his failing marriage. He'd practiced with his teacher for the last two days, until the man walked out in disgust. *A swordsman requires control. We'll spar again when you've regained yours.*

"Did you sleep last night?" August asked, persistent. "Or the night before? Perhaps you ought to go back to the Abbey and try to straighten out whatever's driven you away from Ophelia."

"I'm not sure it's straighten-able." He drove his sword into the dummy's heart for the twelfth time. "My wife hates me. Do you understand? She hates being married to me and never lets me forget it. All of this because I tried to do a good deed, and save her from a bloody fire."

"You slept with her, too," Marlow reminded him.

"Because I thought she was a damned actress."

He drove his sword into the dummy's heart a thirteenth time and left it there. His arms ached and sweat dripped from his forehead. He pushed his hair back and strode to the window, shoving it open to cool his face in the crisp night air. Yes, he'd behaved badly that night. He'd been lustful and lecherous, and taken advantage of an actress he'd rescued, who was really a lady.

But how long must he pay for it? How long would she hate him for that "crime"?

"She won't sing for me," he said. "Did you know that? She's a damned singer but she won't sing a note for me, even though she has a celebrated voice."

"Perhaps her voice is still healing from the fire," August said.

He took up the sword again, stabbing the dummy in the groin this time. "No, it's because she hates me. I've heard her mouthing words beneath her breath when she doesn't know I'm around, as if the songs are trapped inside her. I've done that. I've taken that joy from her. She doesn't sing to spite me."

"Come now," said Marlow. "I don't think she's known you long enough to really hate you, the way the rest of us do."

"This isn't a time for jokes," August said, shoving him on the shoulder. He turned to Wescott. "I'm sure she doesn't hate you."

"She hates me." He stopped flailing at the dummy and leaned against the wall, blowing out a breath. "She's so beautiful. So alluring. I want to do so many things to her."

"Then you ought to. Hurry home to Oxfordshire and spend all your time doing things to her. You did say that was the only time she hated you...well...slightly less."

Wescott answered his suggestive grin with a frown. "If you must know, gentlemen, the only intimacy I've shared with her since our marriage is a handful of spankings—and not the fun kind."

August's eyes narrowed. "I thought you said—"

"I did, but I lied to you. Do you think it's easy to admit you've had no success bedding your own blasted wife?"

Marlow and August exchanged glances. "We've come to the crux of the problem," said August. "The source of all the frustration."

"Nothing *at all?*" Marlow looked shaken. "You were always such a treat for the women at Pearl's. Doesn't your lady know what she's missing?"

"Well, she knows," August said. "Unless things didn't go so well that first time, when you thought she was an actress?"

Wescott stared at his reflection in his sword's blade. "Things went fine, except they resulted in a marriage she didn't want, so now she refuses me."

The men fell silent in commiseration with their friend. He was relieved they didn't rib him, or play it all for a laugh.

"Whatever." He lowered his sword's tip to the ground. "I'll figure it out. I'm just taking some time to think."

"If you'd like to 'think about things' with a more accepting woman," said Marlow, "we'll have to find someplace besides Pearl's. It's still not reopened, though August and I have been making discreet inquiries as to the location of Misses Ellie and Berta while the parlor's being rebuilt."

Wescott dipped a cloth in the water, massaging the back of his neck. "I barely married Ophelia a week ago," he said bitterly. "It's too soon to take myself off to whores."

"Then bed your wedded wife," said Marlow with a shrug. "If you can destroy a half dozen canvas dummies with a sword, you can bed one reluctant woman. Romance her, and show her that Wescott charm. If she still refuses you, spank some sense into her and get on with things. A sound spanking always works with the girls at Pearl's."

"You keep referencing Pearl's." Wescott gave the dummy one last, desultory whack. "I fear you have a vastly misguided view of the marital state. Wait until you marry, and try to treat your wife like 'the girls at Pearl's.' She'll have something to say about it."

"Not with my cock in her mouth." Marlow made a vulgar pantomime of his comment. "I think you're letting her talk too much, and not demanding enough respect."

"Demanding things from women is a tricky business," said August. "Unless you're paying them some amount of money."

"How do you approach her in the bedroom?" Marlow asked, ignoring August's comment. "Are you demanding? Kind? Patient?"

"Damn it, of course the man's patient," August retorted. "He hasn't got relief in over a week."

"I have to hold her at night." Wescott picked up the dummy's head and replaced it on the wooden frame. "She has nightmares about the fire, so I hold her until she quiets. I hold her right against my body." He remembered the close embrace he subjected himself to every time she woke up screaming. "I can feel every curve of her body against mine, every breath. But I can't..."

His two friends waited. Then August said, "Why can't you?"

"Because she doesn't want me to. I..." He tapped the point of his sword into a crack in the floor. "I believe she's afraid."

"Afraid? Of you?" August tsked.

Marlow shook his head. "How strange for her to be afraid. Do you take a haughty tone with her?" he asked. "Do you make her call you 'my lord,' even in the bedroom?"

"Of course I don't."

"Do you make her curtsey when you enter?" August asked. "And insist she speak to you with proper deference?"

Wescott felt his cheeks redden. He might have spanked her for speaking crossly on at least one occasion.

"I'm a perfectly reasonable husband," he said. "I don't know why she fears me, and fights me."

"Does she know your favorite color?" asked Marlow.

August stifled a laugh. "Do *you* know his favorite color?"

"Well, I'm not married to the man, am I?" Marlow turned back to Wescott. "Have you told her you're a swordsman? She'd swoon over that. Have you told her your favorite dishes to eat? The cities you visited when we toured Europe? Have you told her why you wear your hair so long?"

"Why do you wear your hair so long?" asked August. "I've always wondered that."

Marlow affected a pose. "Because Wescott's hair is too thick and lustrous to wear short. Can you imagine him with short hair? It'd be sticking out all over the place."

Wescott returned to the window, looking out at the busy London thoroughfare. What did Ophelia know of him? Nothing. But that was her fault, because she didn't want to know anything. And if he'd been overly lofty or authoritative in disciplining her, well, women needed guidance, didn't they? Otherwise, she'd be leading him around by the stones, strong willed as she was.

"What do you know about her?"

August's question brought him back to their conversation. He turned, ready to tell him off. "I know plenty about her. I know she's a singer. I know she studied in Vienna."

"We all know that," said August. "What kind of personal things do you know?"

His lips flattened in a line. "I know she's the Earl of Halsey's youngest, and that she has a brother and a sister."

"Again, those are things anyone would know."

"I know her favorite color. Daffodil yellow. She told me the night we married."

"What else did you ask her that night?"

He glared at August. "What do you mean? It was our wedding night. I wasn't out to learn her life's story. I spent most of the time trying to convince her to let me bed her." *And spanking her when she did not.* He chose not to admit that fact under his friend's judgmental line of questioning. "But I did ask her favorite color, because I thought I should know something of her."

"Something. One thing. And have you bought her any yellow things since?"

"Damn you, August. What kind of yellow things? What are you talking about?"

"He's trying to help." Marlow stood from his chair, stretching his arms before him and cracking his knuckles. "I think he's saying you could try more friendly conversation with your wife, and less demands for sex."

"If I was demanding sex—" He lowered his voice, trying to hold his temper. "If I was demanding sex, I would have gotten it by now, I assure you."

"You should buy her a yellow frock while you're in town," August said. "Or a hat, if you don't know her dressmaker. I guess you haven't memorized her measurements?"

"Since when are you such a scion of courtship?" Wescott asked.

"I've thought on it a little," he said, his own cheeks reddening. When the silence lengthened, he shrugged. "Why wouldn't I? I'd like to make a decent marriage one day."

Poor August, and his unrequited love for Felicity. It had been so long ago, the rest of them had been young and oblivious to the depth of his feelings. August probably knew a hundred more things about Felicity than Wescott knew about his wife. If he asked him, they'd probably pour out, like Townsend's pronouncements of love for Ophelia.

"Maybe I don't know how to love." The words spilled from his mouth before he even thought to say them. They embarrassed him. "I mean, I don't think I've ever loved anyone in a romantic way, the way my parents love each other. The way you...you cared for Felicity."

August said nothing. Marlow looked uncomfortable.

Wescott felt bereft.

Maybe that was the real problem...that love wasn't inside him the way it was for other people. Was there a cure for that? He was nothing like August, carrying around deep, long-held emotion, or Townsend, entranced to the point of obsession with a woman he'd never met.

What did he feel for Ophelia?

Mainly, he felt frustration that she didn't like him, much less love him. He felt embarrassment and anger because his marriage was such a disaster. Those weren't the emotions of a man who knew how to love. They were selfish emotions.

Fuck and bother. He was doomed, then. Their marriage was doomed. Maybe he ought to go out with his friends to the brothels for the evening, and work out those frustrations between some other woman's thighs. Ophelia would never know.

But that would be giving up, wouldn't it? He wasn't to that point yet. There was more to learn about his wife than the damned color yellow.

"Why are women so complicated?" he muttered.

His friends stared back at him, confused as he was. Weren't they a sorry lot? He'd made himself an expert in swordplay, but forgot about the chivalry, which might have been why all the dummy's limbs were strewn across the floor.

* * * * *

Ophelia received a letter from her husband the fourth day after he'd left, which was, incidentally, the first day that his mother hadn't needed to come rushing to her bed to wake her from a nightmare.

It was pointedly short, and not very sweet.

Dear Ophelia,

All is well in London. I've spent some time with August and Marlow, and attended to some business. Almost all the theaters have reopened since the fire. We saw a comic opera last night, The Barber of Seville. I could not imagine you singing it, but perhaps you have.

I trust all is in order at the Abbey, and that you have not endured too much rain. Be sure to direct the servants if you should need anything.

Yours,

Wescott

What did that mean, that he had *attended to business*? Why could he not imagine her singing *The Barber of Seville*? Was it an insult? A jest? Just a general comment? She had not sung the opera, as it had no soprano role for a performer her age, which he would very well know if he'd actually seen it.

She put down his letter and paced the room that had begun to feel like a prison. Oh, his family was all that was kind. His mother comforted her with cold compresses and hot milk when she woke from one of her nightmares, and his sisters Hazel and Elizabeth kept her company during the day, enticing her to cards or needlepoint, or charades with his parents. One afternoon his sisters brought her on a walk, and when they passed by the Greek temple in the garden, commenting on its beauty, all Ophelia wanted was to run away from the structure and never think about Wescott again.

Another day passed, and another. She threw herself into planning menus, but got distracted petting the cats in the kitchen because she felt so lonely. When she walked the halls, she watched out for ghosts, but they seemed as anxious to avoid her as her husband.

160

What was he up to in London? Dining at his clubs? Engaging in swordplay with his friends to impress all the women who'd wanted to marry him before he was saddled with her? She tried not to think how dashing someone like Wescott would look in a sword fight. According to Elizabeth, there was a secret armory somewhere in the Abbey. Ophelia wanted to find it to irritate her husband. She could disarrange his sword collection, or hide the most lovely, shining ones. She'd do it to punish him for running away from her, probably into the arms of some harlot or mistress.

When would he come home?

When the sixth day arrived with no more letters and no sign of her husband, she searched in earnest for secret panels and hidden corridors, but found nothing. Where would an entire room be hiding in this old pile of rocks? After breakfast the following morning, she sought out a room she'd found early on, one of the largest rooms on the first floor—the Abbey's library.

She opened the heavy door and walked into the high-ceilinged chamber. She had always loved the smell of books and paper. She'd been scolded at her music academy for sniffing every cantata and opera, but it had been printed on such fine, smooth paper, she couldn't resist.

She wasn't looking for music now. She was looking for—

"Good morning, Ophelia."

She spun at the sound of the deep voice. At first she thought it was her husband, and wondered why she hadn't been informed of his arrival. But it was her father-in-law, the Duke of Arlington, who looked very much like his son, only older and more refined. He sat at a table amidst a few disordered stacks of books, spectacles perched at the end of his nose.

"Your Grace." She started to back from the room. "I'm sorry I've disturbed you."

"You haven't disturbed me, and you mustn't call me 'Your Grace' now that we're family."

She blinked at him. "What would I call you, sir?"

"*Sir* is no better, child. Why not Father or Papa as my own daughters do? You're my daughter now, since you've married my son."

She'd as soon be able to call the imposing duke "Papa" as she could go up onto the rooftop and fly, but she didn't say so.

"Come in." He beckoned her forward. "It's so quiet in here. Have you come to find a book to read? There are hundreds to choose from."

"Well, n-no." She stood frozen in place. "Not a book."

He must think her an imbecile, standing and stammering. The duke's eyes were blue, not green like his son's, and at the moment, those eyes looked patient and somewhat amused, so she screwed up her courage and told him the truth.

"I've come to see if there are any house plans here in the library." She scanned the tall mahogany shelves. "Plans of the Abbey. I suppose there aren't, since it was built so long ago, but I hoped someone might have made some newer records of the layout...in the ensuing years..."

"House plans." He pushed the book he was reading away, leaned forward, and steepled his fingers beneath his chin. "Dear Ophelia, you want to find the secret room, don't you? Wescott's secret armory?"

Her cheeks heated as she picked at her dress's sheer organza overlay. "I thought I might attempt it. Elizabeth told me it existed, but she doesn't know where it is."

"Few people know." He raised a brow. "I know, but I won't tell you where it is."

"Oh." She threaded her fingers together in disappointment.

"Because, of course, it would be far more fun for you to try to find it yourself. You might as well amuse yourself, since my son ran off so soon after you were married." His lips formed an intimidating frown as he shook his head. "It wasn't well done of him. I've sent a letter telling him so."

This rather shocked her—first, that he would bring it up with her, and second, that he would chide Wescott on her behalf. "Has he written back?"

"Not yet."

Her throat tightened as she dropped her gaze to the table's varnished surface. "He probably won't." She could feel her father-in-law's eyes on her, and still perceive his frown in her peripheral vision. "I don't think he likes me. At all."

"Why would you say that?"

He left silence for her to fill, though she dreaded to answer. How had things gone so wrong? The more she thought over it, the more she feared it wasn't his fault, but hers.

"I suppose it's because I've been awful," she said, and it felt almost a relief to admit it. "I've been the most unbearable wife, which is why he left me. I've been a shrew and a crosspatch, even when he's tried to be kind."

"A shrew and a crosspatch?" The duke gave a soft laugh that sounded almost like her husband's. "I can hardly believe that. You've been nothing but gracious in my family's company, even after we intruded on your honeymoon."

"We've hardly had a honeymoon, unfortunately. All we do is fight."

"Fight?" He leaned closer. "My son hasn't hurt you, has he? Physically?"

She hesitated, then shook her head. Wescott had spanked her on a few occasions, but she didn't wish to admit that. No, the fights she meant were the emotional ones, the words they snapped at each other.

"You argue then?" the duke asked. "Well, all married couples do so on occasion."

His kind reassurance made tears rise in her eyes. "It's not as simple as that. I've said so many bad things to him. I've said that I didn't want to marry him, that I didn't want this life, this house, his love. I've said that I don't want him to touch me." She could barely get out the last words. "I've said that I...that I hate him." When she stole a look at the duke's face, she expected to see anger. Instead, she saw sympathy.

"That does sound bad." He clasped his hands upon the table, considering. "I wonder, did you mean all those things when you said them?"

The tears in her eyes spilled over. "No, I didn't. I don't. I think I'm only trying to tell him something else. Maybe that I'm...that I'm afraid."

"Afraid of Wescott?"

She nodded, then shook her head. "I think... I think I am afraid of everything." She shuddered, hugging herself beneath the duke's intent gaze. "Since the fire, since everything changed, I have terrible nightmares and I'm afraid all the time. And now I have... I have..."

She sniveled, trembling all over. She shook so violently, the duke reached for her and took her arm.

"I have ruined everything and made him hate me," she cried, "and all my fears have come to pass. I wish that fire had never happened. I'm so tired of feeling troubled all the time."

She hadn't realized until now how much her fears had changed her. She'd been so afraid since the fire, so unsettled and anxious, that she'd pushed away her husband and refused to feel anything for him, even though she desperately needed a friend.

"What will I do?" she sobbed, the words coming out in stutters. "I think I'll be afraid forever. I feel too tired to be brave."

She did feel, suddenly, so very tired and helpless. When the duke guided her against his shoulder, she clung to him blindly, crying into his fine woolen coat. He produced a handkerchief with the same easy grace as his son, and she pressed it to her eyes. "I'm so sorry, Your Grace."

"You mustn't be sorry. Cry it out, my dear. You'll feel better afterward. I know, because I've raised several daughters, all with their mother's stormy Welsh blood. There now." When she stopped shuddering so violently, he released her, but kept hold of her hand.

"May I tell you something?" he asked. He waited for her to wipe her eyes and meet his gaze. "As bleak as things seem now, Ophelia, I have great hopes for you and my son. Your relationship was forged in fire, literally, which can't have been easy, but it shows you're both strong, that you can survive things with each other's help."

"I don't know." She hid her face in her hands, then looked up again. "In some ways, I feel I didn't survive."

"Oh, dear child, things will get better. You've had a traumatizing experience, and you haven't fully recovered yet. Not only the fire, but what happened afterward. My son's trespass, the hasty wedding. And the terror of that night, of the fire, has likely become mixed up in your marriage, complicating matters further."

"It may be so," she said.

"In time, though, you'll begin to heal. It's been a matter of days, really. Barely a fortnight. Things will get better between you and Wescott."

"But how?" She dabbed away the last of her tears, still clutching his handkerchief. "They can't get better when I've ruined everything and acted like such an unlovable fool."

"Let me share some wisdom that comes with age." He released her hand and patted it in a fatherly manner. "Nothing is irreparable. Most of the time, missteps can be fixed."

"No, I've driven him away. He hates me. He's left me."

"Wescott is merely taking a break, Ophelia. He's taking time to breathe and gather his thoughts, as you must, too. It's like the matches at his club, when they spar with swords. When the action gets too heated, the fight master calls a break to the action, so the rivals can recollect their heads."

Perhaps her father-in-law was right. Their marriage had felt like a sword fight to this point, with no one to step between them and make them calm down.

"It's likely my son left to prevent things breaking down further, and to think of a plan to improve matters when he returns. That's his way. He'll come back soon, because you're his. You're his wife." He leaned close to hold her gaze. "And if the two of you can open your hearts to each other, you'll soon be as happily married as his mother and me."

Because you're his. Wescott had used the same type of phrase when he upset her so. *You're mine, you know. I like that you belong to me.* In her fear, she'd interpreted his words as overbearing and evil, but maybe he'd meant them affectionately. Protectively. He'd done so much to protect her, from the fire, from her nightmares, and all she'd done in return was malign him and push him away. Tears fell again, more pitiful this time than sorrowful.

"There, child," said the duke, so patiently. "All will be well."

"You must think I'm the silliest, weakest woman in Christendom." She waved his handkerchief with a self-deprecating sigh.

"No. I think you're a very strong person. So is my son." He thought a moment. "Whatever you have lost in marrying Jack—and I'm sure there are many things—you must look at it this way. You shall not want in safety or security for the rest of your life. A good marriage, with both hearts in order, will bring happiness beyond measure, because you'll always be there for one another, no matter the ups and downs. He will be back, and soon. He is far too stubborn to give up on you."

His serious expression lightened a little, and he took a breath. "Speaking of safety and security, what of this armory you wish to uncover? Come, Ophelia, let's see what the library has in the way of house plans. I believe there were some drawings made in my great-grandfather's time, as they planned some modernizing refurbishments. Let's see."

He crossed to a long set of drawers beneath one of the shelves and started pulling them open. Ophelia joined him, marveling at the variety of contents. There were sketches and drawings, political pamphlets, scrapbooks, household ledgers, and handwritten pages of music she'd have to peek at later. He moved to another set of drawers, riffling through some longer sheets and drawings, and finally made a sound of satisfaction.

"Here we are." He took out a set of plans nearly as wide as the drawer itself, bound together by silver clips. He carried them to the largest library desk, and brought a lamp for extra light. "Sit down, dear. Have a look at them. Do you have much math?"

She shook her head. "No, Your Grace. Er, Papa." Now that she'd cried on the kind man's shoulder, it was a little easier to address him so. "When I started singing, my parents chose to focus my studies on music."

"Ah, but music is mathematical in many ways. Where should we start? The basement corridors? The first or second floor? The third floor or the attic?"

Ophelia bit her lip, getting caught up in the duke's enthusiasm. "I think the basement is too obvious a choice. If they wanted to hide a room full of armor, they'd put it on one of the upper floors. Wouldn't they?"

"Indeed, it's not in the basement." He flipped the pages open, and they looked together at the drawings and measurements. In her music school, she would have felt too nervous to concentrate if she was being tested so, one on one, but the duke made her feel comfortable, even entertained. He made various guiding noises as she pored over the plans, murmuring "warmer" when she looked at certain areas, and "colder" when she seemed to lose the track.

At last, purely by chance, she noticed a discrepancy in the height of the kitchen storage rooms compared to that of the adjacent dining room and the ballroom, which occupied two floors. "Perhaps it's around here," she said, hoping she was right. She circled the areas on the neatly scribed plans. "I think it's got to be here, but they haven't put it down on paper."

"Indeed. Because there was a time, for security, that the lords of this manor kept secrets. The weapons and food stores were kept somewhat close, in case of an invasion or unexpected siege. Shall we go look? Now that you know the general vicinity, you'll find it with no trouble at all."

He refused to give her any further direction, his blue eyes still twinkling with challenge. Ophelia decided to start in the kitchen and work back toward the storerooms, but she got nowhere. She gave her favorite cat a pat on the head as they left the kitchen and walked through the dining room to the ballroom. In past centuries, it had been a Great Hall, and it still had a high stone balcony. She stood in the middle of the smooth floor where guests might dance or dine, and looked up, turning in a circle.

The upper floor was done up with velvet wallpaper and carved wooden panels, alternating to regal effect. She'd never looked at the carvings, not having lived here very long, but now she decided she must. She went up the wide, double curved staircase to the upper walk, with Wescott's father at her heels.

"Who made these carvings?" she asked, as she went around studying each one.

"Sixteenth century craftsmen. Half of them are mythological figures, and half are saints. I'm sure a pagan or two passed along these balconies."

She recognized some of the carved figures, but not many. Some of them were women, perhaps from the Bible, while others were clearly ancient gods, some with multiple heads, or strong arms holding up the sun. She stopped short when she encountered a carved figure wielding a sword. She was almost certain it depicted brave St. George battling his fire-breathing dragon, the flames glancing off his armor, his hefty weapon held aloft.

The armory might be behind the panel, according to her vague calculations. Perhaps St. George was a hint. While the duke watched, Ophelia tapped at the edges of the carved rectangle, looking for hidden notches or levers.

"Don't be gentle, my dear." His voice was warm, perhaps even proud. "Give it a good push."

She stood back and pushed the middle of it with both her hands, and was surprised when the panel popped outward rather than inward, moved by a set of hidden springs. "It's in there, isn't it?" she asked, her voice going soft with excitement. "I've found it."

"I was sure you would. You seem the driven type, when you put your mind to something."

Was she driven? Wescott would say stubborn. "Can I go inside and look? Is it safe?"

"It's safe enough if you don't touch anything. A lot of the weapons are ancient, but his aren't, and he keeps them very sharp."

She stood back to let the duke go first, since he had the lamp. They entered a low, narrow corridor that might have been nothing at all until it took a sharp turn. A few more steps, and a space opened up, higher and more spacious than she could have imagined.

"Jesus and Mary," she breathed.

When her father-in-law held up the lamp, it illuminated dozens of shields, swords, and other battle arms mounted in neat rows upon the walls. Some of them looked very ancient and dull, even rusted, but others sparkled as if they were shined daily.

While the walls were full of pikes, knives, shields, and swords, the center of the room was empty, just a cold stone floor. One corner of the spacious room held an age-blackened fireplace. When she'd sung in *Armide*, she'd worn fake armor and used a fake sword, but the swords around her were substantial and real, their polished finishes glinting by lamplight.

"It's beautiful to see them all lined up and stored so smartly," she said. Even her whisper sounded loud. "I've never seen such a thing."

"Wescott enjoys his hobby," he answered. "He spends many hours here, and often adds to his collection of antique arms."

He lifted the lamp toward another corner, as she wondered how big the room could possibly be. Did the fireplace light up this entire dark, windowless space when Wescott came here to practice at his fights? Then her breath caught. Someone else was here, some ancient intruders, some ghosts advancing toward them. She let out a scream, and it bounced deafeningly off the walls.

The duke laughed, touching her arm to reassure her. "They're only suits of armor, Ophelia. There's no need to be afraid."

He moved the lamp closer to show her the four stately, steel sentries, complete with metal gloves, pointed metal shoes, and conical helms. She blinked at them, wondering that her very eyelids didn't make some sound in the chamber.

For the acoustics were marvelous. Her scream had echoed beautifully.

It made her want to sing.

Chapter Fourteen: The Armory

The note from his father had been short and to the point. *You can't fall in love with your wife if you aren't here with her.*

That was it. He hadn't even signed it. He didn't need to; Wescott knew his father's angry handwriting by now.

He should have started back to the Abbey a couple days ago, as soon as he'd gotten the note. Now the weather had turned as stormy and angry as his father's terse missive, and he was marooned in his luxurious London home, feeling as empty as the opposite side of his bed.

While he walked the halls and ate solitary luncheons and dinners, he tried to find love for his wife, for his tragic Ophelia, but he kept coming up against an impediment. He didn't know her. He hadn't tried to know her. He hadn't done much to understand her, as she'd accused him several times.

By the time the weather cleared, he was no closer to solving the problem of his broken marriage, but he would return to Oxfordshire and keep trying, because once he loved her—if he could love her—

things would get better. Hadn't his parents said so? If they couldn't find love, he'd settle for harmony, or at least cooperation, so they weren't tense with anger all the time.

He finally returned home a week after he'd left, arriving in late afternoon. He went to his rooms first, to bathe away the scent of horse and change into proper clothes to face Ophelia. She wasn't in her rooms, so he went downstairs to find her, and instead discovered his parents in the front parlor having tea.

"Wescott," said his mother. "What a pleasure to see you. Come give me a kiss."

He obliged, then greeted his father.

"It's good you've returned," he said, with only a mild note of censure. "I perceive the weather's been bad."

"Somewhat." He meant no disrespect, but he couldn't sit now and chat about the weather. He scanned the parlor again. "Where is everyone else?"

"Hazel and Elizabeth have gone to Lockridge Manor to visit Rosalind," said his mother, "and your wife's become interested in…other things."

"What other things?"

His parents exchanged a look, then his father spoke. "Believe it or not, she found the armory, and has been spending an inordinate amount of time there."

"The armory?" Wescott was aghast. "And you allowed this? It's not a safe place for a woman unused to weapons."

"On the contrary, she feels very safe in there." His father stirred his tea, unperturbed. "She tells us the room has exemplary acoustics."

"Indeed," said his mother. "My love, you'd never believe it. Her voice has returned. She's been singing like a bird, and smiling again too."

Of course she was singing and smiling, since he hadn't been there in days. He clenched his teeth in agitation. "She's in the armory now?"

"I expect so," said his father. "You ought to go see her. She'll be glad to know you're home."

He doubted his wife would be glad. As for him, this wasn't the homecoming he'd hoped for. Had his parents lost their minds, allowing Ophelia to spend "inordinate amounts of time" in a room full of lethal weapons? He turned on his heel and strode quickly to the second level of the ballroom, hurrying around the balcony to the hidden panel. He found it ajar.

"The armory!" he muttered to himself. "Exemplary acoustics? Are they mad?" The room was full of swords, knives, and axes. What were they thinking, allowing her there? Who'd told her about the armory in the first place? He'd have words for whoever it was when he found out.

He entered the dark corridor and stalked to the bend, then stopped, hearing the strains of a glorious song. It could only be his wife's voice. He'd heard so many times how lovely it was, but his imagination hadn't come close to reality. Her vivid, clear soprano took his breath away, to the point he couldn't move for a moment. Her voice sounded more beautiful than any other singer's he'd heard before. Her tone was as strong and bright as the sun.

He was so taken with the angelic sound, the expression in each note, that he didn't recognize the melody at first. It was an old country lullaby his nurse had sung to him years ago, although her voice could not have been so rich or pure as Ophelia's. *Gentle lamb, shelter here. Gentle lamb, shelter near, quite near in my arms as night falls...*

It was so sweetly sung, so affecting. *An angel's voice. God's gift.* What he'd taken for exaggeration fit her in truth, and she was only singing a lullaby to herself. What did she sound like in full voice, in operatic performance?

He put his hands against the wall, fighting a sudden surge of irritation, even anger. Why had she kept her talent from him? Her voice hadn't been ruined by the fire. It was clearly in perfect working order, but she'd refused to sing for him, perhaps to punish him, or perhaps as a form of disdain, because she didn't want their marriage or his attentions.

173

And when the contrary creature finally decided to sing, it was in his armory, where she had no business being at all.

He went the rest of the way into the room and took in the sight of his wife, his emotions high. She stood in the dead center of the chamber, a light sword held aloft in her hand, the other arm extended for balance. By now, the sweet lullaby had ended, and she'd begun a more strident piece, perhaps an aria of some sort.

He thought, *she's going to maim herself.* He also thought, *she looks like a warrior-goddess of old.*

"You must put that down at once," he said, speaking over her song. "It's not safe."

She turned to him, her voice cutting off, although the last soaring note lingered, echoing off the metal weapons and stone walls.

"Wescott!" She lowered the sword a little. "You've come back."

"It's a damned good thing, too," he said, crossing to her. "What are you doing in here? It's no place for a lady."

She pointed the sword at him as he came, so he was forced to stop.

"Ophelia." Her name was a warning. "Those points aren't blunted. The length of that sword is sharp as hellfire and could easily cut you to bits."

"Or cut *you* to bits."

Was that humor? The corner of her mouth turned up a bit. She held the sword steady. She must have been stronger than she looked.

"Ophelia Lucinda Drake, lower that sword this instant. And be careful!"

Whatever his emotions had been before, they were all coalesced now into one hard ball of worry in the pit of his heart. Not his stomach. His heart. As he stared at his reckless wife, willing her not to slash some part of herself open by accident, he realized a peculiar thing.

He had feelings for her. Strong feelings.

Deep, intense feelings very akin to *love.*

It made no sense, taking into account their marriage thus far, but he was certain it was true. After all his worrying on the topic, he already cared for his wife more than he'd imagined.

When he started toward her to tell her so, and rescue her from her folly, she pointed the sword straight at his heart.

"Wait. Stop there, please," she said. "I have to tell you something."

"I have to tell you something too." He tried to keep his voice level. "Put down that damned sword. You don't know what you're doing."

"I do. Your father told me which ones I might handle, and how to do it safely."

"My father is a meddler, and you can't handle any of them safely. None of them have blunted tips."

"Please, let me speak." She lowered the sword. He watched in dread, waiting for her to slice off a few of her toes. "I have to tell you something very important, and I don't want to lose my courage."

"Speak, then."

He stared at her, his arms crossed over his chest. She wore a gold embroidered gown, impeccably fitted at the top, with delicately layered skirts cascading to her slippers. She looked like a mythic figure with the sword at her side.

"Wescott..." She took a deep breath. "Let me begin by saying that I understand why you left me. I've been a contemptuous person in this marriage. I didn't try to care for you at all. The thing is, I think I was afraid. I don't know why." She couldn't quite meet his gaze. "I just realize now that I was... I was afraid of you. Afraid of everything, really. It was silly of me."

He studied her, surprised by her words. "I'm sorry you felt afraid."

"Your father said perhaps it was leftover fear from the fire that became all tied up in you and me, and our marriage."

He eyed the sword, still worried it might fall on her. "The two of you seem to have struck up quite a friendship over the past week."

175

"Oh, Wescott, your family is so kind, and you've tried to be kind too, although I couldn't see that because I was so afraid of you becoming my husband. I know you're angry that I found your armory, but being in here with all your swords and shields makes me feel braver. It's made me feel better."

"I'm not angry. I just want you to put down the sword."

She looked at the weapon like she'd forgotten it was there. "Honestly...oh, I'm making a muck of this." She touched the back of her free hand to her cheek. "The thing I want to say is, I'm going to try to do better, and not be afraid. I want to learn more about you and be a more pleasant wife."

"I want that too. I mean, I want to learn more about you too, so we can have a happier marriage." *And I already love you. I'm fairly sure I do.* He crossed the rest of the way to her, because he wanted to hold her. He wanted to kiss her. He grasped her sword hand and circled her waist with his other hand, drawing her close. She lifted her face to his, and instead of rebuffing him or twisting to be released, she stood still, trembling a little.

"May I kiss you?" he asked. "I've wanted to for days now."

"Yes." She nodded and bit her lip. "I think… Yes, I'm ready."

Slowly, gingerly, their lips met in the first real, willing kiss she'd given him since they'd shared a bed at the inn. As his mouth possessed hers, his fingers found the sword's hilt and disengaged it from her slackening grasp. He held it at his side, careful not to move it or injure her, even as he clung to her with his other hand and kissed her with weeks' worth of pent up desire.

She was not quite fearless—her hands pressed upon his chest when he deepened the kiss, but she didn't push him away. He dropped the sword to the side to free his hand, so he could embrace her properly. Afraid of him? If only she'd said, he might have done everything differently.

He gentled his kiss, bringing her along with him patiently, even as his cock grew hot and thick against her front. How wondrous, to lust for his own wife so violently.

But he would not make her afraid. When he felt his passions rising to the breaking point, he drew away, for he wouldn't consummate their marriage here on the stone floor of a weapon-filled chamber. It might have been an apt location, considering what came before, but they'd both be sore and scratched afterward.

As she returned to her normal senses in a breathless, charming way, she looked over at the sword, then back at him. "You've disarmed me," she said.

"I love you," he said in return. "That was what I wanted to say when you held me at sword point. I've come to understand that I love you, because you are complicated and moody, and lovely, and more trouble than an armful of kittens."

"Oh." She still clung to his chest. "You love me because I'm difficult?"

"That doesn't mean you must continue to be difficult. I'd rather you didn't, for you've already earned a spanking for pointing that sword at me, and I seem to remember I still owe you one from before."

She frowned. "That's not a very nice thing to say just after you tell someone you love them."

"Ah, but I spank you because I love you. I've figured that out also. Still, let's save that for another time. Ophelia," he said, deciding to just be honest with her. "I want to kiss you again. I want to come inside you and pleasure you as I did at the inn." He felt her tremble again and hurried on. "There's nothing to fear. I won't hurt you. You mustn't be afraid."

"I know, but... The thing is..." She gave a little sigh. "I don't know what to do. I have no idea how to begin, or how to go on, or how to...reach that point we reached before."

"My love, if you come to bed with me, I'll show you."

"Right now? Before dinner?"

He eyed her lips, and the tempting expanse of her décolletage. "I don't think I can wait until after. After all this time, I don't want to wait any longer."

She seemed to understand that, cupping his cheek to drop a shy kiss on his lips. "I've said I would be brave."

Now he was the one who fought a shudder, not of fear, but desire for his wife. "It doesn't take bravery," he said, lifting her into his arms. "Only willingness and enthusiasm, and a bit of stubborn spirit, which you possess in spades."

* * * * *

She'd dreaded going to bed with him since they'd married, because of fear and an unwillingness to be vulnerable to him.

Now he was taking her to her own room, where they would have marital relations, and she held his hand and went voluntarily, even though her heart pounded hard in her chest. She'd wielded his shining swords and found joy in singing again, so she could do this too.

Probably.

When they entered her bedroom, he shut and latched the door so Rochelle wouldn't intrude, then drew her close. "Let me kiss you again," he said.

She liked his kisses more than she'd expected to when he first embraced her in the armory. Her lips didn't know what to do, but his worked very well, and seemed to show her just what would feel exciting. Wasn't that what she'd wished for? Excitement? She'd thought she must travel and have wild adventures to find it, but it was right here, if she was brave enough to accept it.

As he kissed her, he ran his fingers over her hair, and sometimes pressed them beneath her ears, or upon her nape. "I like that," she whispered. It made her feel centered and safe, and desired. His kisses were hot but not messy, demanding but not overbearing. He smelled clean and male, and she sought his cravat, to touch and loosen it. His fingers trailed down to the back of her dress, flicking open the buttons.

She knew this first step, anyway. Both of them needed to undress. As he moved her bodice down over her shoulders, massaging her at every step, she worked clumsily at his buttons, but there were so many. She made a small, complaining noise of defeat as he kissed her shoulders and the curve of her neck. He loosened her stays and petticoat, and somewhere in the process of removing those, his coat was coming off, his waistcoat, his cravat, all undone by his deft hands and tossed across a chair.

"They will wrinkle," she said in a soft voice, as if her own expensive gown wasn't in a heap upon the floor.

"We'll not worry about wrinkles right now." He reached beneath her chemise to tug at her garter strings, pausing to grasp her trembling thighs. "Why must we have so many clothes?"

With a muttered oath, he undid his trousers and shirt, shrugged it all off and let it lie on the floor so he might face her in his proud, muscular nakedness. *Do not be afraid*, she told herself. *This is how men are made, and he looks very fine for all that.* His cock was hard and pointing toward her, as if in challenge, but she would not let it shake her. She untied her chemise and let it fall open to her waist. Drawing in a breath, she let it drop to her feet, so she stood in her stockings.

"By God, you're beautifully made." His praise helped her keep her hands at her waist, rather than using them to hide her body. Still, she rather wanted to hide.

"Shall we go to bed?" she said.

His expression deepened into a broad smile. "It feels like I've been waiting an eternity for you to ask that."

She crawled onto the bed, not gracefully, she feared. He came behind her and guided her back onto the sheets. His eyes were so intent, so green and bright even as daylight faded.

"Don't be afraid," he said, taking off her stockings and setting the garters aside. "You must trust me."

"I'll try." She reached for him even as she turned from his gaze, because they were suddenly so close to one another. "Shall we pull up the blankets? I'm cold."

She meant *I'm shy*, but he pulled the blankets over them as she wanted.

"I don't know what to do," she said again. "Maybe it would be better if you...if you told me what I should do now, before we begin."

He kissed her, tenderly, with feeling. "We've already begun," he said when he drew away. "And your body will know what to do, even if your mind feels nervous. I promise that won't last very long." He pushed his hard shaft against her front, letting her feel his arousal. "But we can go slowly and take our time. We have all the time in the world now."

"Should we put out the candles?"

"Oh, no. I want to see you."

She gazed at him, tangled up with emotions. She was anxious, yes, but curious too, and perhaps a little flustered by his size and nearness. When he held her, her feet barely reached his shins. Her toes curled as he kissed her again, forcing her to open her lips to him and respond. She clung to his shoulders and moved against his front, against the hard part of him, because it seemed the right thing to do.

She was rewarded with a pleased—and tormented—groan. "How lovely you are when you trust me," he said against her cheek, between kisses. "I want to make you feel so good."

She soon remembered he was very skilled at that. His hands roved over her, bringing her body to life. He massaged her buttocks, which made her think of being spanked, but then he insinuated his fingers between her thighs and massaged another part of her that felt sinfully good and sensitive. To her embarrassment, she gave a wanton, avid twitch of her hips.

"Ah, you're understanding now," he said. "What a good, courageous wife you are."

"I should not..." She stopped speaking long enough to gasp as he brushed a finger over one of her nipples.

"You should not what?"

"I should not be like this, should I?" She tried not to squirm beneath his touch. "So wanton. It's not proper for a wife, is it?"

"It's very proper, Ophelia. You are exactly as you should be in your wedding bed, exactly as I hoped you would be. I always wished for you to respond to my touch."

That was a relief to hear, because she couldn't help responding. He slid down in the bed to kiss her nipples as he'd kissed her lips, with passionate force that made her throb between her legs. Then, dear God, he went further still and kissed her right upon her quim, licking and teasing until her hips bucked restlessly.

"You mustn't," she said, even as she gripped his head and tangled her fingers in his hair. "It's too much."

He ignored her half-hearted pleas, caressing and plying her there until the throb in her middle became a pressure she couldn't bear. "Please," she said. "I can't stand much more."

He left off his sensual torment to kiss her lips again, so she tasted herself upon him. Her middle felt drawn up tight, ready to explode. He took her hand and placed it on his shaft.

"You see how I respond to you, Ophelia? I can't wait to come inside you. Are you ready for me, love?"

Yes, I need you. It was a thought at first, but then she voiced it in a slightly hysterical tone. "Yes, I need you. Please..."

He spread her thighs and positioned himself between them. She remembered this from the night of the fire. She'd been carried away then, not knowing where such play would lead. Now she was ready to receive him. Perhaps it would soothe the ache inside her. She hoped so, for every part of her body was tingling now in anticipation.

He pressed himself a little bit inside, stretching her, but she was slick and ready, and he entered into her for the second time since she'd known him.

Oh, the fit was very tight. She had a moment of panic, then remembered she must relax, that men and women were made to fit together so. Still, her shuddery gasp lasted the entire time he slid inside her.

"Are you all right?" he asked, lowering his head to hold her gaze.

"Yes. It only feels so strange," she whispered. "So strange when you're within me."

"Strange and wonderful. You feel so good, so lovely, that I'm about to explode."

"I feel that too. That I might explode."

He didn't answer her wondering observation. She thought, perhaps, he was working too hard to control himself, as his breath had changed since he entered her. His teeth were gritted as he began to move. She stroked his back to soothe him, feeling luscious and wanton, caressing his tensing muscles as he moved in and out of her.

"It feels very good," she said a moment later. "Not so strange anymore." She began to move in concert with him, wrapping her arms about his shoulders as his thrusting hips drove her thighs farther apart.

"You see, you know just what to do." He encouraged her with a deep, demanding kiss, and she responded as he drove deeper, ever deeper inside her.

"You're filling me up, stretching me so. Oh, Wescott..."

His name felt marvelous on her lips, just as he felt marvelous inside her. She rubbed her sensitive spot against him, arching, and he stroked her there with the pad of his thumb until she trembled. Her fingers tightened on his skin, and her legs tensed and squeezed against him, and then the pressure reached a peak that went on and on, pulsing inside her, making her hips jerk against his.

"My beautiful wife," he said. "My beautiful crosspatch." As she shook all over, he abandoned his iron control and thrust deep, groaning against her ear. "Mine," he said, or perhaps he said "Dying." Either one, she'd understand. She felt she'd died a little too, in a very nice way.

He collapsed beside her, taking care not to crush her as he pulled her against him, belly to belly. They were still connected, and her body pulsed around him now and again, making him gasp, and then smile.

"It was better to wait," he said, running light fingertips along her jaw and beneath her chin, "if this was the result."

"It was a fine result, wasn't it?" In the same way she hadn't known how to proceed at the beginning, she was at a loss for words now. She decided a question would be all right, since he held her in such rapt attention. "Since we are married, how often do we lie together like this?"

He smiled. "As often as we wish. It would please me to be inside you every night." He pulled away, his member having decreased in size. "My cock will stand at attention again, never fear," he said at the question in her expression. "You do have a way of arousing my carnal hungers. Speaking of hungers, let's have dinner in our rooms tonight. I'd like to stay in bed with you a while longer. All night, if you wish."

She found she did wish it, even if his parents might wonder at their absence. The duke and duchess had been married some time, and happily, hadn't they? They would probably understand.

He tilted her face up for a kiss. "Are you hungry, Lady Wescott?" he asked when they parted.

"Famished," she said.

Chapter Fifteen:
Not So Afraid

They ate dinner together in her bed, something Wescott had never done with any other woman. He found his wife unlike any other woman, which probably meant he cared for her in more than an abstract way. He loved little things about her, like the way she drew her knees up when she snuggled against him, and the way she licked crumbs from her lips.

"We must ask Cook to make you some Welsh shortbread tomorrow," she said. "Your sister told me it was your favorite thing to eat. She was also the one who told me about the armory."

"Of course she was." He sighed. "I didn't enjoy finding you in there. I worried for your safety."

"I'm sorry if I gave you a start."

"It was more than a start. I had visions of you tripping and impaling yourself, and I wondered how I might explain it to your father."

She laughed, twirling a roasted carrot. "I'm not as clumsy as that. I trained in theater arts as well as singing. I can even dance a bit."

"I don't doubt it." He took another bite of the cook's tender filet. "I was glad to finally hear you sing. Your voice is beautiful."

"Thank you."

He could see a bit of color bloom in her cheeks. "Did you really lose your voice after the fire?" he asked.

"Yes, I really did. Well, the first few days it hurt to talk, much less sing."

"But by the time we married, you could have sung for me."

Her color deepened. "Perhaps. I didn't feel ready then."

They ate in silence a moment, then she spoke again. "I've always had a difficult relationship with singing. There were times I wished I didn't have any talent, because I always suspected...oh, it's ridiculous to say."

"Not ridiculous. What did you suspect?"

She sighed. "Sometimes I felt my mother didn't really love me, that she only loved my talent. My singing was such a great part of her world, and I resented it sometimes because I was the one doing all the work and having to be so proper and well-behaved so I didn't get a poor reputation from being on the stage."

"Hmm. That's sad."

"To make myself feel better, I used to pretend that singing would lead to other things. To fame and excitement. To adventure. I think that's part of why I was so bitter about our marriage. I used to entertain such whimsical dreams and fantasies..."

"Did you?" He handed her a napkin as she took a bite of crumbly cake. "What sort of fantasies?"

"I can't tell you. They're too silly by half."

He blocked her hand when she reached for another forkful of cake. "I can't let you eat anymore until you expand upon these dreams and fantasies you harbored. Otherwise I'll die of curiosity."

"I'll die of mortification if I tell you any of them."

"Might I remind you, my love, you still have a spanking coming. It's a very convenient spanking that I'm continually holding over your head."

Now her blush turned scarlet, but she managed a smile. "Oh, very well. I'll tell you one silly fantasy I had, one that concerns you."

"One that concerns me? Capital. I can't wait."

He pushed the dinner tray back to her, but she'd stopped eating to bury her face against his chest. "This is so embarrassing, and not at all funny considering all that was going on at the time, but the night you rescued me from the fire, when you looked so rough and common, I fantasized about you kidnapping me." She managed a peek up at him. "I was afraid of it happening, but excited by the idea too, because it would take me away from my boring, dutiful life. You seemed so handsome and strong."

He tightened his arm around her. "Kidnapping and ravishment. A bang up fantasy, in my mind."

"Ravishment? I hadn't thought about that side of things. I didn't think much beyond you stealing me away. You see how silly I was? How utterly protected and proper a girl, all the while longing for forbidden things?"

"Well, I've never kidnapped anyone," he said.

"I should hope not."

"But I might enjoy such a caper, if my victim was you."

She laughed, then sobered, meeting his gaze. "Did you mean what you said in the armory?" she asked. "Do you really love me?"

"Of course. You're very lovable, in an irritating way. I did mean it, and I mean it now."

"I imagine I love you too," she said, in utter seriousness. He wished he could kiss her right on her thoughtful pout. "When did you start to love me, Wescott?" He could see her mind working. "What I mean to ask is, did you sleep with other women while you were away, before you realized you loved me?"

"No, my little crosspatch. I was a faithful husband. My irritation with you was all tied up in desire. Another woman wouldn't have satisfied me."

She looked pleased, even though she chided him. "You mustn't call me that anymore. Crosspatch. I'll try to be sweeter."

He stood to clear the dinner trays from the bed. "I'll still call you crosspatch sometimes, as you'll doubtless be one. But you're lovable too." He returned to the bed and pulled her into his arms. Since their recent carnal encounter, she'd become much sweeter and more pliable, to the point he had to try hard not to hoist her upon his cock and take her again. Instead, he held her close, resting his chin against her forehead.

"Do you know why you're lovable?" he asked.

"I can't imagine."

"Because you're kind to my meddling family, as well as the crossest cat in the kitchen. Yes, I know you've made a pet of her. The servants talk."

"Dulcie is only misunderstood," she murmured.

"Dulcie? So you've named the creature? Good for you." He ran his fingers up and down her arm, enjoying her small shiver. "I also love that you sang that lullaby about the gentle lambs in the fields, when you're able to sing any number of fancy arias."

"I didn't know you'd heard that."

"I heard it. It sounded so lovely, I don't think I'll ever forget. Do you know, Ophelia, you've brought some heart to my life that I didn't know was missing, and I'm grateful for that."

She sat back a little so she could face him, her blue eyes wide and sincere. "You've brought something to me, too. You've fallen in love with me for more than my talent and my voice. Your friend Lord Townsend professed to love me, but it was only because he saw me perform. Everyone always goes on about my talent, but I don't think they see me standing there." Her voice broke a little on the last words. "No, I don't want to cry. It's lovely to think that you care so much for me. I think we can be happy together, even though I hated you more than anything a few days ago."

"Goodness. I forgot to mention your brutal honesty in my enumeration of your lovable qualities."

"I will *try* to be sweeter," she said, lying back upon the bed in a show of frustration. "It may take some time."

"And some trips across my knee." He winked at her. "We'll work all of that out."

"I think spankings will make me peevish, not sweeter," she said, sitting up with another pout already in place. If only she knew how it affected him.

"Spankings are essential to a successful marriage." He rearranged his rising cock beneath his bed robe so his arousal wouldn't be so obvious. "There's a closeness that comes from lovingly administered discipline, particularly when we respect one another."

She tilted her head as if to argue, then thought better of it. Or maybe, deep down inside, she understood what he meant.

"Speaking of which..." He stood from the bed and held out his hand for her. "If you've finished your dinner, I believe we ought to make a trip out to the Greek temple in the garden."

"Now? In the dark of night?"

"It's not so late. You're due a spanking, so we might as well take advantage of the temple's, er, atmospheric qualities. And available implements."

She frowned at his outstretched hand. "Why must I have a spanking when we've just been professing our love?"

"Because you earned one, haven't you? Remember your foray to the roof, when I thought you intended to fling yourself from the battlements? Remember when you pointed my own sword at me in my armory?"

She crossed her arms over her chest, over her lovely nipples, barely covered by the sheer nightgown she'd put on. "I think you're too fond of spanking women."

"No, my dear. I'm too fond of spanking *you*." He drew her from the bed and took her into her dressing room. "Come now, put on a cloak and some slippers."

Her eyes pleaded for mercy, but he saw curiosity there too. "You're going to bind me to the whipping post?" she asked.

He smothered a smile. "Perhaps, if you make a fuss. It'll make it easier for you to stand still."

She bit her lip, mumbling beneath her breath, but she did fetch a cloak and slippers and pull them over her night clothes.

"Once you spank me, my slate will be clean, yes?" she asked.

"For now, until you're naughty again."

She thought this over. "The problem is, spankings hurt, and I don't want you to hurt me."

"We've been over this before. They hurt for a reason, but since you've been on your best behavior this evening, I may be kinder than I would have been." He had a sudden burst of inspiration and gave her a rakish smile. "If it makes it easier, pretend I'm your kidnapper, and you're being taken to the temple for punishment. You've been very rebellious and bad, and tried to escape, and now you're to be tied up and made to regret it."

"I'm not sure that makes it any better," she said in a soft voice, but he knew her body well enough by now to see that it had.

* * * * *

Ophelia held her hands where he showed her, gripping the whipping post just at the height of her shoulders. He buckled the cuffs about her wrist so they were too tight to escape from, but not so tight they hurt. His terse orders echoed off the marble walls, and the only light came from the pair of lanterns they'd brought from the house.

Oh, why had she agreed to this? After dinner, civilized people sat in a parlor and talked, or gathered about the piano. They didn't come to a dark sanctuary of erotic punishment, outfitted with chains, benches, and cuffs.

You agreed to it because it's exciting, even though it's going to hurt.

Wescott had made her strip off her nightgown, as he played the gruff kidnapper exacting his due for her disobedient escape attempt. She was going to be spanked, so she shouldn't feel excited, not in that way, but she did. At least her fictional kidnapper did not present any ginger to force into her bottom. He did, however, cross to a set of drawers and return with a supple leather strap affixed to a wooden handle.

"I've not used this one yet. I suppose I've been saving it for a special occasion," he said, forgetting to be the kidnapper for a moment. "You can let me know how it feels."

"I think it will feel awful." Her voice quavered as she clung to the post, for the strap looked like too much of an implement. "You will make me afraid of you again, if you aren't careful."

He stopped and hugged her from behind, pressing his cheek to hers. "Don't dare be afraid of me. I'll never give you more of a spanking than you can bear."

She tried not to feel afraid, but she wondered if his idea of what she could bear was the same as hers. She pushed her bare bottom back against his front, and noted he was quite aroused by her predicament.

"Please, just get on with it," she said.

In answer, her husband slid a hand down between her legs and teased her sensitive center, delaying in a most wonderful way. "Oh goodness, oh goodness," she whispered. "Are you sure what we're doing is proper for married couples?"

He nibbled her earlobe, adding a new layer to her excitement. "It's very proper. Now prepare yourself for your punishment, naughty girl."

When he stepped back, she missed his presence. Or perhaps she missed his protection, for now her bottom was exposed for spanking. She held to the post as the first blow of the strap landed. It stung awfully, propelling her onto her toes.

"Ow, please!" She gasped. "Can't you use your hand instead? The strap feels very hot and unpleasant."

She could swear he was holding back laughter. "I've hardly started with you. I'm only warming you up."

She gritted her teeth as the next blow came, then cried out. "Ouch. *Owww.*"

"Shh." He paused to place a finger over her lips. "I know you're not the quiet type, but you mustn't shriek and scream either. If you like, I can fashion a gag for you. That's something a kidnapper might do."

"No, please. I'll behave."

As her strapping continued, she spent half the time pretending to be a pitiful kidnap victim, and half the time marveling that her husband was so perverse, and that she was so perverse, to go along with him to this secret place.

"Please," she begged, when her bottom felt on fire. "Please use your hand instead."

"Like this?"

He paused with the strap to pinch her nipples, stroke her hips, and squeeze her aching arse cheeks. She was helpless to avoid him, tied to the post, but she found she didn't wish to. In fact, she feared she encouraged his lewd gropings, pressing into his hand when he molested her between the legs. With a groan, he dropped the strap on a nearby bench and poked her backside with his stiff member.

"Untie me," she said, her voice a lustful plea. What was he making of her? He was too skilled a lover. "Please untie me so you can push inside me."

"I think I would rather push inside you when you're tied. How would you like that?"

She hadn't thought such a thing was possible. "Won't we lie on the bench? We must lie down, yes?"

He answered her question by lifting her hips and settling her upon his shaft. As he supported her, he slid deep inside her, eased by her welcoming wetness.

"I did not..." She gasped as he withdrew and thrust within her again. "I didn't think it was possible to make love this way."

"There are as many ways to make love as your imagination allows," he said, pausing to plant a tender kiss upon her lips. "Does it feel good, Ophelia? Shall I go harder, so your toes lift from the floor?"

"Per— Perhaps. Oh, that feels very naughty," she said when he complied. Naughty, but she loved the way it made her feel. She braced against the hard pole at her front, while an equally hard pole drove deep within her, making her lose a bit of her civility. Soon she was pressing upon him like a wanton tart and begging for more when he teased the aching spot between her thighs. It didn't feel like a punishment anymore, even though her bottom still tingled from the strapping.

As her arousal reached a fever peak, she clung to the whipping post, lost in sensuality and the scents and sounds of her husband groaning behind her. When she came off, her whole body trembled with uncontrolled pulsations of pleasure. Wescott reached his crisis just after she did, his groan deepening to a very wild-sounding growl. They'd fornicated like animals, really, but she could not be sorry for it.

"Oh, Ophelia," he said, circling his fingers about her bound wrists. "I'm not sure if that was a punishment or a reward."

"I think it was a little bit of both."

He still fondled her, touching her in all her most private places. The lantern's light flickered off the walls as she leaned into his caresses. She curled her hands into fists and tugged at the cuffs, thinking how exciting it felt to be bound and powerless. Well, with her husband anyway. He'd told her it was proper for married people to do such things together, and she would trust his word, even if she felt a bit embarrassed as he untied her hands.

"I like that you are braver now," he said, in between kissing each of her fingers. "I like it better when you are not so afraid."

She watched as he cradled her hands and thought how confusing marriage was. She still didn't know him well...their acquaintance barely spanned a few weeks. But as soon as he'd opened his heart to her, she felt a sense of connection she'd never felt to anyone else. Not her parents, her brother or sister, or any of the people she'd sung with in her short operatic career. Wescott's father had told her that a good marriage would bring happiness beyond measure.

"Do you think we will be happy?" she asked. "As happy as your parents one day?"

"Of course we will."

His confidence used to rile her, but now it comforted her because she trusted him more. After one last passionate kiss, they fetched their cloaks and lanterns and stole back through the garden to the Abbey. Once they washed and put on fresh night clothes, they reconvened in her room.

"Did you think your parents missed us at dinner and wondered why we never came down?" she asked.

He stifled a laugh. "Probably not."

His smile made her remember the "spanking" she'd just received, and she blushed as they climbed beneath the covers. When he offered his arms, she moved into them and found the perfect spot within his embrace.

"Please stay with me all night," she said. "In case I have another nightmare."

"I'll be happy to. I'm pleased you finally wish me to sleep beside you. I'll be right here if you need me."

He really was quite handsome, she thought. So much handsomer than she gave him credit for, when she was only looking at the things she'd lost. She felt the urge to sing again, but it was quiet in the bedroom, so she only hummed a very quiet melody. *Man and wife, and wife and man.*

"I'll find you some adventure," he said, beneath the lilt of her song. "I've already put my mind to it, Lady Wescott."

She didn't know what he meant, and she didn't ask, for after the carnal events of the evening, she was already almost asleep.

Chapter Sixteen: Kidnapped

Wescott stayed awake long after his wife went limp in his arms. What a turn of events, that he could hold her so after a dreamlike evening of sensual activities. He'd left the Abbey in despair, worried his marriage might never function, and returned to find his wife not only open to a wedded relationship, but keen to enjoy it.

Perhaps it was because he'd decided he must try to love her, or that she'd decided she must be braver. Perhaps it was his father's meddling, or the longing effect of separation. Whatever had opened this connection between them, he was grateful, and he wanted to bask in these post-carnal moments in case she awakened like the old Ophelia and pushed him away.

As he drifted in and out of sleep, he thought of her song, and the way she'd held up the sword like some woman warrior of yore. It came to him then, a place they might go adventuring, a wild, beautiful land where they could learn more about each other away from the strictures of English society. He roused himself long enough to send a note belowstairs, to prepare two carriages and a small retinue of servants for travel in the morning.

After that, he slept very well, and was pleased that Ophelia woke in the same pleasant, accepting mood she'd been in the night before.

"Good morning," he said, brushing back her disordered blonde locks. Later, Rochelle would tame them into a smooth, elegant hairstyle, but now, her wispy messiness was just for him. "You slept well, I think. No nightmares?"

She shook her head. "I haven't in three nights now. I think it's because I've been trying to conquer my fears. I survived that fire—we both did. I'm trying to let go of all my bad feelings about it. Your sister Elizabeth told me that thoughts can be powerful." She yawned, her fingers curled about his arm. "More powerful than any fire, anyway."

"My sister can be very thoughtful," he agreed. "I'm glad you're feeling better."

"Mostly better. My backside is a little sore."

Her impish blush sent heat right to his cock. No, no time for that, if they were to begin their adventure. Not only that, but she was probably still tender from the way he'd ridden her last night.

"Ophelia." He tried to focus on her eyes, rather than her lovely breasts, clearly visible beneath her sheer gown. "Would you like to go on an adventure?"

"An adventure? Yes." She didn't take a moment to think about it. "Where will we go? What will we do?"

"I had a thought of stealing you away to Cairwyn, my mother's corner of Wales."

"Stealing me away?" Her expression grew even more animated. "Kidnapping me after all?"

He thought of the lengths of rope he kept, just in case, in his dressing room. "Yes, kidnapping you and having my way with you whenever I please. If you'll rise and dress, and pack for a fortnight's adventuring upon the moors, we can leave at once. I mean, I can kidnap you at once."

"Oh, yes." She paused in her excited flight from the bed. "What does one wear in Wales?"

"Warm clothes, but nothing fancy. Rochelle will know what to pack."

His wife went to her dressing room to summon her maid, while Wescott lay back with satisfaction. He would need to pack too, but first he would think about how gorgeous Ophelia's eyes looked when they were sparkling with elation. Love wasn't such a complicated thing after all.

When they were packed and ready to leave on their Welsh adventure, he presented the rope to Ophelia, and told her to hold out her hands.

"Is this when the kidnapping starts?" she asked.

He took her offered hands and held them together. "Perhaps." He met her gaze. "Or perhaps it started that night I first swept you up onto my horse. I'm glad you're being so trusting now."

"It's because I know you won't really hurt me."

No, he'd never hurt her, although he'd enjoy spanking her on regular occasions, for that had become one of the greatest pleasures in his life. *Don't think of that now*, he told himself, *or you'll never get this "kidnapping" under way*. He tied the rope securely about her wrists, then swept her into his arms.

"Let the kidnapping commence," he declared.

"May I struggle a little?" his wife asked.

"Of course. I think you'd better."

To his alarm—and amusement—she set up an impressive fuss, squirming and beating his chest with her bound hands. Rochelle stood by the door, trying, and failing, to hide a smile.

"Help me," said Ophelia. "The marquess is stealing me off to Wales."

"Yes, my lady," said the servant, dropping a curtsey. "I believe it is so."

Wescott told her to stop struggling on the staircase, so they didn't both tumble to their deaths, but once they were at the bottom, she put up another token fight. "My parents?" he asked a footman.

"At luncheon in the dining room, my lord."

It was a testament to the Abbey's servants, or his own imperfect reputation, that none of them expressed the slightest unease at their master kidnapping his trussed-up wife. He carried Ophelia into the dining room to find his parents chatting over a light lunch.

"Good morning to you both," he said in greeting.

His father looked up and blinked at Ophelia's bound hands, tilting his head. "Goodness," he muttered to his wife. "The apple doesn't fall far from the tree."

Wescott ignored that comment, and his mother's pink blush. "I'm just letting you both know that I'm kidnapping Ophelia and spiriting her off to Wales."

His mother clapped her hands in delight. "Oh, Jack, what a capital idea."

He frowned at her. "Mama, this is supposed to be exciting and dangerous, so please pretend my wife is in mortal danger."

"Of course she is," she agreed at once, pulling a sad face for Ophelia's benefit. "You poor girl."

"I don't suppose there's any point in resisting anymore," his wife replied. "Wescott won't relent."

"How awful of him." His mother eyed the looped ropes about her wrists. "I pray he is merciful even though he's kidnapping you. Fortunately for you, Wales is lovely at this time of year."

"Mama," Wescott said in exasperation.

His father nodded. "If you asked me for kidnapping advice, son, I'd tell you to take your helpless victim to the cottage. That would be an adventure."

"I was already going to do that."

"Well, then, it seems you have it all in hand. Why don't you stop for some lunch with us before you go?"

"We've asked Mrs. Samuelson to pack us a basket so we can get underway," said Ophelia, who was not very good at playing a kidnapping victim.

"Go on, then," said his father. "Before your arms get too tired, and you let your wife get away."

"Thank you, Ophelia," his mother added, "for being such a gracious hostess to us during our stay. If only we had the capability to rescue you. Unfortunately, those knots about your wrists look too complex to untie."

"They are," his wife replied. "Ah well, I suppose we'll see you all again when we get back."

Wescott ignored his father's grin and his mother's titter as he carried Ophelia from the room. His wife had an odd look on her face. Either she was trying not to laugh, or she was finally attempting to playact the helpless victim. How had he ever mistaken her for an actress?

Once inside the carriage, two days of travel stretched before them. He normally would have gone mad within minutes, but his wife entertained him with some of the favorite songs she'd learned at her school in Vienna. First she sang a few showy arias, her expressions helping him understand the Italian lyrics. Perhaps she was not such a poor actress after all.

After that, she sang some other parts from a German opera she loved, one she'd hoped to perform in London before the theater burned down. They hadn't talked yet about her future career, and some part of him wished to avoid the discussion for fear their newfound connection might come to a fiery end, just like the opera company's theater.

But it was cowardly not to address it, now that she burst into song whenever he asked her to grace him with a performance. He'd told his friends the day of his wedding that he would not allow her to appear onstage again, not if he could help it. But now...now he saw her mother's point. His wife had a God-given gift.

When she came to the end of a rather forlorn song about a lost love, he touched the rope still wrapped about her wrists. "How long will you stay bound?"

"Until you release me," she said, smiling. "There's probably no risk to it. I can't very well escape now, as the carriage is traveling at a fair clip." She cut him a look. "Not that I would try to escape, Lord Kidnapper. I dread your corporal punishments."

"Don't tease me, little crosspatch." He still loved the endearment, even though she complained about it. He took her hands into his lap, working a finger over the knot. "I'm very pleased to hear you singing again. I'd worried your voice was gone for good."

"I worried about that too."

"Will you want to perform again, now that it's back?"

She looked down at her hands as he began to work the knot free. "I'm not sure," she said after a moment. "It would take a great deal of time to perform as I used to, time for vocal practice and theater rehearsal."

"I can give you adventures," he said, unwrapping the rope. "But I can also tolerate a life on stage for you, if that's what you wish. Your voice is magnificent. If you wish to perform before public audiences, I'll support you. Between your august family and mine, no hint of impropriety will stain your reputation."

He could see she was touched by his encouragement.

"I'm not sure," she said again. "I might want to decide later. I think..." Even though her hands were free, she still held them together. The rope had left faint marks on her skin. "Maybe someday I'll wish to do it again." She blinked at him. "Will you be disappointed if I don't?"

"Of course not. If you only ever sing in the halls of Wescott Abbey, I'll be happy. Your voice will make it feel more like home." He traced the marks, emotion welling up unexpectedly. He heard her soul in her voice. It did make him feel he'd found his way home. "Maybe someday, we could have children," he went on. "I can see you being a fiercely loving Mama, as my mother was. I can see you singing to our children, for joy, to make them happy."

"Maybe they'll want to sing too," she said.

"I hope so. But sometimes..." He brought her hands to his lips and kissed each of them. "Sometimes I'll want you to sing just for me."

"You do love me, don't you?" she asked with a sort of awe. "I worried you were only saying it to be kind, but now...I can feel that you love me. It's not an act."

"It's not an act," he agreed.

"We can make a family together, you and me. That's very exciting, an adventure in itself. Can we do that right away? I think I'd rather do that than perform onstage."

He cleared his throat. "Right away? My dear, do you know how babies come?"

She assured him she did, but he could tell she didn't, so he spent the next hour or so clearing up questions about how babies came, and how her anatomy worked. By the time they stopped to change the horses, his wife was far more knowledgeable about her own sexuality—and his. By the time they got to the inn for the night, he ached for her, his lovely Ophelia.

He asked for dinner to be brought to their room. He'd stayed at this inn on numerous occasions throughout his life, whenever they went to visit his mother's family, but it had never felt like this. He was here with his own wife, desperate to bed her now that she'd been awakened to the finer points of her sexuality.

As soon as they were alone, he took her hair down, mussing it up as he kissed her, until she looked as disheveled as she'd looked that morning.

"My sweet wife," he murmured as she clung to him. "I want to be inside you."

"Yes, please." She lifted her face, breaking their kiss. "We are at another inn, aren't we?"

"It's going to be all right," he promised.

"Yes. I'm not that old Ophelia anymore."

He laid her back on the inn's lumpy bed and caressed her all over, and made love to her slowly and thoroughly, until she shook in his arms. There were no nightmares that night, not that he expected there to be.

As she'd told him, she wasn't that old Ophelia anymore.

* * * * *

Ophelia woke to the sounds of the inn and snuggled closer to her husband. "Are we in Wales?" she asked, still half asleep.

"Nearly." He stroked her cheek until she came awake. "We'll cross into the country this morning, if you'll rise and have some breakfast."

He didn't have to ask twice. She was so excited for her adventure to continue; she had only the vaguest idea of Wales, but she knew it wasn't England, and that they spoke another language which her husband also spoke and understood. She knew they were going to stay in a rustic cottage with just a few servants, something she'd never done in her life.

Soon they were on their way. She'd put on a light linen gown of medium blue, along with a plain straw bonnet. She left her gloves off entirely, even though there was an autumn chill in the air. As they passed into Wales, the roads grew a bit narrower, and a bit more rutted. Now and again she was tossed against her husband's side, but she didn't mind that in the least.

He moved his long leg against hers to anchor her, which made her laugh, but also made her remember the way he'd pressed against her the night before, thrusting within her until they felt like the same person with the same beating heart. She didn't say such things to him, not yet. Someday she would. Her courage came in small steps that would add up to a lifetime of togetherness, if she didn't lose her nerve.

"Tell me about your family in Wales," she said. "I would like to know their names before I greet them."

She quickly realized this was folly, as his aunts, uncles, and cousins seemed to run into the dozens. Half the names were close to English names, but half the names were Welsh and unfamiliar. He pronounced those names with an accent, with unfamiliar deep vowels and guttural consonants. When they stopped to change the horses for the last time, he spoke Welsh to the coaching inn's staff, all of whom seemed to know him well.

This impressed her mightily, and intimidated her a bit also, for she didn't speak any Welsh at all, and when she asked him to teach her a few words on the last leg of their journey, her tongue tripped over the foreign syllables.

"You'll learn it in time," he promised. "I'll teach you a little bit every day, and you can practice during the times we visit Lisburne Manor, where my mother grew up." A smile teased the corners of his lips. "I've brought something else along to fill our adventurous afternoons, but it's a surprise."

"What?" She took his hand. "I don't like surprises, Wescott. Please tell me."

"No, my little crosspatch. You'll wait and get your surprise in due time."

A short while later, they passed onto the Lisburne holdings, and Wescott pointed out the low, ancient keep in the distance. "It's not much by looks," he said, "but it's been standing a long while. Most of the families around here have lived on their land for centuries."

In between the cleared fields and farmland, thick forests grew wild. The leaves had already turned, so an explosion of autumn colors rippled in the light breeze. "Can we stop and walk about for a moment?" she asked. "I want to be outside. It looks so pretty."

"No, love, we won't stop yet. It's pretty where we're going, and we're almost there. My parents chose this particular meadow to build a cottage because my mother had loved it so much as a child. They had to pay the miller a pretty penny for the property."

"So the cottage is not as ancient as your family's keep?"

"The cottage is much, much younger, but very charming. Just like you."

Within a few moments, the carriage turned onto a smaller road lined with trees. After a time, the trees became a hedge, and then a crumbling stone wall that appeared to be as ancient as the old keep. She leaned close to the window, taking it all in. Another turn in the road, which was more of a path at this point, and they entered a picturesque clearing. The sun was setting, but it was still light enough to see a neat, whitewashed, thatched-roof cottage in the distance, surrounded by another low stone wall.

"It's like a fairy house," she said. "How sweet and squat it is compared to Wescott Abbey. Not that I dislike the Abbey," she added quickly.

"The Abbey is old and grand. This is a sweet cottage, as you said. My parents always called it their escape. I spent many sunny afternoons in my childhood roaming this meadow with my brother and sisters."

She could imagine him as a brash gold-blond child, playing fantasy games with wooden swords, and climbing the hedges and trees.

"I can't wait to see inside. I've never stayed in such a cottage before." No, this was novel and exciting. An adventure, just the sort she'd longed for, but had never had the foresight to imagine.

They climbed out at the gate, so the carriages could move on to the stables. Now that they were nearer, she saw the cottage was bigger than it looked from afar, but of course, Wescott had come from a large family. She remembered his words about starting their own family, about her singing to their children. Would their children roam this meadow one day?

Why not? They would wish to have adventures too, and she'd encourage it—especially for her daughters, whether or not they inherited her soprano voice.

As her imagination turned, a smiling housekeeper opened the door and greeted Wescott with a torrent of musical Welsh. To Ophelia's relief, she also greeted her in English. *I will learn Welsh in time*, she thought. *I'll work at it, so it will be another thing Wescott and I can share.*

They were welcomed inside and invited to take dinner before they even unpacked their things. Ophelia found she was famished, and the food was simple and hearty, just as she would picture a Welsh country meal. By the time they finished eating and retired to the small, cozy parlor with a crackling fireplace, she almost felt ready for bed. Was it the food? The country air?

"I love it here," she said, pulling her wrap closer about her shoulders. "I can't wait for tomorrow, and the day after that, and the day after that." She turned to Wescott. "How long will we stay?"

"A few weeks, I suppose. Until you've had enough of cottage living and yearn for England again. As for London, we needn't return there until next season, unless you want to go sooner."

"The season? Do you go for Parliament?"

"Yes, I've attended for some years now. My friends haven't much interest, but I try to do my part."

"You're a politician," she said with a smile. "I should have known it."

"Why do you say that?"

"Because nothing shakes you, no matter what happens. I bet you're a very good politician."

He seemed pleased by her praise. "I'm part of the city planning council, and some other organizational committees. I enjoy when things run well."

She knew that about him too. Their abrupt adventure to Wales had come off without a hitch.

"Can I have my surprise now?" she asked.

He took her hand and pulled her over into his lap. "Not now. You're tired from travel and giddy with sleep. Tomorrow is soon enough."

She closed her eyes, wondering what the surprise might be. His warmth made her feel even more tired, and she relaxed against his chest. "Thank you for this adventure," she said, reaching up to touch his faintly stubbled cheek. "It feels like a proper holiday."

"Not a proper kidnapping?" She could hear his deep chuckle in his chest. "Ah, well, I suppose I'm happy with either, as long as we're together."

Together, she thought. *What a wonderful word.*

Chapter Seventeen: Rescued

A few weeks later

Wescott went to his wife's room, stepping quietly so she wouldn't notice him peeking in at the door. Her hair was pulled back, hastily braided, and she wore her exercise togs, a loose tunic fashioned from one of his old shirts, and a skirt Rochelle had transformed into a flowing pair of trousers. She looked ridiculous, and lovely. She leaned down to pull on her stoutest boots, for he'd invited her to practice swords with him before dinner.

That had been her surprise the day after they arrived—a set of blunted rapiers he'd tucked in with the baggage, so he might teach her the beginnings of swordplay. He'd thought she might enjoy a dabble, considering he'd found her brandishing that sword in his armory, but as it turned out, they'd done much more than dabble. His petite wife took to swordplay like some fierce medieval warrior, which was somewhat alarming.

"Bring your gloves," he reminded her as she stood.

She turned with a gasp. "How long have you been there?"

"Not long."

"You've been spying on me." She strode to him, her pert face raised. "I must challenge you to a duel, sir."

He took her face between his fingers and drew her close. "You'll get a kiss instead."

He made good on his words, embracing her and pressing his lips to hers, while his fingers explored the shapely curves beneath her practical costume.

"Anyway," he said when he pulled away, "I've already invited you to duel, remember? We'd better get started on your practice exercises, or we won't have time to spar before dusk comes on."

They left the cottage and took up their usual spots in the meadow out front. He always insisted on a battery of stretches before each practice, lest she injure herself, although he was learning she was much hardier than she appeared. With the warm up done, they ran through the sequences of attacks and parries he'd taught her thus far. Ophelia was a bright pupil, always ready to progress to something new. Sometimes, to his amusement, she sang along to the sequences, an exercise she said helped her remember them.

"I've done well, haven't I?" she asked, when she executed everything with easy aplomb.

"Too well," he said under his breath.

"What?"

"I said you're doing very well. Yes, I'm quite proud of your progress."

"Can we duel now?" she asked.

"Yes, darling. I wouldn't leave out your favorite part."

His stubborn crosspatch loved taking him on at sword point, even though he easily bested her without using his full strength. It was the form and exercise that mattered. They squared up, swords raised, and circled one another, until she decided to make the first thrust.

He blocked it, impressed by her quickness. "A good start. It's always shrewd to use the element of surprise."

A lock of hair had escaped her braid, blowing sideways in the breeze as she grinned at him. "Were you really surprised, Jack?"

"Yes," he lied, then threw his own surprising thrust. She parried it, barely, and centered herself, balancing her body's weight. He began another attack, one she knew well, and she met it with gusto, setting up an impressive defense.

"Good," he said, urging her to greater movement with his sword. "Remember to move with your sword, just like you're dancing together."

"What is this?" A familiar voice came from across the clearing. "Oh dear. They've progressed to weapons, then."

He and Ophelia paused in their mock battle and turned to see his friends Lord Marlow and Lord Augustine walking toward them.

"By God, they are swashbuckling," said August with a laugh.

Marlow raised a fist. "Spear him in the stones, Lady Wescott. That'll take him down right fast."

"For God's sake, have a care for my wife's sensibilities," Wescott scolded.

"That's all right. I know what 'stones' are now," she called to Marlow. "My husband taught me."

Wescott looked heavenward, praying for patience. To their credit, his friends had given them a full month of privacy, but as soon as they showed up again, they brought their chaotic bachelor energy. They must have taken their horses straight on the back path to the stables, or he'd have heard them coming sooner, not that it would have helped.

"Proceed with your skirmish, then," Marlow said. "Don't mind us. We'll watch quietly, and not root for either side."

"Actually, I believe I'll root for your wife." August sketched Ophelia a courtly bow. "Because she looks smashing in her fencing gear, and I'll enjoy seeing the high and mighty Lord Wescott defeated by her sword."

"I was going to root for her too," said Marlow, "but since we've been Wescott's friends for so long, I didn't plan to announce it out loud."

"Why not?" August turned on him. "You announce everything else out loud, like telling Ophelia to stab Wes in the balls."

Marlow snorted, outraged. "Don't say balls in front of a lady, especially your best friend's wife."

"Here, give me that sword," August said to Wescott, "and I'll stab Marlow right where he needs it."

"Both of you sit down." Wescott pointed with the tip of his rapier. "Just sit there and shut your dam—" He stopped himself from cursing in front of Ophelia just in time. "Shut your loud mouths so we can concentrate. She's a capable student, but your yammering will be too much."

His friends sat on the dry autumn grass with an air of chastened insult, leaning back on their arms. When he turned to Ophelia, her cheeks were pink from stifled laughter.

"Do not encourage them," he said. "Their behavior will only grow worse."

"They are silly, aren't they?" She held up her sword, brandishing the tip. "So, will you let me win so they'll be pleased?"

"Of course I won't. You must win fair and square, if you want a true victory."

She lunged at him, and he lunged back, amused by her cheek. In truth, teaching her swordplay had gone a long way to settling the fears that plagued her, just as bringing her to Wales had satisfied her craving for adventure. As he was mentally congratulating himself for those victories, Ophelia nearly disarmed him.

"You must concentrate," she said with a grin. "That's what you always tell me."

"You're not concentrating right now," he shot back. "You're gloating."

He tested her on all the attacks he'd taught her thus far, and she parried every time. Her posture was improving, and her footwork was better than his had been after years of practice at his club. She was so small and light, she could evade most thrusts she couldn't parry. He heard his friends gasp as he went on the attack, but he knew his wife's capabilities, and, of course, both their rapiers were blunted.

"I'm growing tired," she said after his third attack. "I'm not sure I can go much longer."

"Do you wish to surrender?" he asked.

"No, not yet." She strained to defend herself but could barely turn off his next thrust.

He took a step back and decided to go easy on her, so she might save face before his friends. That was his mistake, for the scheming creature had only been playacting her exhaustion. She took advantage of his kindness by lunging for his chest. The dull tip landed upon his breastbone, a clear victory. A stabbing, indeed, if they'd been using real weapons, but there was no chance of that, since his wife couldn't be trusted.

"You little cheater," he said, as his friends surged to their feet and cheered. "You weren't tired at all."

"No, I don't tire easily." She gave him an impish grin. "It's from my voice training. I've got very good breath control."

He couldn't stay angry when she smiled at him that way, although he still itched to turn her over his knee for her cursed playacting. If his friends weren't there, he would have.

"Good show," said Marlow, shaking Ophelia's free hand. "I knew you would best him."

"He's like a great, clumsy oaf beside you," August agreed, "and you so light on your feet, you could fly away."

"I'm not like a great, clumsy oaf," said Wescott. "She cheated by pretending she was tired so I'd lighten my attack."

"And then she stabbed you in the heart," said Marlow with far too much enthusiasm. "Thus is the great, golden-haired Marquess of Wescott brought low."

"Save your poetry for the ladies, you wordy fool."

After a bit more good-natured ribbing, he noticed that his wife was growing tired, for all her proud smiles. She'd also need to change clothes before dinner, and brush out her wild, blonde locks so Rochelle could make her look a proper hostess to their visitors.

"Leave me your sword," he told her, "and go inside to put away your sparring clothes. We'll be there presently for dinner."

"Yes, my lord."

As he took her rapier, he leaned close for a fleeting kiss. "I'm sorry I cheated," she whispered next to his ear.

"You'll be sorrier still, once we get a moment alone."

His quiet threat had the desired effect. By the time he let her go, she was in full blush, her blue eyes dancing with a mixture of pleasure and dread. It took some effort not to stare after her retreating figure.

"Things are better between you, then," said August in a quiet voice. "I'm glad for it."

"I reckon teaching her swords was the best thing you could have done." Marlow reached for one of the rapiers, testing its strength. "Did she ask you to show her?"

"She made herself at home in the Abbey's armory, at my father's urging. She liked the way it sounded when she sang in there. I figured I'd better teach her something of weaponry before she slaughtered herself by accident."

"She's singing too?" Marlow whistled and handed the sword back. "Then I suppose everything's come around."

"It has." He didn't have to go into specifics for his friends to know what he meant. He was sure the look in his eyes said enough. "She's learning Welsh, too. She's made a great deal of progress, for my cousins won't stop chattering at her."

"That's the best way to learn a language," said August. "Although your cousins have chattered at me for years and it still sounds like a load of gibberish. I suppose your wife's a bit more intelligent than me, though."

"A bit?" Marlow drawled, poking his friend.

Wescott set the swords aside so Marlow and August wouldn't use them to turn on each other, then sat on the grass to rest. He'd never admit it, but his wife was a challenging opponent now that she'd mastered the rudiments of swordplay. His friends followed suit; they all sprawled on the grass as they'd done when they were boys.

While dusk deepened, his friends recounted their most recent adventures in London, and told him that Pearl's Erotic Emporium was up and running again in a new location, thanks to a handful of wealthy sponsors. He didn't ask if they were part of that group, but he guessed they were.

Talk turned to family news, who had gone to the country and who was staying in London, and who was adding to their nurseries. They had a dozen sisters between them, nearly all of whom were married by now. Townsend's sister Rosalind and Wescott's sister Hazel would be the last to the marriage market, he supposed, and then Elizabeth, if they could ever get her married off to a proper gentleman deserving of her hand.

As his friends chattered on, he thought with a twitch of surprise that it might be his wife increasing soon, his own son or daughter being added to the long list of Oxfordshire babies.

"Did you hear me?" asked Marlow, waving his hand before Wescott's face. "Are you dreaming?"

"What?" He pushed his hand away. "My mind wandered for a moment."

"We've got news of Townsend," said Marlow. "Nothing dire, just that he's coming back to England soon. His parents have summoned him home."

"Have they?" Wescott kept his voice carefully neutral, and so did they.

August picked at the sole of his boot. "They want him back in England before winter sets in. I think they fear he'll give his heart to some ninny in a far-flung village instead of marrying a proper London girl."

"There are a great many who'd be happy to have him," said Wescott.

"Certainly, with his looks and connections. Anyway, we thought you'd want to know."

Wescott nodded. "I wish him well, for all that recently passed. You must tell him he's invited to Wescott Abbey whenever he returns home."

"We'll let him know," said Marlow. "I think it will help him move on from his *tendre*, to see you and your wife rubbing along so well."

"I don't know." August's voice held doubt. "Towns had it pretty bad for Ophelia. He might need more time."

"He'll be fine once he finds someone to replace her," Marlow said.

August picked at a blade of grass, his lips drawn tight as Wescott and Marlow exchanged glances. It would be good for August to find a woman to replace Felicity too, not that Wescott expected that to happen anytime soon.

"We ought to go back," Wescott said, standing to fetch the swords. He tucked them beneath one arm and held out a hand to his friends. "We eat early at the cottage. I suppose Mrs. Evans has got you set up in your rooms by now?"

"Yes, when we arrived. They've got a lovely view of the back garden," said Marlow. "I've always loved this place, Wes. When I'm here, I always feel a little less..."

"Mad?" August offered, as he dusted grass from his trousers.

He scowled at him. "A little less harried. Yes. What's for dinner tonight, Wescott? Do you know?"

"Rabbit and roast vegetables, I believe. And plenty of Cook's chocolate tarts."

His friends whooped and started toward the house at a run, occasionally trying to trip one another. Bloody children, they were, driven by childish appetites. Silly, Ophelia had called them, and he'd been so much like them only a couple months ago.

How had he changed so fully in only a short time? When had life become more than tarts, the type you could eat, and the type you could bed?

Perhaps it had been the night he followed his wife up to the battlements and realized he must battle for their marriage if they were to survive. Or perhaps it had been the first night they met, when he saw her in harm's way outside the theater, waiting to be saved.

Perhaps she wasn't the only one who'd been saved that night. More and more, it seemed they'd rescued each other as flames tore through London and upended both their lives.

Chapter Eighteen:
In Love

Wescott's friends slept late the following day, so her husband invited Ophelia to a picnic in the meadow by the lake. Oh dear, she saw that glint in his eyes again.

Picnics were easy to plan, as they frequently took their luncheon outside, with warm clothes and shoes to protect them on the chillier days. They were well into autumn now, so the cottage's landscape was changing. The trees grew more spindly looking, stripped of their rich, red-gold leaves.

They walked the well-trod path to their favorite hideaway, a sheltered meadow next to a lake. Even now, the water's surface glittered, alive with aquatic life, and wildflowers blew in the breeze. As Wescott laid out the blankets for their picnic lunch, Ophelia walked amidst the boulders flanking the shore, collecting wildflowers in various colors: violet, pale pink, yellow, and white, even orange.

"You might as well pick them all," Wescott teased as she brought an armful of blooms to the blanket. "They won't last much longer."

"They're pretty, even if they don't smell very nice." She held them to her nose, grimaced, then lay them beside the blanket. If she wasn't careful, she'd begin to sneeze.

"Will it grow cold soon?" she asked, picking up a meat pie.

"I fear so, although, in all honesty, the cottage is easier to keep warm than the Abbey."

Ophelia had written to her parents, describing the cottage and the beautiful Welsh countryside. She did not tell them she was studying swordplay, for they'd probably disapprove, not that their opinion mattered now. She was a married woman and her husband loved her. That was enough.

They ate meat pies, scones, and biscuits until they were full, then packed the rest of the food away for later. Sometimes when the sun was strong and warm, they lay back on the blankets and took a nap, but today they stayed awake instead, watching the birds call across the lake. A pair of hawks soared high above them, weaving back and forth in a pattern that always brought them together again.

"They must be in love," she said dreamily.

"Or planning a hunt together," said her more practical husband.

"Perhaps they're sparring together, like we do. You know, the friendly, loving way, not arguing all the time."

He chuckled. "It wasn't so long ago we sparred together the unfriendly, unloving way. I'm glad we don't anymore. My parents told me that once we understood each other, there would be plenty of room for love."

"Your parents are very wise."

"My mother has a saying. *Ask the heavens for what your heart wants.*" He lifted his hand, drawing it about the meadow. "By heavens, I imagine she means all of this. The earth, the sky, the wind, the sun."

"She doesn't mean God?"

"I don't know. Perhaps God also. When things are so beautiful and peaceful..." He gazed at her. "Sometimes that feels like a prayer's been answered, a prayer you never even thought to speak." He took her hand, tugged off her woolen glove, and brought her fingers to his lips. "It will be beautiful wherever we are, Ophelia, as long as we're together."

"I know. And I don't mind being cold at the Abbey, if you think we ought to return. Our families will miss us."

"They will. The good news is that we can come back here whenever we like, as long as one of my siblings or my parents aren't in residence. Even then, there's room to squeeze in together, to a point." He shrugged. "But there's no rush to return. As long as we're home for the holidays, because..."

She heard the note of tension in his voice. "Because...?"

"Because Townsend is coming back from Europe, and I'd like to be there to see him, and try to make things right between us. It's always been the four of us, you know. Best friends and all that."

She gave his hand a reassuring pat. "If you and I can come to an understanding together, you and Townsend will as well. Perhaps you can tell him what a crosspatch I am half the time, so he won't wish he'd married me anymore."

He cupped her chin with a fond smile. "My little crosspatch. Yes, I'll tell him you're terribly prone to misbehavior, and that he was lucky to escape a leg shackle." His gaze deepened, his eyes vivid green in the afternoon light. "Speaking of misbehavior, darling..."

Ah, that glint. She loved and hated it.

"Misbehavior?" She kept her voice light. "I don't know what you're talking about. I've been a perfect angel today."

"Today has barely begun," he said with a laugh. "No, I'm speaking of yesterday. Shall I enumerate your trespasses?"

"You make it sound so serious. Yes, *enumerate* my *trespasses*."

"Well, aside from mocking me just now, you talked about stones with my friends yesterday, which was quite inappropriate—"

She interrupted him with a gasp. "I never brought it up, though. That was Marlow and his poor manners!"

"And," he continued, holding up a finger, "you also tricked me at swordplay by pretending to be tired, which wasn't very sporting."

"I suppose I *am* guilty of that. And of humiliating you before your friends with a sound defeat."

"A sound defeat?" He gave back her glove and drew her up from the picnic blanket. "I wouldn't say it was a 'sound defeat,' but you will receive a sound spanking in retribution, naughty girl."

He led her across the clearing as her stomach churned with that familiar feeling of anxiety and excitement. He came to a stump that made too perfect a chair, and sat upon it, drawing her over his lap.

"Wescott," she said, trying to sit back up. "What if your friends come?"

"They won't. As hard as I plan to spank you, they'll hear it long before they come into the meadow and stay well enough away."

Goodness, she hoped he was teasing about that. It had been such a pleasant afternoon until now. "I don't know if I'll ever get used to these spankings. Even if I deserve one, I don't want it."

Perhaps that was partly a lie, though she'd never admit it. She did like the way he held her close and handled her with his strong fingers, and arranged her just so across his thighs before he flipped up her skirts.

But the rest of it...

"Oww," she cried as he began to wallop her arse. "That hurts. Please!"

"Please what? Shall I spank you harder? I'm not putting much energy into it yet."

"It feels like too much energy."

She tensed her cheeks and shifted on his lap, her fingers scrabbling at the roots beneath the stump. By now, he'd used a few different implements to punish her, but his hand was the worst, for he spanked her much longer, and the sting grew without relief.

"Please, I must have a break."

"Already? I've just started. Perhaps you shouldn't cheat at swordplay, hmm?"

"I never will again."

Her shrieked promise did nothing to stop the spanking. If anything, the heat increased. When she squirmed too much, he spanked the backs of her thighs, which burned even worse.

"Hold the proper position," he said. "The better you behave, the more quickly I'll consider you punished."

"I feel very punished right now."

She drew out the last word into a wail, but she also understood by now what he wanted, and so she tried to lie still and take the spanking she'd earned. Afterward, he would hold her and make everything better. She had to trust him. She loved him.

But oh, her bottom hurt. She stayed in position and only kicked a little bit, although she cried louder and louder. At last he left off belaboring her bottom, and she gasped for breath. She would never look at this meadow's stump quite the same again. She rather wished it had grown over with ivy many years ago.

"What do you have to say for yourself?" he asked when she caught her breath. His hand moved lazily over her hot cheeks, a soothing sort of threat.

"I'm very sorry I said the word sto—the 's' word in front of your friends," she said. "And I'm terribly sorry I pretended to be tired only to trick you. I'll never, ever do that again, I promise."

As she finished her abject apology, he gave her bottom a final spank, then brushed her skirts down. She let out a relieved breath as he lifted her and set her upon his lap.

"I'm sorry," she said, throwing her arms about his neck, and she meant it. "I'm going to be so good from now on. Well, at least for the rest of today." It wouldn't be hard to remember her manners, with her bottom smarting whenever she tried to sit on it. "I want to be a good wife to you, not a crosspatch."

"I'll love you either way," he promised, pulling her close against him.

They sat that way for long, peaceful minutes. At times like this, she understood what he meant when he said that the occasional spanking was good for a marriage. Although, if she had a choice between erotic punishment and a sound spanking like the one she'd just received, she rather preferred the former. Ah, perhaps tonight...

She leaned back and took in her handsome, loving husband. He wasn't a stranger anymore. He was her rescuer, her heroic Viking with his broad shoulders and long, gold-blond hair.

"I feel like singing," she said. "Shall I sing for you?"

"Always. The answer to that is always yes."

He held her as she sang songs about love in German and Italian, while the hawks flew in lazy circles above their heads. *The world is love, and I shall raise my voice to the heavens. In all the skies, you are the one I see.*

When she tired of singing, he kissed her instead, pressing his lips to hers until she lost her breath.

THE END

A Final Note

Thanks for reading this first book in a new world, with three more stories to come. It took me a long time to dream up the futures for the young children you met at the end of the previous Properly Spanked series. I knew I wanted their parents to be part of the stories, but I wanted the kids to have the spotlight—and the spankings.

If you're new to the Properly Spanked world and haven't read the original series, please enjoy the book descriptions that follow. I hope you'll read all of them as you're waiting for the next Legacy novel. Lord Townsend will be the hero of the next book, and I promise more loving and spankings to come.

Many thanks to wonderful Wendy B. for helping me find a title for this book when I couldn't seem to pull one out of my brain! Thanks also to Tiffany, Lanie, and author Renee Regent for their encouragement and assistance with this novel. If you enjoyed it, I hope you'll leave a review at your preferred site or on Goodreads. As for what's coming up, you can stay up to date by joining my mailing list at annabeljoseph.com, or subscribing to my silly videos and updates on YouTube. (Just search my name.)

In closing, thanks for being a reader. Like Ophelia, your love and support makes me want to sing.

Properly Spanked: The First Series:

Take a rousing romp through 1790s England with the original four Properly Spanked novels…

Training Lady Townsend: The Lady Aurelia has been promised in marriage to the Marquess of Townsend since she was four and he was fourteen. Unfortunately, she grew up into a pillar of propriety while her betrothed grew up into a renowned rake. Of course, no one would expect such an unsuitable match to go forward…which is why they find themselves at a loss when circumstances force them to the altar and into each other's arms.

Hunter, the beleaguered marquess, believes he'll survive the uneven match by continuing to frequent his well-trained coterie of whores and courtesans, but Aurelia's powerful father has other ideas. When he blocks Hunter's access to the only women shameless enough to cater to his decadent needs, the marquess informs his new wife that something will have to be done.

That "something" will be the immediate commencement of her erotic training…whether she wants it or not.

To Tame A Countess: The Earl of Warren never considered himself the heroic type—or the marrying type. Unfortunately, while attempting to save the mysterious Lady Maitland from the clutches of a degenerate fortune hunter, he ends up shackled to her himself.

It was never in the plans, and worse, his bride doesn't want him. Rather than feel grateful, Josephine begs to be released from the marriage so she can accomplish her dearest goal—to be left alone. Troubled by an unconventional childhood, scarred by painful memories, Josephine acts out until Warren has no choice but to begin a disciplinary program to bring her to heel.

Although his spankings are firm, painful, and plentiful, he makes little progress in taming his wild countess. But her wildness pleases him in the bedroom, where they spend hours at uninhibited play, fulfilling licentious and carnal lusts. While Josephine struggles to understand her feelings toward her authoritative husband, Warren must decide if having a tame wife is worth the anguish of damaging her already vulnerable heart.

My Naughty Minette: The Earl of Augustine has always thought of Lady Minette as a sister, but when a nocturnal adventure goes horribly awry, he's forced to make her his bride.

Now his friend Warren is furious with him, the jilted Lady Priscilla is spreading ugly gossip, his father's illness is worsening, and Minette is…well…being Minette. Flighty, exuberant, and utterly irascible, she wants a true marriage, when all August can see is the impish girl he rescued from scrapes as a child.

But Minette has idolized Lord August for years, as long as she can remember, and she's determined to make their union a passionate and fulfilling one. She launches caper after caper in an effort to capture his attention and awaken his masculine hungers. Unfortunately, all she seems to accomplish are repeated disciplinary sessions over his lap.

Can she make August realize she's the love of his life in time to save their crumbling marriage—and her smarting backside? Or will he hold her at arm's length forever, refusing to acknowledge the powerful emotions she stirs in his heart?

Under A Duke's Hand: A duke as wealthy and powerful as the Duke of Arlington requires, by matter of course, an elegant, perfectly pedigreed bride. Unfortunately, he must settle for the king's choice:

Miss Guinevere Vaughn, the rough-edged daughter of a border baron. She's pretty enough for a Welsh hellion, but she hasn't the necessary polish to succeed in London society. When Aidan explains that she'll need to improve her manners—and her disposition—he finds himself locked in a vexing battle of wills.

Gwen never asked to wed a duke. Her new husband is haughty, inflexible, and demanding, and makes no secret of his disdain for her upbringing. No matter how hard she tries to please him, she's never good enough. He disciplines her with an iron hand, and then expects her to submit to his vile whims in bed. Not that his whims are…completely…vile…all of the time. It's only that her husband doesn't love her, and she wants him to love her.

If only her feelings were not so complicated.

If only life was not so difficult *Under A Duke's Hand…*

Other Historical Romance by Annabel Joseph

Disciplining the Duchess

Over five seasons, Miss Harmony Barrett has managed to repel every gentleman of consequence and engineer a debacle at Almack's so horrifying that her waltzing privileges are revoked. If she's not in the library reading about Mongol hordes, she's embarrassing her family or getting involved in impulsive scrapes.

Enter the Duke of Courtland, a man known for his love of duty and decorum. Through a vexing series of events, he finds himself shackled to Miss Barrett in matrimony. But all is not lost. The duke harbors a not-so-secret affinity for spanking and discipline…and his new wife is ever in need of it. Will the mismatched couple find their way to marital happiness? Or will the duke be forever *Disciplining the Duchess*?

The Royal Discipline series

"Absolutely filthy." – Geoffrey Chaucer

"Rather raunchy for a fairy tale, but we liked it." – The Brothers Grimm

"I enjoyed the evil punishments. And the happy ending!" – Vlad the Impaler

"Seriously? I mean, really? He was far too gentle with her." – Marquis de Sade

There's a problem in the kingdom of Hastings: the princess is too headstrong and ill-mannered to carry on the royal line. In desperation, the king delivers his daughter to the darkly imposing Duke of Thornton, who promises to correct her behavior through a course of stringent and lowering physical chastisement.

Despite the duke's harsh disciplinary measures, Princess Violet resists change, and Thornton is soon drawn into an escalating battle of wills with his spirited charge. How far will he go to humble the haughty royal, and put an end to her spoiled behavior?

This series is available at all retailers, and consists of a super dirty and erotic novella, *Royal Discipline*, as well as a free follow-up novellette called *The Royal Wedding Night*.

About the Author

Annabel Joseph is a multi-published, New York Times and USA Today Bestselling BDSM romance author. She writes mainly contemporary romance, although she has been known to dabble in the medieval and Regency eras. She is recognized for writing emotionally intense BDSM storylines, and strives to create characters that seem real—even flawed—so readers are better able to relate to them. Annabel also writes vanilla (non-BDSM) erotic romance under the pen name Molly Joseph.

Annabel Joseph loves to hear from readers at annabeljosephnovels@gmail.com.

You can learn more about Annabel's books and sign up for her newsletter at annabeljoseph.com.

Made in the USA
Middletown, DE
05 March 2021

34886166R00135